1895

Memory Mambo

Memory Mambo

A Novel by

ACHY OBEJAS

CLEIS
PRESS

Published in the United States by Cleis Press Inc., P.O. Box 8933, Pittsburgh, Pennsylvania 15221, and P.O. Box 14684, San Francisco, California 94114.

Printed in the United States.

Cover illustration: Nereyda Garcia-Ferraz
Cover design: Pete Ivey
Text design: Sara Glaser
Logo art: Juana Alicia
Author photograph: Lisa Wax and Robin E. Johnston

First Edition.
10 9 8 7 6 5 4 3 2 1

Library of Congress Cataloging-in-Publication Data
Obejas, Achy, 1956–
    Memory mambo : a novel / by Achy Obejas.—1st. ed.
        p. cm.
    ISBN 1-57344-018-3 (cloth).—ISBN 1-57344-017-5 (pbk.)
      1. Cuban American women—Fiction. 2. Lesbians—United States—Fiction. 3. Cuban American families—Fiction. I. Title.
PS3565.B34M4 1996
813'.54—dc20   96-16120
                                  CIP

In memory of Pedro Javier and Eduardo,
and for all my cousins, whether by blood or exile, with love.

Acknowledgments

I'd like to thank Charlotte Sheedy and everyone at the agency; Frédérique Delacoste, Felice Newman and everyone at Cleis, especially Deborah Barkun; Pete Ivey and Nereyda Garcia-Ferráz for the book design; and my dad, José Obejas, for proofing my Spanish.

I'm obliged to the Virgina Center for the Creative Arts, Illinois Arts Council, Barbara Deming/Money for Women Fund, *ACM* magazine, *Strong Coffee* magazine, and the Columbia College Interdisciplinary Arts program.

Patrick Clinton, Gary Covino, Scott Garman, Cynthia Kinnard, Mark Schoofs, the late Jon Simmons, and Rita Speicher have all been helpful at crucial moments in my writing career.

I'm also indebted to S. Bryn Austin, Sherry and Bernard Beck, Tom Asch and Susanna Ruth Berger, Lynda Gorov, Luisa María Potter, Joan Silber, Gini Sorrentini, Beth Stroud and Nena Torres.

Cathy Edelman and Susan Nussbaum contributed in immeasurable ways.

My cousin Adriana Busot read innumerable drafts and helped give this work its rhythm.

I'm grateful to the late Reinaldo Arenas, for passion and inspiration.

And finally, to Lisa Wax, who read every word of every draft, and gave advice, comfort, encouragement, and, best of all, love.

Oye mi son
mi son mi son
de lo que son
son y no son.

GUILLERMO PORTABALES

I'VE ALWAYS THOUGHT OF MEMORY as a distinct, individual thing. I've read with curiosity about the large parts of our brains where memory resides—how these areas remain vital, as animated at seventy-five as at twenty-five years old. Scientists say that when we think we're losing our memory what's actually happening is that we've blocked or severed connections.

But I don't know. I'm not that old, just twenty-four, and I often wonder just how distinct my memories are. Sometimes I'm convinced they're someone else's recollections I've absorbed. I'm not talking about hooking into past lives, or other links established spiritually or psychically to other times. I'm not talking at all about suppressed memories. It's just that sometimes other lives lived right alongside mine interrupt, barge in on my senses, and I no longer know if I really lived through an experience or just heard about it so many times, or so convincingly, that I believed it for myself—became the lens through which it was captured, retold and shaped.

Sometimes I'm as sure that I couldn't have heard the stories about the memories anymore than lived through them—that both of the experiences are false for me—and yet the memory itself will be so fresh, so fantastic and detailed, that I'll think maybe my family and I are just too close to each other. Sometimes I wonder if we're not together too much, day in and day out, working and eating side by side, sleeping in the same rooms, fusing dreams. Sometimes I wonder if we know where we each end and the others begin.

Here's what I mean. My family and I came from Cuba to the U.S. by boat when I was six years old, in 1970. These are the facts: It was a twenty-eight-foot boat; there were fourteen of us; the trip lasted two days; we were picked up by the Coast

Guard just a few miles from Key West, around *Cayo Sal,* a deserted island that refugees often confuse for the southernmost tip of the U.S. but which really belongs to the Bahamas. I was seasick during most of the trip. My sister Nena, who's three years older and very serious, spent the time with her arm around me, holding me as I leaned over the side of the boat, making sure I vomited into the sea and not onto her lap. My mother was frozen in prayer: head bent, fingers intertwined like wire mesh around my little brother, Pucho. My father, the genius behind the trip, wore loose, improbably white clothes, and stood at the prow of the boat. He would look through his binoculars at the darkened horizon, then turn around and whisper instructions to the two or three men in charge of paddling, or jacking up the motor, or slowing it down.

The whole time this was happening, I didn't know what was going on. I was simply gathered up, like one more precious belonging, and packed into a stranger's bloated car in the middle of the night, then taken down through black, rural roads with the car lights turned off. We huddled at the beach, listening to the fear in one another's breathing, circles of women and children and small men waiting for the sound of the water to break ever so subtly—just a splash or two, an interruption of the otherwise hypnotic lapping—which signaled that our miserable little boat, its planks creaking against one another, had finally arrived to take us away.

So, if these are the facts, why do I remember so much more? Why do I remember foggy meetings around the kitchen table, cigars burning in the ashtrays, their tips glistening, while my father's face appeared and disappeared behind the smoke? My mother tells me there were meetings just like those I remember, but that Nena, Pucho and I were in bed, protected by layers of mosquito nets, a radio on the night table tuned in to a station that broadcast West Indian music from Sint Maarten.

Why do I remember driving around senselessly, for days, in and out of the beaches outside *La Habana* (Guanabo, Cojímar, Mariel, even as far away as San Pedro), combing through tall grasses and dirt, as fascinated by the tiny, translucent frogs on the tree branches as by the malevolent shadows scurrying underneath? My father planned our escape this way, but I never went along on these excursions. So why is it I can see my father's body, gleaming like larvae, vanishing into the water just off the shore? It's a fact that he swam along the coast, checking the bottom for coral and traps, testing the *milicianos*, trying to see how far out he could go before they'd notice. It's true that I've heard the stories, but I never went along, I never saw the motions, so how can I remember my father shaking the water off like a dog, the salt drying on his body, the hurried, nervous way he unearthed the street clothes he'd buried in newspapers in the sand?

If these aren't my memories, then whose are they? Certainly not my father's—he always casts himself as the stoic hero in his stories, unshakable and inscrutable. He would have said his body shone like a blade; he would have quoted compatriots and collaborators applauding his brilliance. If these were my father's stories, they would be wholly congratulatory and totally void of meaningful detail.

My cousin Patricia says this is because his tales are almost always lies.

· · · · • · • · · · ·

Some memories are precise. Ever since I can remember, I've always been surrounded by cousins. My mother says this isn't exactly true, that we hardly ever saw our cousins in Cuba and that our cousins here are a different story. But Nena, Pucho and I have memories of seeing our cousins every day of our lives while we were growing up—not every single cousin, of course, but at least one, and often more. They were always at our house, eating, or we were at theirs, watching TV or using the phone.

In Cuba, when we had birthday parties, there were so many cousins to invite that hardly anybody outside the family came. When I look at those old black and white pictures my cousin

Patricia brought back from Cuba, all the other relatives turn into one big genetic smear but I can identify my cousins at a glance. Most of these—Pedro Javier, Titi, Jorge and Eduardo (the twins), and Tomás Joaquín—are older and stayed on the island. But I know their faces, I know our family. What I mean is, we look exactly alike, with our sallow skin and large, liquid eyes. No matter the memories, we could never deny each other.

In the U.S., Nena, Pucho and I walked to class with our cousins Manolito, Caridad and, later, when she was old enough, Pauli. Patricia, who's U.S. born and much older, gave us tips on how to survive. When American kids called us names or tried to hit us, we fought back or took refuge together. Sometimes we'd just huddle in the playground, listening to them screeching like birds at us.

Just like in Cuba, all the cousins in the U.S. have that unmistakable stamp of kinship. It's all in the eyes—something tragic perhaps; I don't really know how to describe it. Sometimes when I look at Caridad, or even Patricia, who's so strong, their see-through eyes remind me of cats at night.

There are pictures of me in Cuba, right after I was born, being bounced in the air like a rag by my cousin Tomás Joaquín, a skinny blond boy with biceps and bulging calf muscles, even at ten. I don't look scared, but faraway and serious. Tomás Joaquín is looking at me with eyes shiny and black. There is an abyss there, I think.

There are hazy color snapshots of me from when we first arrived in the U.S., a rubbery toddler in the arms of a sloe-eyed adolescent, all proud and beaming. That's Caridad, and in the picture she's holding me all wrong, but I'm happy. My pupils are so bright they look like peacock's coal reflecting light.

The first boy my sister Nena kissed was my cousin Manolito. And the first girl I kissed was my cousin Pauli, not because we liked each other that way, but because we were curious and we could do that with each other.

That's the thing about cousins—they're part of the family and yet they're not. They're like faulty brothers and sisters—

always present, always in on all the secrets, but not pure enough to bring in to the nucleus, the very heart of the matter. They're electrons, just flitting about, connected only by the mystery of their orbit.

Then there's the difference between blood cousins, like the ones in Cuba, and cousins in exile. We're stuck with blood cousins. They're there, recklessly swinging off the branches on the family tree whether we want them or not. They assume they can call on us, just because we crawled out of the same DNA pool, regardless of whether we've ever shared a word with them or not. They figure they can get us to send them food and medicine, to file their papers to get them out of Cuba, even to support them once they're here. They assume we'll tell them our most intimate thoughts, even if we've just met them, because they're family, because they're links in the chain of our history, even the history we don't know.

Cousins in exile are different. They're the cousins we never had, something far more vital than just substitutes for the ones left in Cuba. We know them because they're the only other Cubans in our American neighborhood, or the only Cubans in our apartment building, or, sometimes, even if they're not from the same town as our parents, maybe they're from the same province. We just sort of stumble on these cousins, sorting out coincidences and fate. It doesn't matter how it happens. By the end of the first or second visit, we're related—we're kissing hello and good-bye; before we know it, their parents are *tío* and *tía* and have the power to punish us if we misbehave.

I know a lot of people think cousins in exile are really random relationships, links forged out of loneliness and desperation. And that's kind of true, I admit, but there's more: We have an affinity, a way of speaking that's neither Cuban nor American, neither genetic or processed. There's a look, a wink, the way we touch each other. We communicate, I suspect, like deaf people—not so much compensating for the lost sense, but creating a new syntax from the pieces of our displaced lives.

There are times, I admit, when I can't remember if I'm

related to somebody by blood or exile. It's not often, but it happens now and then. I'll see an impossible resemblance, I'll connect loose branches on the family tree. I'll look into the face of someone who could have been, under different circumstances, a complete stranger, and I'll see myself. These aren't lies or inventions. How else could I explain my family? How else could I explain myself? I don't long for a perfect memory. I don't want to ensnare the universe; I already know that's beyond the flawed connections of my small and curious brain.

What I want to know is what *really* happened.

CHAPTER 2

MY COUSIN CARIDAD AND HER HUSBAND are fighting about whether she should buy a new car or not. My cousin, who's round and sweet and smokes too many cigarettes, feels it's her right to get a new car, since her father (Tío Pepe) died and left her money that was totally unplanned for, so why not? But Jimmy, my cousin-in-law of sorts, says no, they don't need a new car. According to him, their old one (a beat up Ford Escort) is fine, and they have plenty of other debts to pay before buying something that luxurious. Besides, he sneers, where the hell does Caridad think she's going to go without him anyway?

Caridad says she doesn't want to buy a luxury car, just one of those little Geo Metros. She tells him they get fifty miles to the gallon and fit in little itty bitty parking spaces. "They're like baby Porsches and cost just eight thousand dollars. Come on, Jimmy," she whines, "it'll make me feel better about Papi dying."

But Jimmy, who's tired from work (he's still wearing his gray janitor uniform from the hospital) and has been leaning against the kitchen sink, comes right up to Caridad as she sucks on her cigarette and, with his thumb and index finger, flicks the burning ash right off the tip. Caridad winces and I watch the tiny fireball hit the floor and smolder.

"No, and that's final," Jimmy says, then leaves the room. He practically swings his hips on the way out, he thinks he's that cool.

The whole time, I just sit at the kitchen table, playing with the edge of the plastic placemat, which says *Cuba* and has a map of the island, a picture of the flag, and a bouquet of palm trees. On the placemat Cuba looks like a giant brown turd; the flag's colors have faded so that the triangle appears pink. I'm not about to say anything because, while I love my cousin very much, I know damn well she's truth-proof in love with Jimmy and totally immune to reason.

"It's my fucking money," Caridad whispers fiercely. "Papi left it to me to do whatever the hell I want with it and if I want to buy a car, I can do that, don't you think so, Juani?"

What I really want to say is, If it's your money, why do you have to ask him permission anyway? But we aren't having a conversation—that's between her and Jimmy—my job here is to listen. So I just roll the corner of the placemat in my fingers and watch her light another cigarette. She's leaning against the sink now, just like Jimmy did a minute ago. She's vibrating too. When she sees what I'm doing to the placemat, she bends over and swats my hand as if I'm some snot-nosed kid.

"Hey," I protest, then slap down the curled corner of the placemat. "That hurt," I say. There's a big red mark across my knuckles.

But, as expected, Caridad isn't really paying attention to me. She says, "Who does he think he is anyway, huh?"

"I don't know," I mutter.

My ambivalence isn't because I think that, as her husband, Jimmy has any right to tell her what to do. We both know from experience that you just don't mess with Jimmy, because his temper's wild. But—and I hate to give him credit for anything because I've always thought he's a bastard—he does have a point: Living on just one salary in their overwhelmed, over-stuffed one-bedroom apartment above our family's laundromat, they really do have other bills to pay.

"He can't just tell me what to do like that," she says, smoke curling from her nostrils like a ram's horns.

But we both know he can, and does.

. . . .

One time, Jimmy absolutely forbade Caridad to hang out with me and my friends, or just with me, even though I'm family. He said no wife of his was going to be seen all over town with a gaggle of lesbians; what kind of man would people think he was if his wife was always hanging with *tortilleras?*

For the longest time, it's true that Caridad used to hang out with me and my friends, most of whom are lesbians. This was no secret to the family, or the neighborhood, probably. But it wasn't as if anyone ever got confused and thought Caridad was gay. She has always preferred, and enjoyed, her power with men: on top and on the bottom. She likes the dangers that come with men too, especially certain Latino men—that they might not show up for a date, or that they'll be mean, or hurt her. It's not that she likes getting beat up (nobody ever hit her before Jimmy, no matter how often any of her boyfriends threatened to)—in fact, she hates it—but she relishes the role she gets to play in bringing down her bad boys. She likes making strong men weak, not through humiliation or cruelty, but with her hands and mouth and the way she tosses her hair away from her face, winking and laughing.

She has told me plenty of times how, after making Jimmy come, she just loves to look at him, all wet and red and shrunken, as helpless and beautiful as a newborn baby. "I just think, 'I did that? Did I really do that?' and I can't believe it," she says, "I just can't believe it."

Strangely enough, it's exactly this kind of thing which made it easier for her to hang out with my friends and me than with straight girls. With us, there was no competition; we just didn't care. When she told her stories, we laughed and asked questions; sometimes we were incredulous, convinced we'd never put up with what she puts up with and we'd roll our eyes so she couldn't see; sometimes we'd get grossed out; other times we'd slap her shoulder and tell her how right on she was. But mostly, hers was another world. We loved her and celebrated her, but we didn't want her—and there was a certain freedom for her in that too.

That's why when Jimmy said Caridad couldn't hang with us anymore, we really missed her, especially because she's one hell of a dancer. Since she's one of the older cousins, she actually learned to dance in Cuba, where they play the really authentic music—not just Celia Cruz, but Beny Moré, Arsenio Rodríguez, Celeste Mendoza and Los Van Van too—so she got assigned to teach all of us younger cousins how to dance. Patricia's the oldest of all, but she was born in New York, which we joke is the reason she can't dance worth a damn.

Caridad taught us the mambo, the *cha-cha-chá*, the rumba, even the tango. She tutored us in the movement of our hips, how to close our eyes and toss our heads back as if we were in ecstasy and the music had completely invaded us. Since then, most of us have figured out how to really get in the groove with the rhythms, so we don't have to think about looking suave anymore.

Of course, in order to teach the boys how to lead—like my brother Pucho, who's a real flat-foot—Caridad had to learn how to lead herself. This is a unique talent—a girl who knows how to move another girl with just one touch to her lower back, one little glide off her hip, a graceful tug here and there. (Gina, a lover I'm still aching over, dances likes that.) In a lesbian bar, this is a big deal. We loved Caridad—we used to fight among ourselves to see who'd get to dance with her, which she just ate up.

But after Jimmy prohibited her from hanging out with us, we'd see her cigarette at the window just as we drove off on Friday and Saturday nights, a firefly trapped in a mason jar. She'd watch us, all sad and angry with Jimmy, and he'd look out, stupid and satisfied. He'd get a big kick out of screaming at us, "Hey, have a good time tortilla-makers! Suck some pussy for me!"

Then Caridad would yell at him and they'd get in a fight. He'd win by slapping her, or sometimes just threatening to. He has this way of holding his hand stiff, like a karate chop, and checking it up almost to his chin and across his chest, as if only his desire can keep that backhand from snapping.

Another time, Jimmy tried to ban me completely from their house but he wasn't very successful. Pucho, who's considerably bigger than him, heard about the ban and went up to see him. I don't know what they said to each other because my brother does not raise his voice. Pucho's one of those quiet types, the kind that carry knives with which they casually pick at their cuticles, like they're just having a chat and there's nothing wrong in the whole world. Pucho and Jimmy just stood on the stairs up to Jimmy and Caridad's apartment, two black figures with their heads close together. Their shadows fell across a pair of mangy neighborhood cats lapping from a bowl of fresh milk that Caridad puts out (along with expensive all-natural tuna) under the stairs every night.

So the compromise—although nobody says there was a compromise, but we all know anyway—was that I wouldn't spend too much time with Caridad alone, just the two of us. It was ridiculous, of course, because she's my cousin; there's never been any mystery.

· · · , · , · · ·

Caridad told me that she once asked Jimmy *qué carajo* his problem was with me. It was a rhetorical question because she thought he was going to say that it was my being queer, since that's what he'd always said, even the first time I met him and he felt like he had to sit and talk all night about "which one of us has gotten more pussy in our short lifetime." It was the kind of thing only a heterosexual man would consider, and probably only a barrio boy at that.

I've never told Caridad this but that first time she left us alone in the living room at her parents' house, those twenty minutes it took her to get dressed and get her make-up on, Jimmy just sat there on the couch and stared at me, his legs wide open, his hand rubbing his dick until it was practically jumping out of his pants.

"You ever want one of these?" he asked me. He rested his head on the back of the couch, his cheeks all flushed. His penis pushed at his loose dress pants as if trying to erect a tent. "Not inside you, but like, one of your own?"

19

I'm tall, kind of big-boned and flat-chested—tomboyish too—and I've got my father's jawline, so I could see how, in his ignorance, he'd gotten confused. Still, I really should have been ticked off, or maybe scared. Jimmy isn't too big—kind of short really, with a smooth, hairless chest—but he's strong. Yet, when he talked to me like that, instead of telling him what a dumb question that was, or how homophobic and insecure he sounded, I just laughed and told him no, that I didn't *need* one of those.

"I get what I want; know what I mean?" I said to him, all cocky. He smiled from under hooded eyes, then took his hand from his crotch and sighed.

We were quiet like that for a minute or so, him with his eyes closed just letting the tent slowly collapse, me watching intently. It was like a stand-off: dangerous, yes, but also just plain exhilarating. I went home that night and got off a dozen or so times just playing that scene over and over in my head.

So even though he was totally out of line, sitting there rubbing his cock, I couldn't very well tell Caridad about that without also telling her, one way or another, how it'd affected me. She's my cousin, she would have known; I figured, better let sleeping dogs lie. Besides, it would have just confused matters, because she's used to me being a lesbian (and she has very definite ideas about what that means) and she probably would have felt that she had to be jealous, which would have been all wrong.

When she asked Jimmy what his problem was with me—now that they were already married and he had her totally under his thumb—he said, totally serious, "Juani's just like me, we're two of a kind."

"What do you mean she's just like you?" Caridad asked him, incredulous.

So he told her, "She'd do *anything.*"

"Like come on to her own cousin, is that what you think?" Caridad asked.

"Yeah," he said, "maybe, depends on the circumstances."

When Caridad reported all this to me I thought, Yeah, he would do that, that asshole.

· · · · · · · · · ·

On my way home from Caridad and Jimmy's, where the argument about the new car is still going on although it's quiet because Caridad's smoking in the kitchen and Jimmy's taking a shower, I stop downstairs at our family's laundromat and play a couple of quick games of Lethal Enforcer.

The laundromat's closed but I have keys and can let myself in anytime. I'm the assistant manager but since I got back from visiting my sister Nena in Miami, where she now works doing PR for an all-news Spanish-language radio station, I haven't been hanging around here much.

As I step inside, I turn the lights on but make sure the sign outside that reads *Wash-N-Dry Laundry/Lavanderia Wash-N-Dry* stays dark. I'm not looking for customers at this time of night, just a little entertainment, a little distraction.

When Nena was the assistant manager, she thought it'd be a good marketing move to put in pinball and video machines because people got so bored all the time doing their laundry. It took some convincing, though, because my father—the official manager, although it's always been Nena, our Tía Zenaida or me who has really known what was going on—thought the machines would attract gangbangers. But Nena's attitude was that even gangbangers have to wash their clothes (she's a real good capitalist, my sister) and then she figured out the real magnet for them wasn't the games anyway, from which we eventually made tons of money, but the public pay phone, from which we never did pull much. So we got rid of the phone and put in a whole bank of games along the back wall.

After Nena moved away, I took over the laundromat and when it came time to re-evaluate the games, I got rid of Centipede, which she loved but I thought was so inane, all those little beads tumbling down the screen. I replaced it with Mortal Kombat, which is probably even more idiotic, and certainly

21

bloodier, but so popular that the only time nobody's jerking the controls and ripping heads off virtual bodies is when the laundromat's closed. I kept Ms. Pac Man because, even though it's sexist, I like the whole idea of eating a path through the maze. I also brought in The Simpsons and a vintage Fireball pinball machine with the spinning rubber disk in the middle (I once read somewhere that it was Hugh Hefner's favorite machine at the Playboy Mansion, but it's such a great game I try not to hold that against it) and, of course, Lethal Enforcer, which is vicious and which, I admit, I just love. It's just a shoot-'em-up game: You get a gun and a screen full of bad guys and you try to kill them. That's basically it, except that after I play, I always feel really loose, ready for anything.

I'm not doing too well tonight, though. My right arm's a little numb and a line of dull pain circles my breast. I get past the screen with the bank robbery, but I miss all the bad guys in the Chinatown sequence. I try to duck, but I keep getting hit. I twist and turn, leaning into the screen, but to no avail. I'm using the pink pistol but just can't get past Chinatown without being blown away. My wrist's a little sore, as it sometimes gets, and my fingers are tingling so I finally give up and turn off the machine without even finishing my turn. I walk around a little bit, decide to get a Very Fine from the pop machine, toss on my jacket and go outside, where I'm greeted by a crisp and silvery night.

The fact is, I miss Gina.

As I lock the door, I see lights upstairs in Caridad and Jimmy's apartment. It's the overhead light, not a lamp. I hold the Very Fine against me with my arm and feel the cold come through to my breast. It feels good, like a balm. I turn the laundromat door key and walk over to pull the burglar gates together. Even the screeching and scratching against the sidewalk as I drag the gates and roll the chains into a big knot between them doesn't drown out the noise from upstairs. I can't quite make out what Jimmy and Caridad are saying, but they're loud. Every now and then, there's a thud or a crash, things falling and breaking. But after I finish locking up, I just walk away.

When I get home to my apartment just a few blocks away, the light's blinking red on my answering machine. One, two calls. I hold my breath and hope maybe one of those calls is Gina saying she's changed her mind, all is forgiven and she's coming over. I press the review button, listen to the whirl of the tape, take off my jacket and walk over to the fridge, from which I grab a pear and bite into it. I crunch and crunch, listening to all the chewing inside my head, barely making out my messages. The first is from my cousin Patricia, nagging me about stuff I have to do if want to go to Cuba. The other's a hang up. I decide it was Gina, wishing me sweet dreams (I let my breath out, surrendering). Then the phone rings in earnest and for a split second, I'm hopeful again.

"Hey... Juani..." But it's Caridad, sniffling into the tape machine.

I pick up the receiver. "Hey..."

She coughs. "Anybody over?"

"No, I'm alone," I say. Outside my window, a solitary car drives by. It's well past midnight.

"So then, whatcha' doing, huh?"

I shrug, as if she could see me. "Waiting for your call, I guess."

She laughs a little, embarrassed. "You coming over?"

"If you want me to," I say.

"Yeah..." (Sniffle, sniffle.)

"Is Jimmy gone?"

"Oh, yeah..." And she laughs again, a little bitter this time.

I put down the phone, take a last bite out of the pear and pitch the core, in the dark, bull's-eye into the garbage under my old-fashioned kitchen sink.

M Y FATHER BELIEVES HE INVENTED DUCT TAPE. He sees it as the great tragedy of his life because, if the Americans hadn't stolen it out from under him, he'd have been rich, and we'd have been much happier. If things had gone the way he believes they should have, we'd never be running the Wash-N-Dry Laundry/Lavanderia Wash-N-Dry in Chicago.

The way my father tells it, he invented a formula for a strong, durable black cloth tape, ideal for packing, and immune to rain and snow (although this, of course, was theoretical because, never having been out of Cuba in his life at the time of this great discovery, he didn't *really* know). He called his break-through *cinta magnética*, even though it had nothing whatsoever to do with magnetics, electricity or power of any kind.

I don't know how much any of this is true. I have a vague memory of shirtless men in the patio of our home in Havana brushing whole strips of black cloth with some horrible, stinky glue. I remember it as infernally hot, and made hotter by the flames cooking buckets full of my father's goo, and the men, hairy-chested and thin, wearing loose black pants and hard shoes with laces. When they bent over the buckets, we could see the white line of their underwear hanging off their hips, broad elastic bands wet with sweat.

My father, Alberto José Casas y Molina, directed traffic, his reading glasses on the tip of his nose, a handsome, absent-minded fellow with long, fleshy arms. He'd stand in the middle of all the activity, taking mysterious notes on his clipboard, and squinting in the sunlight. To check his masterpiece, he'd stick the little finger of his left hand into the buckets and burn himself. Then he'd curse under his breath and wave his little finger around hoping that somehow the wet tropical air would cool and heal it. He'd instruct the men—always named Felo or Cuco or Cheo—on how to roll the cloth together into big black wheels: They'd stand on opposite ends of the patio, one guy—say, Cheo—holding the tape on a spool and rolling it in, while another guy—probably Cuco—held the end of the tape and walked toward him until they practically touched noses. Then they'd start again, as soon as they disentangled themselves because, inevitably, Cuco would get stuck on the tape, or Cheo's fingers would glue themselves together, so Papi, very frustrated and impatient, would order Felo to cut Cuco free from the tape and get Cheo some Ajax or Lava soap, which sometimes worked and sometimes didn't.

I remember all this, but I don't know if I remember it for real or because I heard the story a million times. My brother Pucho doesn't remember anything, but he was just a baby then. Nena says it's all true, although her memories aren't quite the same as mine, but my cousin Patricia says it's just a fantasy created in exile, a group hallucination based on my father's constant retelling of the story.

Of course, everybody in the family has heard my father's duct tape story at least a million times. And anybody who's ever come to the house has gotten the entire tale, from beginning to end, whether they liked it or not, at least once. Most of our pals are nice about it; they nod and ask a few questions to make Papi feel good, but we know they're incredulous, laughing inside the entire time.

. . . .

I think it's fair to say that, of all our friends, it was Gina, who's a fierce Puerto Rican *independentista*, who had the hardest time with the duct tape story. Mami, Nena and I knew it took an incredible amount of willpower for her to sit through it and not challenge my father, to just bite her lip and say nothing.

"Sweetie, your father's got some serious damage," she whispered to me in the kitchen during a break in the storytelling. She hugged me close to her, not caring if anybody saw us pressed up against each other. "It's a miracle you're sane, honey. It's a miracle you have a grasp on reality at all." She pushed my hair back and kissed my forehead. If she hadn't been a communist atheist, I think she would have blessed me right there and then and gone straight to church to light candles for our family. I swear there was pity in her eyes, which I resented.

"Look, Gina, my father's not crazy," I said, defensively. I had a hideous fear that she'd think it ran in the family, that I might be carrying the same faulty DNA.

"No, no, he's not," she said. "I believe he's not crazy."

"You do?" I was amazed at how quickly she was willing to give him the benefit of the doubt.

"No, of course not," she said. "He's delusional because of what exile has done to him—just look at what life in the U.S. has made of your father!"

I glanced back at him. My father was sitting on the couch in the living room, chatting with my mother and Nena. He had a slight paunch, a robust laugh, a twinkle in his eye.

"He looks pretty okay to me," I said with a smirk.

Gina grabbed a pair of beers from our refrigerator, one for her and one for my father. "You know, you're the sick one," she said, rolling her eyes at me and going back in for the rest of the story. "Your denial's worse than his!"

If Gina had the hardest time, Jimmy had the easiest. My father told him the duct tape story one Sunday afternoon while they lounged around waiting for Mami, Caridad and me to make dinner. My father drank beers with Jimmy and offered him Nicaraguan cigars grown from Cuban seeds and imported through Mexico. Jimmy, perhaps afraid that the male-bonding he sought wouldn't take if he rejected the sleek brown phallus my father offered him, accepted. He spent the rest of the evening looking pretty green, which probably had a lot to do with the ease of his surrender to the story. All the while my father yakked on and on, Mami and I made *boliche, moros y cristianos*, and fried *malanga*, which Caridad had sliced into paper thin chips—one gigantic cholesterol feast.

Depending on who's listening to the story, my father says that either he was a prosperous businessman recruited by the CIA after the Cuban revolution (what he told Jimmy, who he knew was anti-Castro), or that he was unemployed and, when the CIA came calling, didn't have any other options (what he told Gina, because he didn't want to be provocative). But either way, whether he ever implies Fidel Castro was a bad guy or not, in both versions he certainly believes working for the CIA was a good route into the American business community, where he hoped to market his *cinta magnética*.

Apparently, my father was not recruited by the CIA for his invention, but because he had an uncanny ability to procure boats to get people out of the island. He always says this was because, being the son of one of Havana's oldest and most prosperous families, he knew all the boat owners—all members of the Miramar Yacht Club, which was much more prestigious than the Havana Yacht Club—and was in a good position to cut deals. He'd either guarantee safe passage for the boat if they took a hot passenger (artists, government officials, dissidents of all kinds), or he'd buy the boat outright with CIA dollars.

Patricia says this is all invention, that we weren't as high class as my father wants us to believe, and that more likely than not, he was stealing the boats—if, in fact, any of the story is true at all.

"You know, I played an important part in getting Fulgencio Batista out of Cuba on that fateful New Year's Eve in 1959," my father told Gina and Jimmy, both of whom kindly didn't mention that my father would have been just a kid in 1959, or that they knew the old dictator had left the island by plane, not boat.

I remember watching Gina during this part, terrified she'd be unable to keep from laughing. I remember too how relieved I was when she kept a straight face, and the little smile she gave me, as if saying, *Don't worry, I know he's your father, I'm not going to say anything upsetting, I love you, okay?*

I know for a fact my father doesn't do well with challenges.

Patricia, whose father Raúl Fonseca (the rich and famous artist) actually fought with Fidel against Batista, confronted Papi once about his age in 1959 and his alleged participation in the old dictator's escape but he didn't even blink: "Look, I was a very mature teenager—people in Cuba were more mature, everybody knows that—and you're *supposed* to think Batista left by plane," Papi snorted in reply.

Jimmy played along with my father like everybody else, but he went further: praising his courage and asking questions. Were there any celebrities among the people he got out of Cuba? What kinds of boats were they? Did he get paid for his troubles? Mami, Caridad and I watched from the kitchen, amazed at Jimmy's interest and patience. He wasn't just pretending to pay attention: He was really listening.

"But then, you know how it goes with these stupid *yanquis*," my father said, beginning the most frustrating part of the story. "I was doing so much for them, for the CIA, and things were getting hot for me. Of course, I can't say—even to this day—I can't say what I was doing—it's still a state secret, can you imagine?—so I asked them, I asked the CIA to get me out of Cuba, please, before the communists killed me in front of my wife and children."

I remember Gina just nodded at this but Jimmy beamed at him, as if everything he was saying was reasonable. "A sensible request," he said. "After all, you'd done so much for them." He sipped his beer.

"Exactly, Jimmy, exactly!" my father said excitedly. He couldn't believe he had such an appreciative audience in Caridad's boyfriend. I'm sure at that moment he regretted Jimmy wasn't dating Nena or me and on his way to being his son-in-law. "But do you know what the CIA said? They said, 'You're Alberto José Casas y Molina, no? You're the guy who gets everybody out of Cuba, so get yourself out!' Can you believe that, eh?"

"Unbelievable," Jimmy said, right on cue.

According to Papi, once he was abandoned by the CIA, he

managed to prepare one last boat for our family and a few friends, making elaborate plans for a midnight rendezvous at a deserted beach outside Havana. My mother was in charge of getting us to the shore, along with the bare essentials for the trip and life in the U.S.—including, of course, a sample of and the formula for my father's *cinta magnética*—but, somehow, in the madness of the moment, she either lost it or forgot it, depending, again, on my father's audience for the story and how he and Mami are getting along at the time.

For Gina, my father just threw his hands in the air as if he wasn't sure what had happened. For Jimmy, my father pinned our lost fortunes on my mother's nervousness, although he tried to forgive her by adding that hers was not an unexpected response for any woman in that kind of situation and that maybe he shouldn't have left such an awesome responsibility on her shoulders.

"Poof! Gone!" Papi said, sucking on another beer.

"It wasn't meant to be, Alberto," Jimmy said, nearly making a mistake.

"It wasn't meant to be? Are you crazy? Of course it was meant to be," my father insisted. "Don't you realize what happened?"

Even Jimmy shook his head at this one, truly confused.

"The CIA, Jimmy, the CIA!" my father screamed. He was standing up now, hoisting his pants with his free hand, drinking and pacing. "They stole the formula! You know what happened when I got to the United States? The first thing I see in a hardware store window in Miami? Duck tape, that's what."

"Duct tape," Jimmy corrected him softly.

"Exactly, duck tape—*cinta pata, cinta maricona*—can you believe?"

The irony is that it wasn't Gina, but Jimmy, who faltered at the end of my father's story. I think for Gina, who sometimes believes her phones are tapped or that the U.S. government is infiltrating her *independentista* meetings, a conspiracy to steal my father's duct tape formula wasn't all that far-fetched. That she didn't believe my father had a damn thing to do with the development of duct tape didn't stop her for one minute from thinking Uncle Sam could have ripped him off. I took it as a sign of Gina's love for me that after my father told her the story, she thanked him and promised that, in solidarity with him, she'd never use duct tape again.

But Jimmy, hard as he was trying, couldn't really believe my father had lost the rights to duct tape due to a U.S. government scheme. It offended all of his sensibilities. Later, Caridad told me that Jimmy said he thought duct tape had been on the market long before any of us arrived in the U.S. Caridad begged him not to ever mention anything to Papi, for fear of breaking his heart even more.

"You mean the CIA abandoned you so they could steal the formula for duct tape? The CIA is the company that makes duct tape?" Jimmy asked, aghast.

My father nodded smugly. "You see, you young people, you know nothing," he said, still pacing, still pulling his pants up by the waistband. This is a completely unnecessary gesture, because his pants always fit him fine, but he does it whenever he gets anxious. "Why do you think the CIA is called 'The Company', eh? It's a joke, no? Of course they make the duck tape, and they make Pepsi-Cola and telephone poles and all kinds of things. Half of the products in the supermarket are made by the CIA."

That's all it took to get Jimmy back on track. "That's incredible," he said, sitting back in his chair, enjoying the show again. "I didn't know that."

"Yeah, and my *cinta magnética*," my father said sadly, plopping back into his chair and staring at one of Tío Raúl's more tolerable paintings hanging on our wall. "I could have been as rich as that guy," he said, jutting his chin in the direction of the canvas, but Jimmy, understandably confused, missed the reference.

"If only Fidel hadn't come," Jimmy said, "things might have been different. We'd be making duct tape in Cuba and selling it to the Americans."

"Yeah, if only the *yanquis* had not stolen my formula," my father whispered. "If only..."

. . . .

It's not surprising then that, regardless of whatever my father's relationship really was with the CIA, if any, he wasn't the one who pushed to leave Cuba. He's more of a dreamer than a worker, and even though he's no snob, he rather enjoyed the privilege of being a Casas y Molina in Cuba's small society circles. He's harmless enough that he would been able to ride out the revolution without too much trouble and, in his heart of hearts, I'm sure even he knows that.

Frankly, we left Cuba, not because the *milicianos* were after my father for stealing boats, but because of my mother. Not that the revolution had much to do with her reasoning, either. For my mother, the revolution was just the last straw.

It's not that my mother didn't like Cuba—she did. I don't think she's ever been as happy as she is in those dull color pictures of her at Varadero beach, slim and loose-limbed, laughing it up with my father. There's something very marvelously Cuban about them in those photos: My father's in white linen pants and a *guayabera,* my mother's wearing thick dark lipstick and pearl earrings. All around them, Varadero is dense with its unlikely pine trees, and the sun is so bright Mami and Papi are always squinting. In one picture, my father's cocky with his hand on his hips, staring right at the camera, and my mother's swooning underneath, gazing up at him as if he were the biggest star in Hollywood.

In another picture, they're sharing a chaise lounge under an umbrella, their legs tangled in a wildly sensual way that's hard to believe for them. As long as I can remember, they've never been particularly affectionate in public, much less sexual. According to Nena, to whom my mother confides everything, my father didn't even sleep with my mother their whole first year of marriage because, supposedly, he respected her so much; he went to brothels instead—although Patricia, a fervent

31

Fidel supporter until a few years back, always claims that there were no brothels in Cuba in the sixties—one of the real achievements of the revolution—and that the story has to be false on that basis alone.

At the time of these happy photographic scenes, my father didn't have much family money left (most of it having been squandered by his father, a corrupt former government official affiliated with Batista), didn't have a job, and didn't have prospects beyond the *cinta magnética*, but my mother was sure she'd found a prize: My father, after all, is green-eyed and very light-skinned. For my mother—Xiomara Ruíz y García, a *café con leche mulata* from Guanabacoa—marrying a guy this pale was a big deal. Her older sister, Zenaida, Patricia and Manolito's mother, had married Tío Raúl, a brown-skinned character who'd moved them to New York with a nutty dream of becoming an artist. Since then he'd dumped Zenaida and taken off to have adventures with Fidel all over Oriente province, Costa Rica and Mexico. Their whole relationship, including the eventual divorce, was considered a horrible family disgrace. My mother was sure she could do better than that, especially with the prestigious Alberto José Casas y Molina.

Before my mother met my father, she'd been told during a shell-throwing divination session that she'd marry the next man she met who had green eyes. She was delighted at this news because, though my mother is clearly a mixed breed—just touch the *pasitas* on her head—and my Abuela Olga is obviously of African descent, my mother will do just about anything to deny her real lineage. When she saw my father, sipping a *cafesito* at an outdoor café just outside the house of her favorite *babalao*, she was sure their kids would be colorless and beautiful.

Alberto José Casas y Molina wasn't just light-skinned though: He boasted a splendid ancestry. As we've always been told, we're direct descendants of Bartolomé de Las Casas, better known in Cuban lore as "The Apostle to the Indies." Las Casas got this name because of his alleged work protecting the island's indigenous population from the Spaniards' bloodlust.

My mother always professes admiration for Las Casas' humanitarianism, although, perhaps more importantly, I think she likes the way the whole legend around Las Casas positions the question of race between white and Indian, consigning most of the issue of blackness to silence. In fact, my brother Pucho's real name is Bartolomé. At one time, Pucho tried to get his American friends to call him Bart, which horrified my parents. Some people did call him Bart for a while, but the neighborhood kids—mostly Appalachians, Poles and Jews—called him Pooch, which wasn't that much different from Pucho.

I was named Juana, I've been told, because my father always liked the name. All the great Cuban songs mention a Juana, he'd tell us, but we could never think of any that did, and then he'd just say, "Hey, what kind of Cubans are you anyway?" He'd make something up, a little chorus or funny verse about *Juana La Cubana* and how she danced in Havana and we'd all laugh. My name has its own legacies, though: A dissident sister of Fidel's is named Juana, as was the unhappy and somewhat mad daughter of Ferdinand and Isabella, the Spanish monarchs who set Columbus on his way to Cuba and for whom the island was originally named.

But, Nena and I have never believed either one of us got named simply because of the way our names sounded, or for religious reasons or any of that. Nena (whose real name is María Victoria) and I have always believed I was named after a girl in Varadero my father liked as young man, and that she was named for a woman nicknamed Marivi who we heard from Pucho was Papi's "regular girl" at that alleged brothel in Havana.

Curiously, that Bartolomé de Las Casas was a Catholic priest sworn to celibacy is always left out of the family stories so how, exactly, we're supposed to be directly related to him is a bit of a mystery, even to us. My parents usually say our bloodline dates to prior to his commitment to God, although there seems to be little—even in exile literature—to indicate Las Casas was ever married. (There is a governor Las Casas that shows up about two hundred years later in Cuban history, a rather productive but boring fellow who paved the streets of Havana and invented the concept of one-way streets, but my family has never expressed much interest in being related to him.)

Patricia, who has traveled to Cuba to cut sugarcane with various communist brigades over the years and tried to research the story, says that the whole Bartolomé de Las Casas tale is one elaborate lie. She told us that one of the ways Las Casas "protected" the Indians was by making the first suggestion to the Spanish governor that Africans might be better suited to work in the tropics than the Indians. This, Patricia said, is what started slavery in Cuba. I still remember the look on her face when she gave us that bit of news: her eyebrow arched, a smirk barely contained on her mouth.

Whenever Patricia spews this, my parents get hysterical, making the sign of the cross, telling her she's been brainwashed. Wherever she got her information, they say, it's obviously pure communist propaganda. But what really kills them is when Patricia tells them that, if indeed we're descendants of Las Casas, chances are we're the spawns of an illegitimate child conceived with some Indian woman he probably raped. My mother practically faints over this—not because it so tampers with the historical image of our supposed ancestor but because it would mean that, in spite of my mother's better efforts, we're not so white after all.

When we were little, my mother was always after us: *"Caminen siempre por la sombra"*—always walk in the shade. She was terrified that too much sun would somehow reveal our real heritage, whether Indian or black.

As it turned out, I am pretty light-skinned, and Nena got my father's green eyes. But Nena's actually kind of yellow-colored, with a propensity for darkness after any exposure to the sun. The truth is that Nena is more beautiful the darker and browner she gets. And my brother Pucho, with his kinky hair and full lips, obviously got my mother's genes instead of my father's. (To my mother's chagrin, Patricia and Manolito, the children of her sister Zenaida and the brown-skinned Raúl, are both pale and Anglo-like, with blue veins visible just under rice-paper skin.)

When the revolution triumphed in 1959, nothing stunned my mother more than the fact that that crazy Raúl and his black friends were riding on tanks with Fidel through the city, shooting rounds into the air and getting drunk together. When she saw him, she looked away and hid, sure she was not going to give him the satisfaction of having won this particular battle. In that instant, my mother—who'd been struggling to pass her entire life—could see that the order of things had just been altered.

Years later, after she'd landed Alberto José Casas y Molina and we were born, her immediate goal became to get us out of Cuba, out of Latin America, out of any country where we might couple with anybody even a shade darker than us: We had to get to the United States, which was close by and chock full of frog-eyed white people such as Joe Namath and President Ford.

Each time Mami remembers the moment when Raúl, Fidel and his supporters waved and laughed at the multi-colored masses lining the streets of Havana on that historic New Year's Day, she's reborn as a counterrevolutionary.

CHAPTER 4

"**H**EY, CARI...IT'S ME," I whisper through the door of Caridad and Jimmy's apartment. A circle of cats are devouring a bowl full of tuna Caridad has left for them under the stairs. I'm a little cold so I hug myself and wait, looking across the street at the second floor above Polonia Furniture.

When we first moved here shortly after coming to the U.S., we were some of the first Latino immigrants in the area (a lot of Puerto Ricans, like Gina and her family, were already here) and the Poles who'd made Logan Square their neighborhood weren't very friendly to us. The guys who owned the furniture store would routinely shoo us away whenever we lingered too long around their windows. The owners used to live above the store: We would see work shirts and underwear strung along clotheslines inside the apartments, little babies with food smeared on their faces who'd lean perilously out the windows, and sometimes a few skinny stems growing out of old soup cans set on the sill. But that was a long time ago.

As I wait for Caridad to open the door, I can't help but think that those old Poles are probably wishing there were more of us Latinos from back then still in the neighborhood. At least we always bought their feeble furniture—the vinyl dinette sets, the bureaus made of pressed wood, even the framed pictures of clowns. It was because of us that they were able to make enough money to move out of the upstairs apartments and into houses of their own in the suburbs.

Eventually, the Polish guys sold the building and the new people who live upstairs knocked down the walls between apartments. The new people don't buy furniture. They're mostly Anglo artists, long-haired and cool, who eat standing up and sleep on futons. Day or night, they have their lavish lights on. Through the windows you can see huge canvases with swashes of color and the flickering of computer and TV screens. Downstairs, the Polish guys wander aimlessly around the store during business hours, worried about their long-term store lease and their suburban mortgages. They've gotten so desperate they've even hired a Spanish-speaking salesperson—a Marielito named Chacho—in the hopes of luring us back to Polonia Furniture. I think our brood's one of the last of the original Latinos—not the new Hispanics who've moved in, driving German compact cars and recording English-only messages on their voice-mail. Anyway, we're buying mostly at Sears and Homemakers now, and I don't know what Polonia Furniture could offer to get us back.

"Hey, you coming in or what?" asks Caridad, standing at the door of her apartment and acting annoyed, as if she's doing me a favor by letting me in instead of me doing her one by coming over in the middle of the night.

I step inside where it's dark; Caridad won't look at me. She pulls her worn pink robe closer to her body, swats the hair dangling in her face and walks into the kitchen where there's a small light on. I follow but she doesn't pay any attention to me. She grabs the broom she left leaning against the kitchen table and carefully sweeps around a small pile of debris in the center of the floor. There's glass and coffee grounds and bits of food. Caridad keeps her head down, not letting me see her face, not because she's bruised there but because she's been crying, and she's ashamed, and she's not ready to talk about it just yet.

· · · · · · · · ·

Caridad met Jimmy at our family's laundromat. We all knew Jimmy—all of us who worked there—because he always came in by himself on Monday nights and did exactly one load of laundry. He didn't separate his clothes, just tossed them in all together and sat very quietly, not reading, not playing pinball, not really talking to anybody. He'd sit with his elbows propped on his thighs, fingers entangled together, foot tapping restlessly.

The vein in his head would vibrate, in and out, threatening an aneurysm at any moment.

When his wash was done, he'd take all his clothes in his hands—never a cart—and deposit them all together in a dryer, then go next door to the *bodega* and make a phone call. Nena thought he was dealing drugs, as did I, but my father volunteered that he thought Jimmy was just calling his mother—or a brother or girlfriend or something like that—to say the wash was almost done. My father was sympathetic even before they'd been introduced and wanted to believe Jimmy was the responsible type who would check in without making a fuss about it.

But the rest of us—Nena, Pauli, me, all the women who worked in the laundromat at that time—we knew Jimmy wasn't making a personal phone call. We believed he lived alone, because when the drying cycle ended, he'd carefully pluck out each piece of clothing—his hospital janitor uniform, T-shirts and jeans, Jockey underwear and long black socks—then carefully fold them into a neat little pile on one of the tables. There was never a bra or a blouse, a towel or a sheet of linen. We couldn't figure the guy out at all. Later, after Caridad started with him, we found out he was temporarily living with his sister Adelaida and her family, and that the phone call was just to check the Little Lotto winning number, which is always announced Mondays at six. Jimmy, like my father and practically every Cuban man I've ever known except my Tío Raúl, plays the lottery every week and dreams of winning—of being delivered from his life's drudgery with one magical combination.

Jimmy started coming in to the Wash-N-Dry when Nena was in charge, while she was still finishing her B.A. and before she had moved to Miami to work at that Spanish-language all-news radio station. Back then, she was always trying to think up new things for us to do at the laundromat, new ways to draw more customers and keep the business fresh. The pinball machines, of course, were very successful. But some of her other ideas were real flops.

There was, for example, the time she got some flyers about

the laundromat translated into Korean and put them up at a nearby Korean grocery. It turned out there was a mistake in the translation which said our machines would transform clothes into charred meat. It was a big joke: For months afterwards Korean people kept coming into the laundromat, peering uneasily into our Speed Queens and just cracking up. Nena would shoo them out with a broom, embarrassed and angry with herself. The rest of us would just try to stay out of her way, containing our laughter until we were well out of earshot.

Like the rest of us, Pauli, Caridad's younger sister, had to put in time at the laundromat too, but she didn't work out. It wasn't that she was lazy. To the contrary, we could always count on Pauli, who's all muscles (she was once a dancer at a club in Mexico City where they play *rock nacional*), to do the really hard work—refilling the Very Fine machine, scrubbing down the bathroom, re-stocking the supplies. She likes to keep busy and she was very strong, even then, so she really got quite a bit done. But the problem was that all her boyfriends would visit during her shift, causing fights and scandal. We had to have my mother or one of our aunts come in all the time, just to keep the boys at a distance. Tío Pepe and my father concluded that if somebody else in the family needed to be around to chaperon her anyway, then there was no benefit in having her work, so they fired her. That caused quite a sensation. Cubans don't fire family, but we fired Pauli. It was Nena, of course, who did it: Even though they made the decision, neither Tío Pepe nor my father could bring themselves to face Pauli, the family's most difficult child.

Of course, Caridad worked with us too. She loved it actually: The gossip from the neighborhood's always fresh, the pinball machines are fun, the radio's going all the time. Caridad loved playing with the little kids that mothers always bring in, flirting with all the guys and sitting around reading *Glamour* and *Vanidades* in her spare time. She wasn't especially good at money. Her register was always a little short but nobody would have ever accused her of stealing—besides, she always offered to make up the difference, which both Tío Pepe and my father, embarrassed, would decline, but which Nena would gladly accept. Caridad wasn't especially good at doing the drop-off laundry either—she'd forget to move the clothes from the washers to the dryers, or she'd take an eternity folding things. Customers would show up hours later to pick up their laundry only to discover it all in a pile on top of a washer, wet and wrinkled. Caridad would charm them, though: Nobody ever got mad enough to complain. She had such a sweet way that everybody loved her—even Nena—and we kept her on.

Caridad could have had that job forever but shortly after they married, Jimmy forced her to quit—even though that was just about when Nena and Pauli both left and the business needed Caridad most. For a while, she'd come down and do her laundry and just hang around, working informally, but that stopped when Jimmy, in a fit my Tío Pepe said was just to spite us, bought her a Maytag portable washer and dryer for the apartment. At first, I thought Tío Pepe was exaggerating, his alcoholism finally manifesting itself as paranoia, but when I saw the look on Jimmy's face as the Maytags were hauled up the stairs, I realized my uncle had read him right all along.

· · · · ● ● · · ·

When Jimmy first started coming in to the laundromat, Caridad didn't pay the slightest bit of attention to him. It was Nena who was obsessed with him. "See the way he just sits there, all tense like that?" she'd whisper to me as we watched Jimmy and his vein vibrating in front of a washer. "It's like he's a dealer or serial killer or something, you know?"

Nena'd shadow his every step and ask the neighbors about him (but nobody knew anything, which was strange because, in our neighborhood, if people don't know something about somebody they just make it up—except I think Jimmy's so scary nobody dared, just in case he found out). Nena even went through his clothes once while he was at the *bodega* making his Lotto call, desperate for any clue about who he was or why he always seemed so tense, but all we got was his name from the patch on his hospital janitor uniform.

"I just don't like him in here," she said. "He's creepy. He seems dangerous. I'm trying to run a family laundromat."

Of course, Tío Pepe agreed that Jimmy was spooky but even he didn't think that was grounds for tossing him from the premises, which is what Nena wanted to do. "So he's a *comemierda*—you can see that, the way he sits there thinking he's so important," Tío Pepe would say. "But he's paying. And he doesn't bother anybody."

"What are you talking about?" Nena would protest. "He scares people. He looks like he's going to blow up any minute. You're just afraid of him, that's all."

"Oh yeah? Oh yeah?" Tío Pepe would yell. Then he'd get huffy and walk out of the laundromat, offended—a perfect excuse to avoid the question of Jimmy and go get drunk somewhere.

Mami, Tía Zenaida and Tía Celia, Caridad and Pauli's mother, had another theory: They thought Nena was attracted to Jimmy and was bugged because he didn't seem to notice her. They'd laugh and tease Nena until she got so angry she'd threaten to fire them—which, given the combination of her steely temperament and Tío Pepe and my father's lack of spine, she'd have been able to do easily.

"Ah, c'mon, Nena, you sure you don't like him just a little bit?" Tía Zenaida would say. "He's awfully handsome, and mysterious too—like in a *telenovela*."

Mami and my aunts would laugh and laugh as Nena glared and stomped off to the back room where she'd immerse herself in tax forms and public relations textbooks. Out front, Jimmy would stare intently at the clothes whirling in the washer, oblivious to the havoc he was already causing in our family.

· ' ' · * · ' ' ·

My cousin Caridad is beautiful—that is important to say. She's more beautiful than her sister Pauli, more beautiful than

41

Patricia or me, and even more beautiful than Nena, which is hard for me to admit because Nena is my sister and a real stunner. Caridad doesn't have Nena's fine cheekbones or stature, Pauli's hard stomach, Patricia's elegance, or eyelashes as long or thick as mine, but here's what's all hers: the blackest eyes, skin like butter, lips as juicy as a slice of *mamey*, and the sexiest way about her of anybody I've ever met—which makes her choosing Jimmy as a husband all the more puzzling. She really could have had anybody in the neighborhood but, to everyone's dismay except my father's, she picked him.

Caridad took note of Jimmy because of Nena. The day it happened, she was busy hanging out, laughing with customers, reading a letter from Pauli who was then just vacationing in Mexico. Since everybody in the family seemed to think Nena had some bug about Jimmy, Caridad finally decided to check him out.

I was there when she did it. I was at a folding table, carefully creasing a pair of long cotton pants for Emilia Fernández, who always dropped off her clothes with us even though—especially after she was appointed the first Dominican on the school board—she could easily afford a more expensive laundry service, one that would pick up and deliver clothes to her door.

Caridad strolled over to Jimmy, his elbows nailed to his thighs, watching his clothes tossing around in the washer as if this were the most compelling thing he'd ever seen. She just looked at him for a moment, studying him, I think, and understood right away how ridiculous the situation was. In anybody else, this realization might have provoked laughter but not in Caridad—because what she saw as absurd was not Jimmy, but our making fun of him, our focusing on him as an object of fear and ridicule.

I watched from across the room, still folding Emilia Fernández's clean laundry (a beautiful black negligee, a pair of black tights, a lacy pink bra), as Caridad spoke to Jimmy and he answered, his eyes never leaving the washer, his vein quivering as his entire face flushed red. And I realized, watching as she leaned into the washer and partially obscured his view, that this was probably the first time any one of us had ever actually spoken to him. I watched as he twitched and twisted his fingers, looking at the floor, then finally up at Caridad. When they made eye contact—and I saw it, so nobody can tell me any stories about it—she was already enchanted by him and his nervousness, and he was practically on his knees, hypnotized by her.

Neither of them remember it quite this way. Caridad says he was flirting with her from the go, winking at her from across the laundromat, all cocky and sure. According to her, he made the first move by complimenting her on her skin when she walked by which, she says, "is a very different, very observant kind of compliment from a guy." He denies this, of course, insistent that it was her who was cruising him, walking back and forth in front of him and "showing off the merchandise."

All I know is that Caridad didn't work much the rest of her shift. She sat by Jimmy as the washer kicked into the rinse cycle, then into spin. I finished Emilia Fernández's laundry and started cleaning filters on the dryers, all the while watching them laugh, with Jimmy occasionally blushing, and Caridad twittering and tossing her head back. They were so hooked on each other that Jimmy's washer stopped and neither of them noticed. Later, when Jimmy went to make his call at the *bodega*, Caridad rushed over to me, as giggly as a teenager.

"I can't believe we've been so mean to him," she said.

"We haven't been mean to him," I said.

"Well, we've had mean thoughts," she said. "He's just lonely. He doesn't have any real family here, that's all. He's a little scared."

"And scary," I added. "I mean, Cari, he's kinda weird."

"Nah," she said, smiling. "He's like a lost little boy, like a little stray kitten."

Then Caridad told me—and, later, all of us—how Jimmy had been sent to the U.S. by himself on the Mariel boatlift, how he'd nearly died from dehydration and had to be hospitalized for weeks. Caridad said that as soon as he got better, the Catholic

Church helped place him with an American family in Indiana. They were kind to him but different from everything he'd ever known, and though Jimmy never felt that he was a part of their family, he got so Americanized without even realizing it that when his real sister showed up from Cuba years later and he came to live with her, he didn't know her, and didn't know how to be with her. He'd say "excuse me" all the time, preferred Folgers and eggs to Bustelo and toast for breakfast, and couldn't dance to save his life.

"See, he doesn't belong in either world, Cuban or American," Caridad said, shaking her head in pity, patting her heart with an open palm. "And his parents are still back in Cuba. *Me da tanta lastimá.*"

I didn't say anything after that because I knew then what had happened. Of all of us, Caridad's the one who always feels the most for the miserable people of the planet, *los infelizes*. She's the one who won't take the L downtown in the winter because she can't bear the sight of so many cold and homeless people. She's the one who sends fifteen dollars a month through Christian Charities to a Peruvian orphan who lives in the mountains (his name's Rafael and she writes him letters and has his picture in a place of prominence on her bureau). And what had happened was that Jimmy had tapped Caridad's strongest emotion—not love but sympathy. From that moment on, he could have anything he wanted, including her.

· · · **.** **·** · · ·

It's about one in the morning and Caridad and Jimmy's apartment is humming, like mine was when I got home earlier in the evening. After a minute or so of watching Caridad sweep, I take my place at the kitchen table and sit in silence. Caridad sweeps around the perfect pile, and me, then stops, sighs heavily and pulls a pack of cigarettes from her robe pocket. She extracts one, lights it on the stove, then leans against the kitchen sink. She takes one giant toke and lets out a slow cloud of blue and white smoke that obscures her face completely.

"Why do I put up with this, huh?" she asks, but she isn't talking to me. This is a conversation with herself, with the ghosts of all the previous fights she's had with Jimmy right here in the kitchen. "Why, huh? Why?" she asks again, this time covering her face with her hand. "I mean, I'm not stupid. Am I—am I stupid? No."

And, of course, I agree she's not stupid. And I say so, but it comes out in mumbles. What can I—of all people—possibly say to her? I cross my arms across my chest, momentarily touch my scarred breast, and remember Gina. Caridad just stands there, not quite crying, not quite angry anymore.

"You know what'll happen now? He'll show up and say he's sorry and that he'll never do it again, but that I made him do it and that if I stop, he'll stop," she blurts out. "And you know what? It'll work—I don't know how, I don't know why—but I'll feel sorry for him and I'll promise I won't provoke him anymore. And then, for about a week, he'll treat me like a queen, give me everything I want. And he'll tell me he can't live without me and that I'm the only person he loves, and the only person in his life—"

"I know, Cari, I know," I say, annoyed, my hand in the air. "Please stop." I've heard all this before but repetition never dulls my discomfort. (I need to talk to Gina, I know.)

"But this is the problem," she says, smoking and pacing now, her face all serious. "Because I'll forgive him, and then I'll forget it happened, and I'll start seeing him in a good light again, and as soon as that happens—bam!—he'll do it again." She hits her fist in the air to make her point. "What the fuck is my problem, huh, Juani?"

And I think, Maybe it's genetic, this ability to see only certain things. Tía Celia, Caridad's mother, managed to never notice how often Tío Pepe cheated on her, or the frequency of his binges or, sometimes, even that he'd disappeared. Once, my father actually suggested Tía Celia file a missing persons report because Tío Pepe had been gone ten days, a record then. But Tía Celia got offended, so much so that she didn't talk to my father for a month. Tío Pepe eventually showed up, unshaven, stinky, and fast asleep on the living room couch. How he got back there, where he'd been—nobody ever knew. Tía Celia never mentioned it; she made breakfast for him as if it were just another day.

Amazingly, the all-time denial queen in Caridad's family isn't her mother, but her maternal grandmother, Nivia. Patricia once told me that, back in Cuba, Nivia's husband Felipe was notorious for womanizing. Felipe didn't drink like Tío Pepe but they both shared a penchant for mistresses, quite an accomplishment on Felipe's part because Gibara, where they lived, was a little spit of a town. In other words, everybody knew; it was impossible not to.

According to Patricia, who heard it during one of her canecutting trips to Cuba and then secretly confirmed it with Tío Pepe, the story goes that Felipe met death while in the throes of passion with one of his mistresses. She called the police in hysterics, creating an incredible scene, and the town coroner took away the corpse. Although very embarrassed, the town authorities were forced to ask Nivia to come in and claim the body—the rest of the immediate family was already in exile and there was no one else to do it.

Unfortunately, Patricia told us, the coroner was a revolutionary from another part of the island and a stickler for rules. He told Nivia the circumstances of Felipe's death before letting her in to identify him. So when Nivia finally got her eyes on Felipe's cadaver—naked and waxy, something of ecstasy about his face, and his formidable member stiff and pale on his thigh—she didn't blink: She told the coroner there had been a mistake and that this was not her husband. Needless to say, the coroner was aghast. But Nivia's resolve was such that he felt he had to go along with her. In fact, everybody went along: the newspaper, the neighbors, even the mistress in whose arms Felipe had died.

Of course, this was not a simple lie; it caused tremendous headaches. Because Felipe was declared missing instead of dead, it took years for Nivia to collect on his pension, leaving her dependent on friends and relatives in exile for a long time. The mistress bore a child she named Lazaro (for obvious reasons) and didn't even bother to try to legitimize him. Felipe's body, left unidentified in the morgue, was eventually buried in an unmarked grave.

Later, Nivia began to claim that Felipe hadn't exactly disappeared, but had escaped from Cuba by boat, and that he was living in southwest Miami in a big house and trying to get the paperwork together to get her out of Cuba too. Once, Tía Celia suggested that, to please Nivia, who was still in Gibara, the family should pretend they had contact with Felipe in Miami, but Tío Pepe—who had supported Nivia for years until she got Felipe's pension and had since run out of patience with the whole matter—said that if he ever heard about such a scheme he'd give Tía Celia another disappearance to make up stories about.

· · · , · · · · ·

"Juani, are you even listening to me?" asks Caridad, now kneeling in front of me, her cigarette drowning in a glass on the table.

"Yeah, of course I'm listening," I lie, because it's true that I'd drifted off. I'd been thinking about Gina, about our last embrace, and about the pain in my chest. Everything ended so horribly between us, so shamefully. A glance outside the window tells me dawn is upon us, and I suddenly feel tired.

As I stroke Caridad's hair I listen to the hum of the apartment again: It's the machines—the refrigerator, the clock, the blinking VCR in the living room, the Maytags. The only sounds that break through the drone are from a couple of cats screaming, the female in heat and enraged. Caridad laughs.

"She's not having a good time," she says, meaning the cat.

"How do you know, huh?"

" 'Cause cat weenies have tiny little spikes that rake the female cat's vagina," she says. "Of course, by morning, she'll forget, she'll share her stupid tuna with him, whoever he might be."

And then she laughs again, bitterly, just like before.

· · · . • • · · ·

When Caridad opens her robe, we both see the greenish bruises on her shoulders and the bloody red spiders under her skin; there are purple blotches on her breasts, which are tender even to her own touch, and just below her neck. There's a huge scrape from her thigh up to her hip from when she raced too fast around the kitchen table and got cut on the corner. I cannot bear to look—I have my own fresh memories to run from.

Because the fight is over, because she's too tired to be angry anymore, Caridad's adrenaline is down now and just taking the robe off is an effort. I run a bath for her. The water splashes hard into the tub and steams up the mirror on the medicine cabinet. As the tub fills, I drop in chamomile tea bags which turn the water yellow and fill our nostrils with its familiar sweet smell. A few tea bags I merely dip in the water and hand back to Caridad, who sits naked on the edge of the tub. She holds the tea bags to her breasts and groans.

"Can I get cancer from this?" she asks, dropping her feet slowly into the nearly scalding water. She pulls them out quickly; they're red. "I mean, I know I ask every time but I'm getting worried, you know?" She's holding her breasts with a pair of tea bags in each hand.

"Well, do you have any lumps or anything?" I ask, unbuttoning my shirt and rolling up my sleeves because it's gotten so hot. My right arm feels heavy.

"You mean now or when I'm, you know, normal?" she asks, and tries to stick her feet in the water again. She grimaces but keeps them there this time.

"Ah...normal," I say.

"I don't know," she says, smiling ironically. "I haven't been normal in a while."

"You got lumps now?"

"Everything hurts now," she says. "I got ninety-eight wounds now, just like Jesus." She stands in the tub, holding herself up with a hand on the tile wall. "Or is it ninety-six wounds?"

"It's 'Ninety-six Tears'," I tell her, smiling. "Question Mark and the Mysterians."

"He was Mexican, you know," she says, lowering herself into the water.

"Chicano, actually," I say, "but trying to pass, don't you think?"

"Well, then, he wasn't Chicano," she says, laughing. "Chicanos, Juani, don't pass—they're *raza*—they're cool. Besides, he's so dark what's he going to pass for—Arab? Armenian? Puerto Rican? Big improvement, huh?"

We laugh. She's all the way in the water now, floating among all the tea bags. The purple blotches look like faces, spirits on her flesh. Her hair spills out from behind her head like ink from a squid. Caridad sucks in air, then forces her head under as well. It's only for a few seconds—only long enough to get all her hair and face wet—but I feel my stomach start to turn. I grab her hand and pull her out of the water. She jerks away, wiping her hair from her face.

We look at each other. Then, together, we start singing: *Too many teardrops/ for one heart to be cryin'.* I drum on the edge of the tub. *"You're going to cry/ ninety-six tears...."*

CHAPTER 5

THE NEXT MORNING, I'M AT THE LAUNDROMAT bright and early, making sure all the coin slots are operable and double-checking the machines that dispense single-wash detergent boxes when Emilia Fernández walks in, her hands empty.

"Juani, *mi negrita*," she says, all skittish, her eyes already telling me she's embarrassed about whatever she has to say.

I've always liked Emilia Fernández, in part because she has a soft round face that's so inviting, and in part because she's a lesbian, even though I know that isn't public information. Normally, I don't care for people who are in the closet, a subject that Gina and I debated intensely because she's always been somewhere on the threshold. Emilia Fernández, however, is an absolute exception to my rule: She's sweet and from a generation in which coming out meant much greater risks than what we deal with these days. I know from stories around the neighborhood that, even in her twenties, when she was pressured by her father (a mafioso precinct captain with the old Democratic machine who used to have an interest in jukeboxes), she never tried to pass by parading with a make-believe boyfriend or inventing elaborate lies about her life. Even though she's been named to the board of education, which is very high-profile, she talks in neutral pronouns (as much as Spanish allows), and, according to all the newspapers, pushes a fairly progressive agenda. In fact, every time something even vaguely gay comes up, such as family planning or AIDS policy, Emilia Fernández does the right thing, unlike the other gay member of the board, a swishy closeted white man who, in trying desperately to throw the scent off his own trail, consistently backs the most homophobic proposals the board ever comes up with. Once, he even considered a suggestion to pull HIV-positive kids out of the schools.

"*Ay, Juani,*" Emilia says with a sigh. I cringe. I can tell she's not here to give me good news. "Juani, Juani." She shakes her head but doesn't say anything other than my name. I try to pretend it's one of our regular mornings but it's difficult because she's just standing there repeating herself, empty-handed. This means I have no laundry to fold, so I dig out the Windex and some paper towels and begin wiping down the counters. As my arm stretches across the surface, I feel the weight of my breast, which is swollen today.

"*¿Qué pasa, Emilia?*" I ask, making an effort to smile.

"Well, you know how life is," she says, shaking her head, her ears glowing red. "*Es que...*"

Just as she starts to talk, I notice Jimmy hanging out by the laundromat door, glancing over his shoulder out to the street, then at Emilia, then at me. His hands are stiff at his sides; he's practically goose-stepping in and out of the laundromat. Every time he comes in, the temperature in the laundromat goes up a bit. Our eye contact's minimal, an infinitesimal measure of time, less than a second, but I feel suspended in mid-air by it, as if I were hanging by the thinnest thread above the most horrible, darkest hole.

"...So you see, Juani, although it really pains me, I'm going to have to stop," Emilia finishes saying. She looks at me expectantly but I don't have a clue what she's talking about. I'm still hanging over that hole, trying to defy gravity. "Do you understand?" she asks me.

"*Claro, claro,*" I assure her, but I know I'm unsteady. In the instant I focus back on Emilia Fernández, Jimmy disappears.

"It's no reflection on you or your family or my deep affection for all of you," Emilia Fernández continues, her voice relieved, almost excited. "But the new house does come with the Maytags—we didn't even order them, really, they just came with. Isn't that something?"

That's when I register the finality of her bare hands, and that there will be no laundry of hers to separate, no fine fabrics to admire, no lacy underwear to imagine her in. In that moment, I realize why Emilia Fernández, with her tender curves and velvet breasts, has been so important to me.

Emilia Fernández is annoyed. "Juani," she says, sighing again, "haven't you been listening? I just told you I'm moving into a new house with my friend Adriana and it comes with a new Maytag washer and dryer so I won't need to bring my laundry down here anymore."

I can't help but think, What is it about Maytags that has everybody buying them? Whatever happened to Kenmore, Whirlpool, or GE? Every time I hear about a Maytag, I picture Jimmy's face the day the delivery people hauled the machines up their stairs: He was just so sure of himself, a triumphant general watching his soldiers bringing in the spoils. Caridad stood numbly by his side. Jimmy put his arm proudly around her, but she didn't respond, just stared off into space like a mental patient.

I remember seeing that strange face on Caridad once before, when we were kids: She'd fallen through the ice at the lake and though the water was only about three feet deep, she couldn't move. The shock was such that, though there was nowhere to go, Cari began to sink, little pieces of ice like crystal around her shoulders and neck. I was standing right there the whole time, watching her descend, not moving. I watched her drop into that black and white hole in the lake, imagining the water seeping in slow motion through her clothes, piercing her with spears of brittle ice. In my mind, Cari splintered into a million pieces right there. It wasn't until the water touched her lips that I reached over and yanked her up, suddenly screaming and yelling and causing everybody to come help. Everyone in the family remembers me as a hero that day—including Caridad, who seems clueless about my actual behavior—but I know better: I'd watched, mesmerized, until she had almost disappeared and drowned.

"Juani, I'm sorry," Emilia Fernández says, waiting for me to respond.

She has little crow's feet around her eyes, but no lines at all on her pink, plump cheeks. I want to tell her—with real words, not just by implication—that I know what's really going on, that I'm happy for her, and that I couldn't possibly begrudge her doing her laundry at home with someone who will help her sort and fold and love her all the while. As I picture her and Adriana, my mind transforms the figures into Gina and me, impossibly happy, folding cotton undershirts and jeans. But because I know all too well the rules of my understanding with Emilia Fernández, what I say comes out quite different.

"A new house? That's wonderful, that's great, I'm sure you and Adriana will be very happy, with your own washer and dryer and everything. We will miss you here but, hey...life goes on."

But then, for the first time ever, Emilia Fernández falters. "Well, we're just roommates, just two friends," she says with an unexpected defensiveness. "I just thought it'd be better if I came down and told you myself that I wouldn't be coming by anymore rather than just have you notice and wonder if I was mad, or if you'd done something wrong—which you haven't, not at all."

I realize I've never seen her quite so nervous, so animated. She talks in a rush, her fingers pinching the air, eyes everywhere but on me. I quickly scan the laundromat to see if maybe Jimmy's back and that's what has set her off, but he's nowhere to be seen. I instantly wonder how much similarity there is between her response to me and what Gina might have said about us in a moment of doubt.

"*Felicidades*," I say, barely able to disguise my disgust. "I'll explain to my family." But I can't look at her anymore, and I turn away before she can open her mouth again.

When Emilia Fernández finally leaves, I ball up the paper towels I've been using to clean the counters and toss them into a trash can by the front door. My breast bops up and down and sends sparks all over my right side. I cup it immediately with my hand. A Mexican woman folding the last of her husband's shirts eyes me for an instant. I resent Emilia's denial of her lover. But more importantly, I'm upset because, in spite of everything, I know I'm going to miss her. I put the Windex away, grab a handful of quarters from the cash register and head for the Lethal Enforcer machine. I know I need a few rounds to feel okay again. I just hope it won't be too painful this time.

· · · ˎ · · · ··

"Let me make this perfectly clear, okay?" Jimmy's saying, standing as close to me as he can get without bumping me, poking the air in front of my face with his finger. We're like angry ball players, shaking bitter sweat off on each other, daring the umps to eject us. "Just stay the fuck away from my wife, understand? Just 'cause I said it was okay for her to come by a few times while you were down doesn't mean you can hang all over her again. I don't want you alone with her, get it?"

I want to ask the bastard what he's afraid of, but instead—and as usual—I say absolutely nothing. I stand there, awkward and useless, trying not to let him know how angry he's made me. His vein throbs like a pneumatic pump. Luckily, it's a very slow afternoon at the laundromat, so we can have our little family fight without the whole world as an audience. There's nobody here, not the Mexican woman who'd been folding her husband's shirts, not even the usual cluster of kids at the video games.

"Did you fucking hear me, you little dyke?" Jimmy asks, hissing between his teeth. Then he does it—he bumps me—except instead of using his stomach or chest the way ball players do, he uses his pelvis: He leans over, for a second practically standing on his toes. The lump in his pants reaches out to me, but I arch my body, and he misses. Then I push him back, hard.

"Leave me the fuck alone," I tell him. "And get out of my fucking business."

He falls back a bit, surprised, and bumps up against a counter. He smiles that smug smile of his, eyes all muddy. "Oh, right, Juani, like you're going to do what? Call the cops to throw me out? Like they'd believe you, right? Call your brother again? Is he gonna hit me for you, huh?" He grabs his dick through his pants, as if it's some kind of power tool. "Like I care," he says. "Besides," he adds, licking his lips in an exaggerated, disgusting way, "I'm your favorite guy in the whole world, remember?" He's laughing, wearing loose sweats and wagging his thing at me.

"If you want me to stay away from my cousin, Jimmy, then quit hitting her," I say, surprised at the steadiness of my own voice. I look him square in the eye, my jaw tight.

But Jimmy doesn't flinch, and his dick continues to bounce up and down. "*You* are telling *me* not to hit somebody? *You?*" Jimmy stands there, acting like Robert DeNiro in *Taxi Driver*, his face askew. "What happens between Caridad and me is between Caridad and me," he finally says. "And besides, she's not your cousin; you're not family. I'm the only one here who's *really* family, understand?"

"You're just her husband," I say, defiantly. "Husbands can be divorced, husbands come and go. I'm family, I run the laundromat—get it?"

"It's 'til-death-do-us-part with us, babe," he answers, his hand still around his dick. "And you're nothing. You're just decoration here anyway. You're all nothing. Who cares about this fuckin' laundromat, okay?" I know from the look on his face that he could just spit on us. "I've got my own job, I don't need you people, get it?" he says, letting go of his dick long enough to tap his finger on the place on his chest where his name tag would be if he had on his hospital janitor uniform. "You hear me?" he says, his hand immediately encircling his cock again. "Stay away from her, got it? If you don't...well, who knows what could happen if you don't, okay?"

"Will you cut that out?" I say, annoyed, looking straight at his crotch so he knows what I'm talking about. I'm as fascinated as ever with his brazenness, but this time, because we're in a public place, I'm not sure what might happen—and I'm disgusted with myself for being so hypnotized.

Jimmy laughs. "Oh, Juani, I think you're forgetting a few things," he says, running his tongue around his mouth again. "I mean, who the fuck do you think you are telling me how to deal with my wife, huh?"

"Eat shit," I say. I grab a pair of pants from a nearby pile of clothes and start folding.

"Oh, big time memory failure!" Jimmy laughs. "Don't you remember how much you owe your favorite cousin-in-law? I mean since you insist we're all family and everything."

I say nothing, trying to avert my eyes from him in general and from his dick in particular. His huge hand caresses it through his sweats.

"You jealous, Juani?" He asks and smoothes his pants with his fingers so I can see he's not wearing underwear and that his penis is swelling.

"Of what, huh? Of what?"

"Of this, babe, this," he says, his hand stroking his growing erection through the fabric. "Maybe things would have worked out with you and Gina if you could have given her one of these, huh?" He laughs and laughs.

"You fuckin' asshole," I say, turning away from him. I can see him in my peripheral vision, grinning, eyes blurred, leaning with his back to the counter. He holds out his pelvis so anybody can see the bulge in his sweats. He's just hooking his thumb under the waistband—the slimy slit of his cock is just peeking out—when the front door of the laundromat pops open, exploding with noisy traffic from outside. Then Caridad walks in, smiling, waving an airmail letter. Jimmy's eyes suddenly become shiny and he turns around fast, leaning his body across the counter. The way he's wrinkling his forehead, you can almost see football scores playing along it, a Herculean effort to soften the erection he's hiding under the counter. His vein, my heart, pound.

"Jimmy, *aquí*, another letter from your cousin Vicky in Cuba," Caridad says, oblivious to the tension clearly etched all over her husband's face. She's covered up nearly all her bruises from the night before but there's one still visible on her neck; the cuts on her hands are unavoidable. "You need to take care of this, you know," she says, smiling at him as if nothing is, or has ever been, wrong. "Hey," she says shyly to me, perhaps even a bit embarrassed, then turns back to Jimmy.

I'm embarrassed too, but unable to turn away: It's like watching a train wreck about to happen.

Jimmy takes the airmail envelope with an expert move of his arm, not lifting his body one centimeter from on top of the counter. I imagine his dick, still bobbing up and down, underneath. "I don't see what I gotta take care of," he says, his eyes hooded now. Sweat slowly emerges on his upper lip.

Caridad sighs. "Jimmy, she's family," she says.

She looks over at me for confirmation of what that means, as if I could, if called upon, enumerate the duties and obligations of that. I'm amazed: How can Caridad not know something's wrong?

"Juani, *negrita*, are you okay?" Caridad asks me.

I quickly glance at the round mirror above the door behind her, one of the four that allows us to have a quick overview of the entire laundromat. My reflection stares back: pale, my shoulders slumped.

"Your mouth is hanging open, stupid," Jimmy says with a laugh as his hand slaps up on my jaw. He turns around, leans on his side, his crotch calm and level. He's wholly unrepentant. I realize Jimmy, that sly train engineer, has just steered the locomotive away from disaster.

"*¿Qué te pasa?* Are you okay?" Caridad asks. She goes to touch me but catches herself, putting her arm stiffly behind her own back instead.

"I'm fine, I'm fine," I say. My mouth feels sticky.

Jimmy snaps his index finger at his cousin's letter. "She wants me to send her money and shit," he says, wiping his lip with his sleeve. "Like it's my responsibility to make sure she eats and gets her ass over here."

"Jimmy, you and your sister are her only relatives in the

U.S.," says Caridad. "How else is she gonna survive when things are so bad down there, huh?"

Jimmy arches his eyebrows. "It's not my concern," he says, stretching his arms above his head. He yawns. The envelope flaps in his hand. "I didn't see her give a fuck about me, write me letters to see how I was doing when I was in Indiana."

"Jimmy, you know she said she wrote—you know she said the letters probably got intercepted," Caridad chimes in. She's talking to him as if he were a little boy.

"Funny," he says, wrinkling his nose, "my mother's letters got through, my sister's letters got through. Just not my cousin Vicky's, whose kids are suddenly all out of school and jobless on that miserable island and it's sure nice to have *primo* Jimmy in the United States to send care packages and try to get visas for everybody."

Caridad crosses her arms across her chest. "See what I mean?" she says to me. "See how he's so American about some things?"

I keep thinking of her in the tub the night before; I realize I know the exact location of every single bruise on her body.

"I already got one charity case in this family with Rafael in Peru," he says, snickering. "I'm not going to start sending fifteen dollars a month to those *descara'os* in Cuba, okay?"

Caridad snatches the letter from his hand. "She's your *cousin*," she says, "your *blood cousin,* your *prima hermana.*"

I stare at them. Everything Caridad predicted the night before, everything she feared, is true: Jimmy has worked his magic, obliterating all trace of his prior terror and destruction. It doesn't matter now—again—that every move Caridad makes will cause dull pains all over her. She might as well be dead, animated only by the bolts of lightning that come from his eyes, Jimmy Frankenstein.

CHAPTER 6

MY COUSIN PAULI, Caridad's younger sister, never thought Jimmy was a potential serial killer, the way Nena had. Nor did she think he was a petty hustler, like I originally envisioned. Pauli didn't even think he was a *comemierda,* as Tío Pepe always described him. For Pauli, he was simply Jimmy Frankenstein (pronounced Fran-khen-ess-tein, since life in Mexico produced a sudden accent in Pauli's English), but her reference was not to the hapless monster, whom she regarded as an innocent, but to the scientist, the evil Victor who pieced together cadavers and animated them in his own earthly hell. As far as Pauli was concerned, Jimmy had found a way to kill Caridad and then bring her back in his own distorted image, compliant and anesthetized.

"You guys don't notice because you're around her all the time and change is so slow, so tiny, that it's hard to see," Pauli said when she arrived from Mexico for Caridad and Jimmy's wedding. She'd just started working at the Mexican rock club and the family was still in shock. "But I haven't seen her in almost eight months—I mean, I can really tell—and I'm telling you, that's a zombie, that's not my sister in there."

Pauli nodded in the direction of her parents' house, from which Patricia, Nena and I had just rescued her. After spending a chaotic afternoon with Caridad and her parents, all of whom were trying desperately to get her to quit her go-go dancing job and come home, Pauli wanted dinner somewhere "away from everything, *por favor*" with just the girl cousins.

"I'm telling you, man, something's wrong," she said climbing into Patricia's VW Rabbit (which Patricia and her American Jewish husband, Ira, insist was built by American workers in Philadelphia, not Germany). "That Jimmy Frankenstein has done something to my sister. He's drilled holes in her head, he's poured chemicals in her brain." Pauli and I were squeezed so miserably into the back of that VW that she refused to go home with us after dinner, opting to take a cab back to her parents' house instead.

Even Patricia, who prides herself on her ability to see the family from a measured and civilized distance (she's a political science professor at the University of Illinois who uses her mental health benefits for therapy twice a week), didn't exactly disagree with Pauli's assessment of Caridad. Although we might not have had the benefit of Pauli's distance, among the cousins we'd all commented on the changes in Caridad.

"I think it's a few things," Patricia said as she maneuvered the VW into a spot in front of the restaurant, a pizza parlor with thick-stuffed pies that Pauli adores and the rest of us hate. "One, I think, it's timing: after so many years—I mean, Caridad's thirty and, feminism and all that aside, the fact is she's still living at home and probably just got lazy—and, whether we're willing to admit it or not, Jimmy does love her. Two, there's something disgustingly Cuban about him, and I think, in a way, that appeals to her, like a primordial memory."

When she said this, we laughed aloud. The concept was typical Patricia: She always sees a connection to Cuba. "No, really, think about it," she insisted. She shut off the ignition and turned to face us. "Cari came to the U.S. when she was—what, seventeen?—right smack in the middle of her prime, as far as Cubans are concerned. Just as she was at the age to have formal relationships, she was dropped into the barrio, where everything was scary and she didn't know English, and the men were all potentially dangerous. Don't you remember how Tía Celia would always tell you guys not to get on CTA buses if it was only you and the driver because he could be a rapist?"

We all laughed again, perhaps even louder. Certainly, we had all been overprotected girls: Every one of us had had a chaperon on our first date, all of us had gone out in groups for years, and it was only recently that any of us had dated Americans (except Patricia, whose parents emigrated to the U.S.

before the revolution and always had different ideas about everything).

"Your father hates Jimmy," Nena told Pauli as we crawled out of Patricia's VW and headed for the pizza parlor.

"I know," Pauli said, smiling. It was a cool night in the city, with just enough moisture in the air to make everything shiny.

Nena and I looked at each other. Pauli seemed uncharacteristically smug.

"It's *really* killing him," she said. "The wedding's killing him more than I'm killing him, and that's the first time that's ever happened."

· · · · • • · · ·

All our lives, Pauli had been Tío Pepe's pearl and headache—something to marvel at, with her snappy wit and flexible limbs, but also something to fear in many ways. When she got mad, she didn't yell like the rest of us, just shut down cold; we used to call her the Fortress of Solitude. With her straight *A*'s and cool temper, Pauli was often unpredictable to us, especially to our parents.

Caridad, by contrast, was Tío Pepe's comfort. If Pauli annoyed him with the long line of tough admirers she always attracted and the troubles they caused, Caridad assuaged him by asking his opinion of the men in her life, seeking his advice for her problems and often having dinner out with him. We'd see Tío Pepe and Caridad out by themselves for a bite at Maria's Kitchen, Tío Pepe laughing and relaxed, proud and cocky. He'd raise his drink and wave through the window whenever any of us drove by and honked. Caridad didn't mind his drunkenness, and she seemed not to notice his infidelities.

Pauli, though, was a whole other ball game. There's a story the cousins tell among ourselves (except around Caridad) about Pauli when she was about twelve, just as she first realized her father was a philanderer. She and Tía Celia were out running a few errands when they saw Tío Pepe across the street, flirting shamelessly with another woman. ("A saucy, red-haired woman," Patricia always says when it's her turn to tell it.) Tía Celia didn't say anything, of course, just endured, biting her trembling lower lip and taking deep breaths all the way home. Pauli, though, understood everything: her mother's pain, her father's indiscretion, her own humiliation.

Later that same afternoon, Pauli tracked down Tío Pepe's mistress at the counter of the Busy Bee, an old Polish diner at the corner of North, Milwaukee and Damen. But instead of trying to appeal to the woman's better sentiments by explaining Tía Celia's dismay, or even her own anger, Pauli—never letting on that she was Tío Pepe's daughter, not just some street urchin— told the woman she'd been looking for him to no avail.

"Do you think you're gonna see him later?" Pauli asked her. She spun mischievously on a stool as she spoke, a small paper bag in her hand. "I've looked all over and I just can't find him." She gripped the bag with white knuckles, glancing at it now and then, underscoring its mystery and importance with every spin on the diner's stool.

"Who wants to know?" Tío Pepe's mistress asked while smacking her gum and clearing some dishes from the counter. (She was a saucy, red-haired woman, all right.) Amazingly, she took Pauli's bait hook, line and sinker: Every time the bag danced by the counter in Pauli's girlish hands, the woman would anxiously stare at it.

Pauli shrugged and sighed. "It's just that..." She hesitated, then looked around the smoky diner. In the corner, two uniformed cops were on break having some blood sausage soup. "I'm supposed to...no, never mind, I can't tell you," Pauli said, starting down off the stool. "I'm just gonna have to find him myself." She leaned on the counter, the bag teasingly floating above its surface for just an instant.

"What, honey, what?" the woman asked. She had huge breasts which sat on the counter like loaves of bread when she bent down to talk to Pauli.

"Well, he asked me to bring this to him and...no, I can't, he'll get mad at me," she said, shaking her head. As she stood up, Pauli put the paper bag on the counter to use both hands to zip up her sweat jacket.

"What's this, huh?" asked the woman, smacking her gum as she grabbed the bag.

"Hey, give it back!" Pauli exclaimed loud enough for the cops to look up. As if on cue, the mistress peeked inside where Pauli had placed a well-labeled tube of Pucho's herpes ointment. The woman's eyes widened in horror and her mouth opened, an audible gasp escaping from between her cherry-red lips. Pauli grabbed the bag from her. "I told you I can't say," she said, indignant. "He asked me to pick it up for him at the drugstore and if he finds out I let you see, I'm in big trouble. So don't go saying anything, okay? You understand?"

It was brilliant: Within a matter of hours, the saucy, red-haired woman confronted Tío Pepe with one sensational, screeching outburst that was heard for several blocks. People gathered across the street from the fight to watch as she threw her shoes at him. Above Polonia Furniture and all the other stores along Milwaukee Avenue, women and kids leaned out their windows to get a view of the scandal.

Although the incident didn't stop Tío Pepe's womanizing, it effectively ended that relationship—and it also forced him to be more discreet. No more flaunting his mistresses in the neighborhood, no more risking being seen by his family. If Pauli could think in such conspiratorial terms at twelve, it was hard to imagine what she might do as she got older.

· · · . · . · · ·

In American terms, Pauli refused to enable her father. In Cuban terms, she was an ingrate.

When she got home from school and Tío Pepe was dead drunk, sprawled on the floor of the living room, Pauli would walk around him. She'd make herself a pot of American coffee, watch the news or MTV, do her homework—whatever she needed to do—without acknowledging her father's body reeking of alcohol and sweat on the floor.

"I've tried to talk to him," she'd say, "and he won't listen. Well, fine. I can't do anything to help him, but I'm sure not going to contribute."

When Tía Celia got home from work, she'd find Tío Pepe in whatever position Pauli had left him. Sometimes he was balled up, cold or in pain; sometimes he'd spread himself out like a giant starfish. Tía Celia would help him up, direct him to the shower or the bed, make dinner and go on with her evening's routine. But for all the attention Tía Celia gave Tío Pepe, she'd be nearly as indifferent to Pauli as her daughter had been to her father. She and Pauli would pass each other in the hallway or kitchen, kiss hello and talk briefly about the day's events without a single mention of the bloated body on the bed or in the shower.

Caridad, however, couldn't take what she called Pauli's "coldness." For Caridad, the sin lay in Pauli's detachment, not her father's addiction. If Caridad beat Tía Celia home, Pauli was assured a lecture and a fight—a physical fight, in which they'd push and shove each other, scream like cats, and leave little moon-shaped cuts all over each other's wrists. All the while, Tío Pepe would continue to lie on the floor, sometimes drooling or moaning, waiting for Tía Celia to save him.

Although anxious and tired from the continuing conflict with Caridad over how to deal with their father, Pauli would try to hold up, to carry on her day at home as normally as possible. Pauli believes in routines, in small rituals. She carries a list of things to do, wears only black and gray and deep reds, and spends twenty minutes doing visualization exercises every night before she goes to bed. But for all Pauli's efforts, the fights with Caridad eventually wore her out. Instead of coming home after school, she began avoiding Caridad and going to the library or a friend's house; sometimes she'd just hang out at the park or at some of the neighborhood coffeehouses where the people who live above Polonia Furniture also pass the time. We'd see her through the coffeehouse windows, reading and writing, scratching things off her lists.

Of course, Pauli's wanderings in the neighborhood led to all kinds of trouble. First, there were the boys. Pauli may have attracted little nerds with pencils in their pockets, but we never noticed them. We were too busy with the wackos and the rowdy boys. Guys twice her age would get obsessed with her and call the house hundreds of times a day. Tía Celia had to change their phone number so many times we finally just got her a personal pager (she hated it, saying it made her feel like a drug dealer, but she endured it until Pauli moved to Mexico). Boys would hang out at the laundromat from opening to closing in the hope of catching a glimpse of her, playing pinball and video games so we wouldn't accuse them of loitering. (Nena, of course, thought this was great because Pauli made us money just by being her luminous, impossible self.)

Curiously, Pauli never gave a damn about any of these guys. Her idea of love and romance has always been particularly tragic. Put off by what she always saw as an imbalance in her parents' marriage, she made a promise to herself never to marry, never to have their kind of relationship. So instead of commitment, Pauli looks for impact: Back then, she had affairs only with what she calls "impossible" men (and a few women). These were not married or incorrigible lovers (because Pauli's not into hurting other women, or adding to anybody's reputation), but people for whom having sex with her was a transgression, a triumph of desire over all else. This meant Catholic priests, Orthodox Jews (especially Chassidics), Moslems, beautiful young boys, or men so old they thought yearning was a thing of the past. Once, Pauli spent six months with an octogenarian named Mike. When he finally slipped into a coma and died, she told us it had been her longest, most satisfying relationship. In the end, Mike left her about six thousand dollars— just about all the money he had—which is what she used to go to Mexico.

For Pauli, the whole point was memory. "I just know they'll never forget me, ever, no matter what else happens in their lives," she told me once about her lovers. "And that way, I'll always, always be special." Even then I thought, she doesn't need to do that: Who wouldn't always remember Pauli?

I know how resourceful she can be, but I still worried. Pauli was young when she started having sex—fourteen, the earliest of all of us—and she didn't always use birth control. She told us that kind of preparation took away from the spontaneity, the sacredness of those memorable moments.

Eventually, her after-school activities caused some trouble with the police. These were minor skirmishes—charges of loitering, disturbing the peace, nothing serious like drugs or assault—but the family as a whole felt great worry and shame. And even though Pauli held her head up, even though she asked for nothing and was possibly the best worker we ever had at the Wash-N-Dry, as she grew older the family developed an uneasiness about her. When Pauli brushed wordlessly by an intoxicated Tío Pepe at work, Mami would stare off after her and shake her head. "He *is* her father," she'd say. "That should be enough to get some respect, no?" Or Tía Zenaida: "What Pauli doesn't realize is her father's pain, or how hard he works. The girl takes it for granted that there's a roof over her head and food on the table every night."

But the cousins knew whatever Tío Pepe's grief, Pauli matched it with her own sullen soul. When she worked at the laundromat, I'd watch her sometimes as she lifted heavy boxes or hauled equipment from one place to another in complete silence: She seemed like a prisoner fulfilling a sentence. When Nena fired her—after two boys got in a fistfight over her which caused about a thousand dollars worth of damage to the Wash-N-Dry—Pauli looked her straight in the eye and nodded, saying nothing. We watched as she packed her backpack and walked out of the laundromat, wholly composed; how she strolled through the door out to Milwaukee Avenue, not once looking back at the lights bouncing off the shiny washers and dryers, not once looking back at us.

· · · · · · · · ·

Tío Pepe suffered plenty because of Pauli. He was visibly pained by her emotional distance, by her refusal to be around the family, by the trouble she was always getting herself into. He had a sense of her perverse sexuality too, and you could just see the torment in his eyes when Pauli, who seemed to give off light after each encounter, would wander back home. But nothing—*nothing*—caused him as much despair as Caridad's relationship with Jimmy.

It wasn't just that Caridad loved Jimmy and was giving him time that might have otherwise gone to Tío Pepe. In fact, Tío Pepe had hated Jimmy on sight, before Caridad had ever laid eyes on him, back when we thought he was a mere nuisance and someone Nena might have liked. "Who's the *comemierda?*"— those were Tío Pepe's first words about Jimmy, spoken as he came in to work one night when Jimmy was sorting his laundry.

It's not as though Jimmy didn't try to win over Tío Pepe and the rest of us. When he and Caridad were still dating, he'd come over, his black hair slicked back and smelling of violet water, never wearing jeans or gym shoes. He'd never curse, and always bring a bottle of wine or a six-pack of beer to bribe the men, especially Tío Pepe. Jimmy would be extraordinarily polite, using *usted* on everybody, even after we'd tell him to stop. He'd bring flowers for my Tía Celia and be quite respectful to all the cousins.

But in spite of all this, Tío Pepe never liked Jimmy. My mother said it was because Pepe knew his own kind, but she was wrong: Tío Pepe never hit anybody in his life.

And unlike Tío Pepe, Jimmy never drinks and he's never cheated on Caridad. Jimmy's actually rather proud of his fidelity; in fact he's turned it into a badge of honor. "If you're sure about your manhood," he tells the cousins, "you don't have to prove it all the time, you know?" Jimmy takes pride in his work as a janitor at the hospital, in his steady paycheck and small promotions. He loves that he can take care of Caridad, and he promised Tío Pepe that she'd never go without so long as he's around.

It didn't matter, though: Tío Pepe couldn't stand him. He'd call him names practically to his face. *"Ese tipo es un comemierda,"* he'd say, sometimes dragging out *cohhhhhhh-meh-mierrrrrrr-da* as if it were some rotten tripe he'd pulled out of a dead dog. Jimmy would wince and pretend he didn't hear.

Everybody laughed and said Tío Pepe just couldn't handle the idea of his little girl finally falling in love, but Caridad wasn't so little when she met Jimmy, and she'd certainly had other boyfriends before—even serious ones she almost married—and Tío Pepe had never just plain hated anybody the way he did Jimmy.

. . . .

The day of the wedding was especially disastrous. It had been planned as a small ceremony, just family and a few friends at Saint Ita's in Uptown, an old church with stained glass and a wondrous pre-Vatican II altar where all the Cubans in Chicago get married. As it happened, my Tío Raúl came in from New York—so the wedding became a community event. A photographer from *La Raza* snapped our famous uncle with Patricia in her bridesmaid dress nearly as often as he shot pictures of the groom (surprisingly handsome and happy) and bride (breathtakingly beautiful) for the paper's society pages. Tía Celia and Tía Zenaida jumped right into the frame, as did my mother and father, but Tío Pepe, who was curiously sober as the photographer shuttered away, refused to join them.

"Perhaps," I whispered to Pauli and Nena, "he's discovered secret Indian roots and believes, like they do, that cameras can steal your soul."

"That," said Pauli in her newly accented English, "presumes he *has* a soul."

"*Ay,* Pauli, please, don't talk like that," Nena said, giving Pauli's arm a squeeze. "It gives me the creeps, okay?" Pauli laughed and nodded as if in agreement.

In the meantime, Tío Pepe, ignoring all pleas that he get in the pictures for *La Raza,* paced in the church vestibule, smoked cigarettes on the church steps, and shot Jimmy menacing looks, all of which Jimmy ignored and Caridad didn't register.

Under normal circumstances, one of us would have tried to talk to Tío Pepe and figure out what he needed to play along but, frankly, we were too busy with the wedding itself. Pauli, resplendent in a white lace dress, was the smart-ass maid of honor. (It may have been the only time any of us had seen her in anything other than black, gray or deep red since she was a kid.) Nena, Jimmy's sister Adelaida and I were bridesmaids in matching outfits. Jimmy's American stepbrother, a lanky white boy from Indiana named Garth, was the best man. Since Jimmy didn't really have any close friends, there were no ushers other than Pucho and Manolito.

There were maybe three hundred guests, including a few of Jimmy's janitor colleagues from the hospital, Emilia Fernández, and Tomás Joaquín, one of our cousins from Cuba who got a visa just in time to attend. He's a skeletal fellow with a stringy mustache on whom everything appears awkward, but Pucho lent him a suit for the occasion in which he didn't look half-bad. A Fidel sympathizer, Tomás Joaquín insisted on pulling up his trouser leg to show off his bulging calf muscles to whomever he happened to be talking to at the time. This, he assured us, was one of the benefits of riding his bike during the "special period," the economic crash after the Soviet Union's subsidies to the island vanished and there was only a little fuel with which to run cars or public buses.

For Jimmy and Caridad's wedding, the church was covered with yellow roses (in honor of the Virgin of Charity, Cuba's patron saint). Mario Varona, a young fellow of Cuban and Puerto Rican heritage, was hired to play guitar and sing Cuban songs during the ceremony. My mother, however, was not pleased with Mario's hiring.

"Now every picture of the wedding is going to have a Negro in it," she said, rolling her eyes, as if Mario were actually black instead of *mulato,* or the only black person invited—and as if any of that mattered to anybody but her.

"Tía Xiomara, just think how white we'll look by comparison," Pauli told her, winking at us. My mother groaned.

As it turned out, my mother and Tío Pepe weren't the only ones who were miserable on Cari's wedding day. If it weren't for the publicity for the Wash-N-Dry my father was sure would be generated by the photos in *La Raza*, he probably wouldn't have cracked a smile all day either. He'd gone ahead to check how things were going at the church's banquet hall, where the reception was scheduled to take place, and discovered that the band hired for the occasion—a group called Mercy, put together by some of Pucho's friends—had made liberal use of duct tape to hold down its cables and cords. Papi had come back from the banquet hall pale and despairing, hoisting his pants up unnecessarily and mumbling at a little piece of duct tape stuck to his fingers.

"*Mira,* Juani, look at this," he said to me, his eyes watery, his lower lip flaccid, "what should have been our future. The gods, they mock us at every turn, no?"

He turned away, sobbing. I put my arm around him and told him not to think about it anymore. I tried to get Pauli's attention, hoping she'd tell him a funny story about life in Mexico or in some way get him out of his dark mood, but she was too busy flirting with the priest, a handsome, red-haired American named Father Sean who became utterly flustered in her presence and spoke a rather broken Spanish (learned while on a mission in Nicaragua during the Sandinista years, which we kept a secret from our parents, who would not have approved).

The night before, at the rehearsal dinner, Pauli and Father Sean (our parents all pronounced his name "Chong," as if it were Chinese) sat side by side. A dismayed Tomás Joaquín later told us they talked and laughed until almost two in the morning outside her parents' house (Tomás Joaquín, a *chivato,* as my mother would say, was staying over at their house for the wedding). Nobody heard what Pauli and Father Sean were saying during the rehearsal dinner, but we did notice that he kept blushing and covering his mouth with his palm. By the end of the night, Nena and I had bets on whether Father Sean and Pauli would beat Jimmy and Caridad to the nearest honeymoon suite.

· · · · · · · · · ·

I was still comforting Papi about the duct tape when Nena came in, totally agitated. "Has anybody seen Tío Pepe?" she asked. We all shook our heads. We were all sitting around an anteroom, waiting for the wedding ceremony to begin. "Look, it's only about ten minutes until we're supposed to start, and I can't find him anywhere," she said.

"Have you checked under the chalice?" Pauli asked sarcastically. Father Sean giggled inappropriately, then caught himself and began flipping through his prayer book and notes.

"Listen, we've gotta find Tío Pepe, wherever he might be," Nena said. Already Patricia was out the door, looking both ways, a woman on a mission. As Father Sean, Papi and I headed out in search for Tío Pepe, we noticed Pauli wasn't moving. I turned around, but it was almost as if she'd read my mind.

"I'll stay here," she said softly. "In case he comes back, so he doesn't find an empty room."

We searched everywhere: Pucho and Manolito scanned the congregation from the balcony; Nena and Patricia looked for Tío Pepe at a couple of bars on the same block as Saint Ita's; Papi and I checked out a nearby liquor store and a *bodega;* and Tío Raúl and Tía Zenaida, divorced but friendly, drove around the neighborhood in his rented car looking for our lost uncle. Not only was Tío Pepe not to be found, but everyone we asked claimed not to have seen him. Finally, with Caridad and Tía Celia growing more anxious by the minute, Jimmy starting to really look like Frankenstein, and the congregation whispering so loudly that it sounded like a swarm of bees had invaded Saint Ita's, Nena took over.

"Here's what we're going to do," she said, ordering Father Sean onto the altar and Caridad onto Papi's arm. "If Tío Pepe shows up, great, but right now our concern is going to be getting Cari married. Everybody got that?"

We all nodded as if we were trained dogs. Tío Raúl grabbed Tía Zenaida and a sobbing Tía Celia and led them up to the front of the church to signal the wedding was about to begin. Jimmy beamed; he couldn't have been happier to be rid of Tío Pepe. We lined up accordingly and, with the first few notes of the wedding march, proceeded. Jimmy and Garth, the bridesmaids and ushers, the ring boy (Jimmy's little nephew Fidelito) and the flower girl (his niece Yoli) filed out, and finally, Caridad, wondrous even through her worry about Tío Pepe and his whereabouts, led to the altar by my father, who held his pants up with one hand and rolled that little piece of duct tape between his fingers during the entire ceremony.

The service itself was simple but poignant. Father Sean, who kept looking up and smiling at Pauli as if there were already a secret between them, managed to get through the service in English and Spanish without major gaffes. At Caridad's request, he included a modest verse written by Rafael, the Peruvian orphan to whom Cari sends monthly checks through Christian Charities. To everyone's surprise, Father Sean also recited a little poem by Jimmy about how much he loved Caridad.

"*You are my home,*" Father Sean read, concluding Jimmy's piece.

As the words floated out, Jimmy looked intensely at Caridad, who, unable to withstand the force of his gaze, looked away. Nena and I were actually moved by the moment—Nena even got a little sniffily—until we looked over at Pauli, who was enjoying Father Sean's attention a little too much (her dress strap had actually fallen and she made no attempt whatsoever to fix the situation, standing there teasing him). They were so obvious, and so ridiculous.

Just then there was a commotion in the back of the church. We all turned, thinking perhaps Tío Pepe had reappeared. But though Caridad swears she saw his figure going back out the door, no one else saw a thing. Later, Tomás Joaquín said he'd gotten his trouser leg caught in one of the little hooks on the pews that hold the day's missal; he said the noise we all heard was his knee banging against the back of the bench. Apparently, he'd been trying to show his calf muscles off to another wedding guest. He had Pucho's torn pants to prove his embarrassing story, but Cari never forgave any of us anyway, especially Nena. She was convinced we all acted too soon, that Tío Pepe had in fact come back and that he cracked when he saw the ceremony under way without him.

As it turned out, Tío Pepe disappeared for three days after the wedding. During that time, Caridad called every day from her honeymoon in Miami Beach to see if he'd returned. She was crying each time; we all knew Jimmy couldn't have been very happy. When Tío Pepe finally re-appeared, he offered no explanations, as usual. But it was different this time. For one thing, he never spoke to Caridad or Jimmy again—not one single, solitary syllable. Caridad begged and pleaded, threw tantrums and hung off his arm, but Tío Pepe offered nothing. (As Patricia pointed out, we all suddenly understood where Pauli got her ability to turn into the Fortress of Solitude.) Eventually, Tío Pepe stopped speaking to Nena, Patricia and me, and then our parents and Tía Zenaida, and finally to Tía Celia. One day, she came home from the laundromat and found him in his pajamas, tucked into bed, a rosary tangled between his fingers. Ten months after the wedding, Tío Pepe was dead. Mami said it was his heart that broke.

It was just as well. When Pauli came up from Mexico for her father's funeral, she shocked everyone by bringing along her baby daughter, Rosa—a luscious little brown thing with no resemblance whatsoever to Father Sean. Of course, she refused to name the father. If Tío Pepe hadn't already been dead, the sight of Pauli bare breasted and nursing the fatherless baby at the funeral home would have certainly been enough to kill him.

CHAPTER 7

F OR EVERY CUBAN I'VE EVER MET in the U.S., there is at least one relative left on the island. This is the relative who sends coded messages in letters, who describes how long the lines are everywhere, and all the new ways of making *cafesitos* from used coffee grounds and crushed red beans. The stories they tell are always slightly incredulous, but those of us who are here have no choice but to believe them.

We have several relatives—mostly cousins—in Cuba, all with different relationships to the revolution. Some, such as Tomás Joaquín, are happy within it. A government bureaucrat, he considers every hardship a righteous struggle and rationalizes Fidel's every absurdity. No matter how difficult things are in Cuba, he will never leave, he will always live in Cuba.

Some cousins, like Titi, hate it there and are constantly trying to get out. Titi has applied for visas to the U.S., Mexico, Spain, even Israel (she claimed to be a *marrano,* a Catholicized Jew, and tried to sneak in through the Law of Return, but Israeli authorities saw the sham in her request pretty fast when she also claimed to be a descendant of the distinguished Bartolomé de Las Casas). She tried to get on a boat at Mariel in 1980 but fell off and the people already on it refused to turn around for her in spite of her cries. Once, she tried to pass as the great Mexican singer Lydia Mendoza and board a flight out of José Martí airport, but she was immediately caught when she didn't know any of Mendoza's songs (she also apparently didn't know that Mendoza, in spite of her youthful appearance on the album covers in her apartment, was about fifty years older than her). Last we heard, Titi had attempted to get out through Cojímar during the great summer exodus of '94, but everything she tried to use as a *balsa* (at different times: an inner tube, a bus roof, and a covered lounge chair) sank within a few feet of the rocky shore.

I know about Titi only through stories, most of them told by Tomás Joaquín, who travels fairly frequently to the U.S., and re-told by relatives. I've seen photographs. I've seen her crazy hair, her crazy eyes. I've seen the way she leans into a door-frame, wearing only a loose print housedress, and the despera-tion etched into her brave and weary face. I know just from the pictures—Titi at the beach grinning and straddling a raft, Titi with her arms around her friends at work, Titi smoking like Bogart and staring intently at the sea from the gray and crum-bling *malecón*—that Titi's a lesbian. There's no androgyny, no fashion statement, no political button or secret hand signal to give her away. There is nothing other than her particular mad-ness.

I know everything just by gazing at her; I know it in my heart, which reads and decodes her every gesture and look. More importantly, I also know that the damage in Titi's soul—and it's there, clear as the blue skies in every one of those pho-tographs—is connected to how she loves, or more precisely, how she's not allowed to love. Her face, with its thin lines and bloody red lips, is a map of a sealed island, surrounded not by water but by an invisible, electrified barbed wire.

I also know how dangerous all this is to say—how suggesting a correlation between being queer and being nuts throws out more than thirty years of civil rights and all the goodwill built up by Martina Navratilova's Wimbledon records and Pedro Zamora's MTV love affair.

Titi's problem is not, of course, that there aren't other queers in Cuba—there are, and always have been, plenty. It's not that there isn't a gay society within all the political sloga-neering and the official silences about homosexuality, because there is. There are long-term, happy couples all over Havana—many of whom live openly but wordlessly about their love. It's not that Titi hasn't had lovers, because between the lines of Tomás Joaquín's stories—in which Titi's "best friend" changes from time to time—I know from the shadings, omissions and insinuations, that she's been loved and has loved, powerfully

75

and jealously. But what none of the women who wrapped themselves around her body during those sticky nights could satisfy, what love could not erase, is what's evident only on my radar: My cousin Titi's need to be loved in daylight—to walk down the street arm in arm with her lover without the pretense of a mere friendship, to be utterly and ordinarily in love.

When I hear the stories about Titi—about her wild escape attempts, about the way she gets into deeper and deeper trouble because she can't keep quiet—I'm always fascinated by how the family has imbued Titi's persona with a great craving for a near mystical freedom and democracy. "She wants to be free," my mother exclaims, "who could blame her?" But free to do what? No one says.

What my relatives see in Titi's relentless unhappiness is the archetypal would-be exile, the heroism alive in her because of her great heart, and because of her insanity. "She says what she thinks," my mother tells us, "because she doesn't know any better, because communism has made her crazy."

What no one will say—not even Patricia, who can say almost anything at this point without shocking anyone in the family— is that Titi's addiction to the notion of escape, her desire to come to the U.S., has nothing whatsoever to do with any of that patriotic crap, but with a whole other, perhaps even crazier idea—that once here, she might be free to be queer.

I'm the only one—*the only one*—who knows it's that unquenchable romantic desire—and not Fidel, not communism, not shortages of rice or limited hours of electricity— which has her twisted.

. . . .

Even though I'm here, in what is supposed to be the land of the free, I share this desire with my cousin Titi. Every lover I've ever had has been closeted, has always instantly looked over her shoulder when we've kissed on a street corner or train station platform. This was especially, and most painfully, true of Gina.

It wasn't as if she pretended to be heterosexual. There were no boyfriends, no allusions to men, in anything she did. And she certainly determined that some places—mostly bars, some restaurants and parks on the north side of the city—were safe enough for her so we could hold hands, or so I could put my head on her lap while sitting on the beach on a sunny day, or so she could sit me on her knee and nuzzle my neck.

But Gina created a fog that got thicker the closer to home we were. Whenever she introduced me to anybody, she had no word for me, not *friend* or *lover*, just *Juani*. She'd greet me with a kiss, but always on the cheek, and squeeze my hand, then always let go. I tried hard to understand and to respect her boundaries, but they were so different from mine—and to make things worse, Gina refused to talk about any of this.

"It's nobody's business," she'd say. "Why should my life be an open book to complete strangers?"

"Yeah, but why deny your life in the process?" I'd ask, except that I'm not good at political discussions, and she always was, so I'd inevitably lose these arguments.

For money, Gina usually works as a strategist for community-based political candidates, not exactly what one would expect from a Puerto Rican *independentista* but she isn't like anybody else. That her socialist and communist buddies think elections are a farce, a pillar of the oppressive colonial system that keeps Puerto Rico enslaved, doesn't faze her. Gina contends that by working local campaigns she is in the belly of the beast, learning all of the enemy's tricks. When we argued, no matter the topic, I always felt her expertise.

"Look, I'm not interested in being a *lesbian*, in separating politically from my people," she'd say to me, her face hard and dark. "What are we talking about? Issues of *sexual identity*? While Puerto Rico is a colony? While Puerto Rican apologists are trying to ram statehood down our throats with legislative tricks and sleights of hand? You think I'm going to sit around and discuss sexual identity? Nah, Juani, you can do that—you can have that navel-gazing discussion."

And though she never quite said it, I felt the sting: I knew part of the reason why I was pinned with this topic as personally important was not because it was valid, but because I'm Cuban, and in Gina's eyes, automatically more privileged—as if my family had ever been privileged, as if we were doing anything except trying desperately to stay afloat.

Later, after the fight was long over, I'd come up with all the snappy answers: Lesbians weren't her people too? And all this about sexual identity—if it was that meaningless then why did it have to be such a big secret? Weren't a lot of these things inherently contradictory?

It's not like I'm an activist. It's not as though I'm out there carrying signs and smashing windows for gay rights, or any other cause, for that matter. For me, being out is a simple matter of convenience: I just don't have the patience, or maybe the brains, to lie, to dodge the truth, to try to make people think I'm something else. But for Gina, being a public lesbian somehow distracted from her *puertorriqueñismo*.

"That's so white, this whole business of *sexual identity*," she'd say, while practically undoing my pants. "But you Cubans, you think you're white…"

And was I going to argue? No, not at all, at least not then. At moments like that, when she was fiddling with my belt or running her hands up and down my thighs, I didn't care if we had wildly different views on the world because what I wanted was to be smashed against the wall, pinned by her fingers inside me. What I wanted was to taste her, to smell her, to rub her all over my body. I really didn't care if she was a raving communist or a self-hating queer. Nothing mattered, nothing except the urgent, slippery sweetness between us.

· · · . · . · · ·

Knowing what my family says about Titi, the way their words coast around the truth to project and protect their own fears, their own yearnings, I have often wondered what my name turns up when I'm not in the room. I know I'm the mystery child, the one born premature (just six and a half months in the womb), who should, by all rights, have had balsa bones, a heart of chalk. I'm not the proud success that Nena has become, or a genius like Patricia, but neither am I the trouble baby that is the sinewy Pauli, nor as helpless as Caridad. I'm something else entirely: my own island, with my own practical borders, seemingly ordinary on any map but, for all the burnt earth and barren mines, the least likely to be swallowed and disappeared by the waters.

What I mean is this: I am as marked by genetics and exile as everyone else, as comfortably a part of any family portrait as the others. But though nobody much notices, I'm also a stranger in my own family, whether my connection is by blood or experience. I run about ten degrees hotter than they do—not to a boiling point, but to a simmer. Unlike Nena, I don't fight to get my way. Unlike Patricia, I don't prosletize. Unlike Pauli, I don't shock. And unlike Caridad, there's a real weight about me.

What does my family want for me? My mother would say happiness, but she couldn't tell you what that means, not really. My father would say, "Whatever she wants"—because he has no idea whatsoever what that might be, and it would shock him to realize that. If asked, Nena and Pucho would look at each other nervously, dismayed by their own lack of knowledge.

Right now, I hold on to myself, sometimes literally. I hold on to my sides, my arms, my stubborn ankles, because in this house of nostalgia and fear, of time warps and trivia, I'm the only one I know about for sure. I keep my own space, a journal with the right dates, photographs with names and places written on the back.

My lesbianism is not the cause of my alienation, but it's part of it. My mother knows about me; we've talked about it. These are unsteady, clumsy conversations. Her basic reaction is Catholic: she is mystified but defers, both to her vague knowledge of the church's condemnation, and to the fact of my existence. I think in her heart of hearts she wonders, if this is supposed to be so morally disfiguring, why do I seem so clear and reliable? My mother meets my friends and lovers and cannot hide her confusion: She wants to dislike them but can't. Even Gina, the communist *independentista,* won her admiration, her love even, for the time that we were together. My mother wants to warn me about something, but she knows—and in a way, hates—that I might know the way better than she does. Embarrassment is part of our tension, and of our ever increasing silences.

My father knows too but we don't talk about it. This doesn't mean there are any pretenses between us. To the contrary: My father is as aware as anyone could ever be. He avoids not just the topic of my sexuality, but any subject that could inadvertently lead us there. My father's worst fear, I think, is that'll I'll say something to him about it. Because he can think of nothing worse than having to look me in the eye and make a decision about whether to accept or reject me, my father creates an illusion of normalcy about the emptiness of our interactions, our meaningless chats. If anyone at a family gathering or party starts in on when I'm going to find the right man and get married, I can always count on my father to rescue me with a quick comment about women's liberation, or there being no man alive good enough for his daughter. His motivation isn't to spare me discomfort but to save himself. Because he's afraid I won't lie, it's vital to him that I not be provoked into the truth.

In my family, this is always the most important thing.

· · · , · · · · ·

The very first time I was inside a woman, I was confused. I didn't recognize her, or myself. I didn't know what flesh was hers, what was mine. I thought I was swimming, but in air. Maybe flying, underwater. I opened my eyes in a flash, sure I was drowning.

The very first time I pulled my fingers out from inside a woman, I watched the tendrils of cum catch the light. They seemed as strong as spider's silk, as impossible as morning. I took the string of her wetness and laid its end on my nipple. We toppled, folding onto ourselves, smearing it all over us.

Her mouth touched mine. "Kissing," she said, "is a happy accident between two women who have already exhausted all words."

CHAPTER 8

I DIDN'T INVITE GINA TO CARIDAD and Jimmy's wedding because we were still too new for such a family occasion, but by the time Tío Pepe died, she was in my life to the point that the family would have been surprised, and disappointed, if she hadn't come to both the wake and the funeral.

I met Gina at a political meeting for an aldermanic candidate. Nena and I had become increasingly worried about gang activity in our neighborhood and we thought that, as businesspeople, somebody might actually pay attention to us during an election season. We were sick of cleaning graffiti off the walls in the alley behind the laundromat and we'd gotten freaked out over a shooting just outside Polonia Furniture one afternoon a few weeks before.

Gina, as it turned out, was running the campaign of one Rudy Canto, a former FALN sympathizer (in our neighborhood, nearly every Puerto Rican who runs for office has some kind of link to the FALN or some other Puerto Rican independence group) turned community activist, turned aldermanic candidate. Rudy was earnest and hardworking. Under Gina's tutelage he opened up a campaign office two years before the election, which ended up serving the community as a kind of default ward services office. It was brilliant in a lot of ways: Some people actually thought Rudy had already been elected and seemed to accord him a quasi-incumbent status. But there were drawbacks to it too—after all, he really *wasn't* in office and sometimes there was only so much he could do, so he inevitably let down a few people who sought out his help.

I noticed Gina the minute Nena and I walked into Rudy's office for the meeting. She's hard to miss: mid-thirties, brown like Nena, muscular like Pauli, eyes so dark the pupils disappear, eyebrows that meet in the middle like Frida Kahlo's, and the kind of style that lets her wear jeans with rips at the thighs and still look totally, and formally, in control. When Nena and I strolled into that community meeting and saw her for the first time, my knees turned to guava.

"Juani, *por dios,* don't be so obvious," Nena said to me, but she was laughing and pretty amused; I'm usually cooler than that.

We took seats up near the front to hear about Rudy Canto's plans to fight crime in the area. During the presentation, I tried hard to concentrate on what he was saying, but at the end of it all I couldn't have described a single proposal he made or any of the questions asked of him from the floor. I was just too busy trying to figure out how I was going to meet Gina, and what in heaven's name I would say if I actually finagled an introduction.

"My god," Nena laughed, "look at you! You're sweating! You're nervous!"

And, sure enough, I was a wreck. I couldn't concentrate. I felt inadequate. I worried about the clothes I was wearing and whether I needed a haircut. I wondered if my upper lip was glistening, the way Jimmy's does when he's stressed out, or if there were any veins visibly vibrating on my head.

I'd had lovers before Gina, of course. I'd had wild crushes and obsessive sexual trysts and I'd conquered and been conquered in a thousand ways. By the time I met Gina, I'd already enjoyed the sweet exhaustion that comes from satisfaction, and I'd endured the inevitable and tiny dramas of relationships that don't work out: the phone hang-ups, the nasty letters, the jealousies and indifference too. Up until I first saw Gina, I'd felt quite experienced, quite a woman of the world, even if that world revolved mostly around Milwaukee Avenue, the north side, and a few brief and ecstatic forays to Miami. But the thing that was missing from my life at that point was plain and simple, and what I wanted most: love, rapture, and surrender.

After Rudy Canto's little talk, Gina went up to the front of the room and gave her own speech. It was much briefer, and much more direct—she was simply firing up the troops and trying to draw out some volunteers to stuff envelopes for a campaign mailing—but she was so serious, so ardent and so in the moment, that Nena and I immediately looked at each other, registering the same thought at once.

"My god," Nena said as she leaned over to me, "why isn't she running instead?"

Yet, even then, I could come up with a few reasons right away. For one, Gina is an out and out communist. Although the fall of the Soviet Union and Eastern Europe threw communism into disrepute with most people, among some Latinos and Latin Americans it still seems to hold sway and it can still inspire or terrify. It's Fidel, of course, and the fact that he hangs on against all odds, which makes it possible for so many people to continue believing in it, one way or another. In neighborhood politics, though, Marxism scares the gentrifiers and local businesses, the families that just want their garbage picked up and the cops to answer their 911 calls on time. And here was Gina, using the word *proletariat* and practically giving a power salute. I didn't need Patricia's political science education to know that wouldn't have mass appeal on Milwaukee Avenue.

But there is something else altogether about Gina which makes her totally unelectable in our neighborhood. With those long, strong strides across the room, Gina withers most men. As a campaign manager, that can be described as tough, but if she were ever a candidate, sexism would dismiss that same confidence as just plain bitchiness. Besides, she clearly prefers women. I don't know how I knew but she registered that way immediately, just like my cousin Titi, clear as day on my personal radar. I also knew immediately that she's closeted, and that that would never bode well for a political candidacy. I really believe people can tell when you're lying or hiding something, even if they don't know what it is. The fact of the secret can hurt as much, sometimes more, than whatever the secret may be.

"Juani, raise your hand," Nena whispered to me. She poked me in the ribs with her elbow.

"Huh?"

Nena nodded in Gina's direction. "They're stuffing envelopes at her house for a mailing," she said. "*Raise your hand.*"

I was still deciphering what this meant, and taking in the fact that my sister was actually trying to set me up, when Gina walked right up to us, all business-like, and, without glancing up, began scribbling on her clipboard.

"Juani Casas," Nena said, volunteering me by pointing at me and nodding at Gina.

I started to raise my hand ever so meekly when Gina glanced up. "Don't worry," she said with a wink, "I already got you down."

· · · . * . · · ·

It was funny how it happened, how one minute Nena and I were concerned citizens up for grabs in the political game—a couple of loose Cuban-American votes that could have gone to Rudy Canto or any other candidate in our ward—and the next we were passionate partisans doing campaign work for Rudy. I really don't know how Nena justified it for herself (she got drafted into working the phone bank)—it seems pretty clear to me that the only reason I had for ringing Gina's bell that Sunday was that I was falling in love with her (although I really didn't understand that at the time).

That Sunday, those few seconds between pushing the button on the bell and hearing her on the speaker were an interminable hell. I'd misjudged the temperature and overdressed, with too many layers that now threatened to drown me. It was a lovely morning, about seventy degrees, with the birds chirping, squirrels rustling through the trees, and the vague sounds of a gospel choir from a big church a block or so away. I was wearing a sweater over a T-shirt, long black jeans, and boots. I could feel perspiration running from my arm pits down to my waist.

"Juani Casas," Gina said when she opened the door, wearing a smile as sure and warm as if we were old friends. "You're late," she said while leading me up the stairs to her apartment, but I could tell she wasn't mad.

"Am I *too* late?" I asked as we reached her door and were greeted by two other volunteers, both dressed in light summery prints and loose fabrics. I could tell by the spent, golden glow on their faces that they were leaving rather then arriving.

"We're working in shifts," Gina said, then turned to the others and hugged and kissed them good-bye. Suddenly, stuffing envelopes didn't seem like such a waste of time.

I looked around. Gina's apartment struck me as a museum dedicated to Puerto Rican independence and Latin American liberation movements. There were posters of Albizu Campos, maps of Puerto Rico, bookshelves stuffed with tracts by Oscar Lopéz Rivera and poetry by Amparo Maure, worn out records by Lucecita Benítez, Pablo Milanés and the whole *Nueva Canción/Nueva Trova* gang. Over her desk in the dining room, I noticed a picture of Harry Truman outlined in a bull's eye, a macabre allusion to the 1948 attempt on his life by Puerto Rican *independentistas,* martyred when most of them ended up spending the rest of their lives in jail.

There were, of course, lots of tributes to the Sandinistas in Nicaragua—a signed photograph of President Daniel Ortega as if he were a rock star, one of poet and minister Ernesto Cardenal (embracing the American singer Holly Near, the once and future lesbian). Posters commemorated celebrations of the fifth and tenth anniversaries of the Sandinista triumph, of debuts of revolutionary plays, of sports achievements. Nora Estorga, who allegedly slept with one of Anastasio Somoza's generals to get information for the Sandinistas then slit his throat, obviously held a special place of reverence for Gina, who placed votive candles under her image. Scattered on different walls were photos or drawings of César Chávez, Angela Davis, Frida Kahlo (lots and lots of Frida, actually), and Ché Guevara.

Eventually, I came upon the one hero I knew Gina's museum couldn't exist without: Fidel Castro. There was a collage featuring pictures of Fidel grinning, a cigar in his mouth clenched between strong, white teeth; Fidel with a pigeon or dove on his shoulder while giving a speech; Fidel surrounded by a bevy of bathing beauties, a photo taken, I later learned, by Gina Lollabrigida, the Italian actor, for her *World's Most Interesting Men* series. There was a framed photo, obviously cut out of a magazine, of a young Fidel wearing sneakers and chinning himself on the support beam of a *bohío* in the Cuban countryside. It's a silly photo: In it, Fidel is shirtless, you can see the roundness of his body, and that his tummy is soft and practically hairless.

"You're a fan of the young Fidel," I said to Gina, noticing there were no pictures of the latter-day Fidel, the gray-templed lion.

She smiled. "Well, I liked Fidel when he was a revolutionary," she said. "I don't like Fidel the dictator, Fidel the bureaucrat."

There was hope then, I remember thinking to myself. There was a possibility we could bridge the gap between us—not because I give a damn one way or another about Fidel, but because I know all too well how the world of politics, with its promises and deceptions, its absolute values and impersonal manifestos, can cut through the deepest love and leave lovers stranded.

· · · **·** **·** · · ·

Gina's apartment was excruciatingly hot. As we sat down to stuff envelopes and stick them with little pre-addressed labels, I felt sweat beading up on my brow. Without my asking, she opened a window in her kitchen, but it didn't much matter. There was no breeze. The heat was like a haze, it hovered around the kitchen table with its stacks of propaganda papers, blurred the revolutionaries on the walls, and made my mouth sticky. Gina offered me an ice cold Materva, which I accepted, but it didn't help. The bubbles floated into my nose, made me sneeze, and gave me only temporary relief from the temperature.

"I didn't realize it'd be this warm," I said, pulling my sweater over my head. I was standing there, in a black T-shirt with its sleeves rolled up, looking, I suspect, like something out of *West Side Story*. Gina smiled—I saw it—but not too much, for which I was glad. "I dressed all wrong," I said.

"Do you want to borrow a pair of shorts?" she asked, but she didn't wait for my answer. She shot up out of her seat, disappeared into her bedroom, and returned with a pair of gym trunks from Northeastern Illinois University, a school notorious for its radical Puerto Rican politics in the 1960s and seventies. "Try these," she said, holding them out to me.

I was a little taken aback with her efficiency. But more than that, I was really nervous. The fact is that Gina just stood there after I took the shorts from her, staring at me, not exactly showing me the way to the bathroom or bedroom or anywhere I might undress privately. Unsure about what to do, I bent down to pull my boots off. Then Gina made some sort of sound—a gasp, a click—I don't know.

"God, I'm sorry," she said, then flew out of the room.

I looked around the kitchen, boot in hand. Everything was cramped, lived in. Worn steel pots and pans with a Rorschach of old burns hung from hooks on the wall. The *cafetera* was practically black from use. There were potholders scattered about the counter tops, one dangled from a hook on the stove. And yet everything was clean, scrubbed. There wasn't a crumb to be found. Even the slit of space between the side of the stove and the wall was spotless.

"You ready?" Gina yelled from the other room.

"Ah, not quite," I yelled back, hurriedly dropping my other boot, pulling off my jeans and stepping into her shorts one leg at a time. They were a little big on me, but comfortable. I hadn't shaved my legs for months and I wondered if the curls on my ankles would turn her off. "Ready," I announced.

She came in, tried not to look too hard, and sat down to work while I folded my jeans. "You look good in those," she said, not looking.

"You think?" I said, standing back, pulling the legs out a little with my fingers. I was trying to give her permission to look, to make the moment as casual as possible. The truth is that I'm a little vain sometimes; I mean, I know I'm good-looking, and solid. "They're a little big, no?"

She glanced up but didn't make eye contact at all. "No, no, you look fine, just fine," she said, her hands continuing to slide papers into envelopes. She pressed the envelopes down on a wet sponge sitting in a small dish, then up, sealing them with a pair of pinched fingers. She tossed each of them into a plastic postal basket under the table.

"Yeah?" I asked, again, because I wanted more and didn't quite know how to go about getting it.

Gina stopped working, sat back in her chair and laughed. "You're something, aren't you?" she said, bringing her legs up on the chair and putting her arms around them.

"What do you mean?" I asked, but I was smiling back, posing with hands on hips.

"You're showing off," she said, laughing outright now. "So okay—yeah, you look great, okay? I see the muscles on your arms, I see the muscles on your calves, the cute little hairs on your legs—cool, all right? Now sit your ass down and stuff some envelopes. That's why you're here, remember?"

I dropped with a thud into the chair, my ears burning red, unable to look up. I immediately grabbed some papers, folded them and stuffed them into the nearest envelope.

Gina got up, casually, chuckling. "Juani Casas," she said, squeezing my shoulder. "You're adorable."

Then she bent down, kissed my cheek, turned around, opened the refrigerator and offered me another Materva as if nothing had transpired.

· · · . · · · · ·

This is how it actually happened: We were standing awkwardly by her front door, hours later, our hands smelling of ink and glue. I had my sweater folded over my arm, my boots on my feet. Gina was barefoot, yawning, her eyelids dropping. It was three in the afternoon and it felt like the whole world was taking a nap. We could hear an ice cream truck jiggle-jangling on the street.

I thought about apologizing for keeping her up, except that it was her who'd kept me here long after my so-called volunteer shift. We'd started talking about our lives, about growing up in Cuba and Puerto Rico, about our families, about women, about past lovers and first times and heartaches and everything in between. I'd had two Matervas and an interminable number of *cafesitos*. I was wired.

"Thanks," she said, sleepily, "for helping us out."

I nodded but didn't move, just stood there. I smiled at her.

"What?" she asked, smiling back.

"I don't know," I said, "you tell me 'what.' "

"Do you know why I wanted you to volunteer today?"

"Ah…because you needed another convert to stuff envelopes for the future alderman?" I was pretty cocky.

"Nope," she said, swaying from foot to foot, playing me now. Her whole expression turned lazy, teasing.

"No?"

"No. Guess," she ordered.

"Ah…to show off your altar to Nora Estorga?"

She laughed. "I asked you here because I was hoping you'd stay."

"I have, for hours," I pointed out.

"I meant, the night."

Just then, even though my sweater was dangling off my arm, I felt the heat again, like steam rising off the ground. Had I really heard her? Was my mind playing tricks? I re-wound the videotape in my head, played it over and over, all in a matter of seconds that seemed infinite and suspended.

"Well?" Gina said, but she was totally into her rhythm, her skin taut and moist and calling to me across the couple of feet of air between us.

"I'm not very good at this," I said, which was true. What I meant was that I'm not very good at finessing these moments. When it comes time for the kiss, or the touch, or the sigh, I inevitably stick my elbow in the other person's ribs, or bite her lip by mistake, or step on her foot when I try to stride up to her. I was sweating again, my T-shirt glued to my back, my jeans like heavy canvas against my skin.

"Well, let's try this," she said, pressing her body against mine and pulling me toward her, her hands spread across my back like mighty wings. Her lips were top milk, and perfect, and my own arms went around her, suddenly expert.

· · · · . · · · · ·

When I woke up later that night, I didn't want to open my eyes. For an instant, I couldn't tell if I was dreaming or breathing in the dark. I was afraid if I lifted my lids, I'd look out to the old, familiar view of my apartment, with its toppling bookcases and artless walls. And then, when I realized I recognized the steady heartbeat behind me, the tender flesh that spooned the length of my body, I shut them even harder, wanting the moment to last forever, afraid that I'd break down and just cry.

CHAPTER 9

WHEN PAULI CAME BACK TO TOWN after Tío Pepe died, she stayed with Tía Celia. Then everything changed. Tía Celia, who had seemed so lost those few days between Tío Pepe's death and the funeral, suddenly came back to life. Mami and I commented on how worried we'd been—Tía Celia had a blank look about her without Tío Pepe, as if she could miss a step and fall down the stairs or forget to eat. But as soon as the burial was over, as soon as the funeral stickers were peeled off the car windows on the way back from the cemetery, Tía Celia emerged from her haze. She was not her old self—not the humiliated wife with infinite patience and blind loyalty—but a whole new person. At the reception after the funeral, we were all awed by her, tossing her hair and rolling her new granddaughter on her lap.

Although Cubans don't normally have people over after funerals, Father Sean had explained to our family that this was an American tradition that made some sense. At first it sounded too much like a party to us. Cubans prefer to hold an all-night prayer vigil and bury the body immediately. Mami was concerned that Tía Celia would think the kind of gathering Father Sean suggested might be offensive to Tío Pepe's memory. But Father Scan said, "It's a healing thing. It's not a celebration, but a reassurance." I thought it was a good idea, as did Patricia, who'd actually been to a few American funerals, so we decided to try it.

After the burial, after Tía Celia had tossed a handful of Cuban dirt on the casket (brought from the island by Tomás Joaquín for precisely this purpose) and the neat line of cars that had followed Tío Pepe to the cemetery had scattered all over the roads, we gathered at Tía Celia's house, where the windows and mirrors were all covered with black cloth. People from all over the neighborhood brought plates of black beans and rice, guacamole, *yuca con mojo,* freshly baked breads, baskets of fruits, flan and *tres leches,* and about a dozen other kinds of dessert. I realized most of us were Latino, awkwardly trying to perform an American custom, and didn't really have much sense of what to do. Luckily, Patricia played host to the crowds, directing people to Tía Celia, who sat on the couch as if on a throne. As folks came in, Nena would grab whatever food they'd brought and determine if it needed to go directly to the buffet table, to the kitchen for heating, or into the fridge.

"Do we play music?" asked my father anxiously. "Mozart or something like that, soft?"

"No, no music," said Ira, Patricia's husband. He's a tall, skinny fellow with frizzy hair. "I mean, I think no music..." He shrugged his shoulders and walked away.

Papi shook his head. "What kind of an American is he?" he asked, incredulously.

"He's Jewish, Tío Alberto," Patricia said, as if that meant anything in particular to my father.

While we greeted people and ripped tin foil off casseroles and pulled things in and out of the oven and the fridge, Tía Celia tried on her new role: savvy, delighted grandmother to Rosa, Pauli's plumb little baby. "Isn't she beautiful?" she'd ask of everyone who came to her with condolences. "Yes, yes, of course," they'd say, confused because they'd been expecting a shattered widow and were instead being greeted by this glowing woman. When Rosa grabbed her hair—coils of braids expertly placed on her head—Tía Celia laughed, reached up and undid the pins, letting a cascade of dark brown and gray curls fall to her shoulders. "Isn't she gorgeous?" Tía Celia exclaimed yet again about her granddaughter, her eyes sparkling.

Later in the afternoon, when the men's ties had loosened and piles of used paper plates mounted on the buffet table, Tía Celia got up from the couch where she'd been receiving guests and went from mirror to mirror, window to window, quietly removing the black cloths and letting in the light. All the while, Rosa nestled sleepily on her shoulder.

Although no one would admit it, Tío Pepe's passing seemed to free Tía Celia. She foundered a bit at first. For instance, she said she wanted to re-decorate the house but didn't know how, then felt guilty and worried that people might think she was trying to erase Tío Pepe from her life. Eventually, she bought new curtains and painted the bedroom an off-white that showed off the new pictures of Rosa on the wall and on her bureau. Tía Celia hadn't had citrus fruits for more than thirty years because Tío Pepe was horrifically allergic to them and now, without him to worry about, she gorged on oranges and pineapples, grapefruits and mangoes. When she served water at her house, lemon slices floated with the ice.

But what really seemed to animate Tía Celia was the presence of Pauli and her baby. The two of them gave Tía Celia things to do: cooking and laundry, shopping and cleaning, singing Rosa to sleep, sewing little jumpsuits for her to roll in around the house and the laundromat.

No one was surprised that Tía Celia took Rosa in as her grandchild. No one was surprised that, with Tío Pepe gone and Caridad married, a part of Tía Celia clearly relished having someone new to care for. That had always been her style, to press her loved ones, literally and metaphorically, against her ample bosom for protection and nourishment.

What no one expected was that Tía Celia would become Pauli's champion and Rosa's mentor. Suddenly, Tía Celia shone with pride about her daughter, the previously problematic child who had so often embarrassed her. Pauli's intellect—which no one had ever doubted—became a badge. Tía Celia talked about her as if she were a genius. Even Pauli was a bit embarrassed. And her crazy independence, her sexuality and vigor, all these became medals of honor. To hear Tía Celia, Pauli was a kind of new woman, a pioneer who did not need men or approval. And she was the first to defend Pauli's right to silence about the identity of Rosa's father.

"It took Pauli nine months to have this baby," Tía Celia would say in Pauli's defense. "The father? It took him nine minutes. Who cares who he is? Right now, he will only complicate our lives. Besides, it is Pauli's business, that is all."

Because of Pauli's stubbornness, it was impossible to tell just what new blood had been injected into the family. Rosa, with her round black eyes and lashes like arching spider legs, had the thickest, blackest and straightest hair. Mami thought Rosa's father was *un indio*, a Mexican or Guatemalan perhaps, with a heavy indigenous heritage, but Patricia and I thought Rosa had a whole other look about her, something even more ancient than Aztec or Mayan, something both serene and cruel that was new to us as a family. Nena was sure Rosa looked like a man she'd seen Pauli talk to once at a Middle Eastern restaurant but nobody else could remember him so we weren't sure if it meant anything.

When Pauli came home, I asked her about Rosa's father. She shrugged, telling me I'd probably seen him, but that she had no intention of telling me who he was. "It's not that I don't trust you, Juani, because you know I do," she explained. "It's just that I'm not ready to talk about it with anybody, and I'm afraid if I told you who it was, eventually the whole family would figure out you knew—you know how these things just get out sometimes—and then I would have put you in a terrible position, trying to figure out who you should be loyal to, them or me."

I wanted to tell her I was pretty sure I could withstand the pressure and, more importantly, that I had no conflict about my loyalties when it came to her, but the truth is that I wasn't certain what I'd do if Gina asked me. I could resist telling my parents without effort, but I knew withholding from Gina would be critical. How could I ask her anything then? How could I expect her to tell me things *en confianza*?

· · · . • . · · .

Curiously, Tía Celia's new embracing attitudes did not extend to Caridad. Or rather, they seemed to recast Caridad, especially in her marriage to Jimmy. Where once Tía Celia would shrug her shoulders about Caridad and Jimmy's tempestuous relationship, she now rolled her eyes and openly disapproved. It was as if she'd taken on Tío Pepe's disapproval, but where he had surrendered, she had a harder, more judgmental edge.

"Being loyal to your husband does not mean letting him hit you," she said to us one day at the laundromat.

Mami and I glanced at each other. Tía Celia's pronouncement seemed to come out of nowhere.

"You know what I'm talking about," she said. She stopped folding clothes. "Where does it say that a woman has to be a punching bag for her husband? I don't know where she got the idea that was all right."

"Well, Celia, I think Caridad and Jimmy have had their troubles but they're trying to work things out," Mami offered.

"How is that?" Tía Celia asked. "They're not going to counseling, they're not going to see the priest. They're not even talking about the problem, okay? They're just taking a break. I ask Cari about it and she tells me to mind my own business. I say, okay. But you'd think she'd understand what killed her father, you'd think she'd throw Jimmy out in the streets by now—if nothing else, to honor her father's memory."

"Celia, Celia," Mami said as she tried to hug her. "Cari has to live her own life, make her own decisions."

"Of course!" Tía Celia exclaimed, pushing Mami away from her. "But that is not what she is doing. She is living Jimmy's life, being his slave. He is really Jimmy Frankenstein, just like Pauli says." She grabbed a pair of pants from the folding table and began to crease them. "You know who's leading her own life? Pauli. I don't say I approve, but I admire. Everything she does is her decision, good or bad. How many of us can say that, huh?"

As Tía Celia talked, I looked around the Wash-N-Dry, with its immaculate whiteness and shiny features. For how much longer would this be my life? I loved running the business, making decisions, having the respect of my family. But in my heart, I could not see myself here, doing the books, refilling the Very Fine machine and picking out new video games, for too many more years. It'd get old, it'd become a trap I could never undo if I overstayed. The problem was, unlike Nena, who'd always wanted that PR career she was now off to in Miami, I had no clue what I could, or wanted, to do.

"Not many people are that independent, it's true," Mami said, "but I'm not sure, Celia. Pauli is happy about the baby, yes, but I don't know how happy she is about being here, about being back."

Tía Celia shook her head. "You don't understand," she said. "Pauli is a very different creature. She is doing exactly what she wants, all the time."

I pictured Pauli at Tío Pepe's funeral, pale and exhausted. Everyone had said it was because she was overwhelmed by grief, but I wondered if that could be true. Pauli had never been close to Tío Pepe—could barely even look at him, she disliked him so much. At the funeral, she cried and cried until her eyes became red-ringed and puffy. Could she really have been that traumatized by her father's death?

I remembered a few days ago, her thin frame bent over a stuffed garbage can in the alley behind her mother's house. She was trying to cram yet one more bag in it and the weight and force of her pushing finally caused the bag to break, spilling trash all over her feet. I was on my way to the Wash-N-Dry when I saw her, standing over the mess and shaking her head. When I ran over to help her, Pauli seemed embarrassed, frustrated.

"*Don't,*" she said without even looking at me. Her shoulder was half turned away as she bent over to pick up diapers and rotting food. I stopped in my tracks. "I can do this," she said. "Go back to work, okay?"

Ordinarily, I would have brushed aside her comments, rushed to my knees and picked up every last grain of rice for her, but this time, I stepped back. Pauli, her hair falling in her face, her lips trembling as she grabbed handfuls of garbage from the ground, looked doomed.

· · · **,** **·** **·** · · ·

While Mami and Tía Celia continued their discussion about Pauli and Caridad, I wandered up to Cari and Jimmy's apartment. It was time for a break anyway and I thought it might be good to check in with Cari. She'd been a mess in the weeks since her father's death, but in a totally different way than Pauli. After the funeral, Caridad had remained a zombie. She sat in front of the TV all day, staring aimlessly while the remote idled on the coffee table, untouched. Cari's only movements were to get a cigarette, light it and then sit back. Other than that, she just sat there, eyes wide open, her mouth slightly open, as if she were a corpse propped up for a macabre joke.

When I knocked on their door, Jimmy answered. He was wearing his hospital janitor uniform and his hair was wet from a shower. "Hey," he grunted, letting me in. His face was worried, wrinkles all over his forehead. "God, I don't know what to do." His voice cracked a little bit as he nodded in the direction of the living room.

I noticed Caridad's head bobbing above the couch like a target at a carnival. She was going for a cigarette. The room had a blue haze.

"I've tried everything, Juani, I'm not kidding. I'm so fucking worried, and I can't take any more time off work," Jimmy said, pacing in the vestibule.

"I can stay for a little while," I offered, hesitantly, knowing he wasn't fond of me being alone with Caridad, "but not for long. I mean, I've gotta get back to work."

"Nah, that's not so good," he said. "But I swear she's going to light the place on fire. All she does is sit there and smoke and smoke and smoke. And she doesn't care where the ashes land. She's burned holes all over the couch and the rug. I don't know what to do, man, it's just crazy."

"Maybe she needs a change of scenery," I suggested. "Maybe being here, with the family and everything, isn't so good."

Jimmy shook his head, smirked. "Don't get any ideas," he said, grinning malevolently. "If she goes anywhere, it'll be with me."

I ignored him. "Maybe she could go to Mexico with Pauli," I said. "Pauli's gotta go back and get her stuff if she's staying here, and maybe the trip would be good for Cari—you know, time with her sister to talk about their father and everything. It might be good for Pauli too, I think she's kind of fucked up about Tío Pepe's dying," I added.

"The only way Pauli's taking Caridad from here is if she leaves Rosa as ransom," Jimmy said, laughing now. "And you know she ain't gonna do that."

With that he spun into the living room, kissed Caridad on top of her head, said good-bye and pushed me out the door with him.

"Hey asshole, I didn't even get to say hello," I said as he pulled on my arm and tried to take me down the stairs with him.

"Missed your chance," he said, grinning, triumphant as usual.

CHAPTER 10

I N EVERY CUBAN FAMILY, there is also—no matter how much it may be denied—at least one person who at one time ardently supported Fidel Castro and the Cuban revolution. My Tío Raúl, Patricia and Manolito's father, was that person in our family. He fought alongside Fidel, or more precisely, drove with him to the Moncada attack.

Previously married to Zenaida, my mother's older sister, Tío Raúl was a struggling artist living in New York when he was approached at a fundraiser by Haydée Santamaría, one of the original rebels. Although he's never admitted he fell in love with her, we have always suspected it. Since he had no money to give, and his paintings were not yet yielding enough for anyone to guess what an investment they would later turn out to be, Raúl offered the beautiful Haydée the only thing he had—his body. Haydée didn't accept in the way Tío Raúl had hoped and signed him up to do battle alongside the *barbudos*. He would grow a beard too and fight, Tío Raúl announced after his recruitment, because that was all he could do. He returned to Cuba to plot Batista's demise, leaving Tía Zenaida in New York.

Curiously, Tío Raúl doesn't talk much about his time with Fidel. Most of the time, he says, it was so long ago, he just doesn't remember anymore. When he does tell stories about his years as a revolutionary, they are always comic and absurd, painted with a brush of youthful mischief and meant to be indulged that way. He is no doubt embarrassed by his part in the revolution. Because of that, he rarely even admits to strangers that he ever had anything to do with Fidel, even though, at one time, those tales were his greatest triumphs.

We've heard other, varying versions of the stories from Patricia, who for years and years shared the same revolutionary zeal her father once had, and from her brother, Manolito, who has never believed a word his father has said, preferring to see all his stories as products of a supreme and despicable artistic imagination.

Patricia, who has met Fidel on several occasions and, in spite of her current disillusionment, works feverishly to re-establish diplomatic relations between the U.S. and Cuba, originally saw her father as an idealistic but weak man who didn't really understand the process of change and revolution.

"He wanted everything to happen overnight," she'd say. "He was selfish and had no patience for others and their revolutionary development."

Back when Patricia was enamored of the revolution, she'd tell the stories as glorious adventures, exempting her father from the heroism, as if his presence there was some sort of accident. Nena said she thought Patricia, who wanted so much to be heroic, probably envied the fact that he had so effortlessly taken part in something so historically vital. But later, as Patricia's own disappointment with the revolution grew, and as her own patience began to dwindle, her take on Tío Raúl began to shift: Now an old man with a peppered beard and paintings in the Museum of Modern Art in New York, Tío Raúl has become sympathetic, sometimes even courageous in her eyes. He never reminds her of the times when she dismissed him because, I suspect, he's too grateful for their new, more serene relationship, especially now that he's an old man.

Manolito has another view: Tío Raúl was a *comemierda* during and after the revolution, before and after his art made him rich. Manolito, who works like a mule on a chain with his American father-in-law rehabbing and selling urban properties, hates Raúl's accent in English, his effete ways, and the dumb luck he has always had with everything, but especially with money.

Nena and I have talked about all this, trying to sift through it all. We like Tío Raúl a great deal but the truth is that we just don't know what to believe.

The story goes that when my Tío Raúl returned to Cuba to join the revolution, prostitutes on Virtue Street in Havana called out to him but he refused them all—not only was he broke, but he was saving himself for Haydée Santamaría. Short of Haydée, there was always Zenaida, who wasn't sure what she thought about Fidel and his cohorts, but was sure she didn't like the idea of her husband, the delicate artist, running around in the mountains with a loaded gun and risking parasites.

Unlike my father, whose greatest assets were his white skin and fancy surname, Tío Raúl was a plain joe, but my Tía Zenaida adored him anyway. He was skinny and doe-eyed, golden tanned and flat-footed. Tía Zenaida was plumb and pretty, with a spark in her eyes. When I look at the pictures of the two of them when they were young, they're always laughing and beaming at each other. I just know they were great friends once.

After they got married, Tío Raúl and Tía Zenaida moved to New York to start a new life. He was going to be an artist, although I don't know that Raúl ever thought of himself as museum material. He's pretty modest and probably only imagined that he'd do well enough to live comfortably. Zenaida was going to be his agent and secretary.

It didn't quite work out that way, though. Tío Raúl got himself a small studio but he also had to drive a cab and work as a dishwasher at a downtown hotel to keep up with all their living expenses. Tía Zenaida worked as a maid at another hotel and, with her faulty English, tried to sell Tío Raúl's canvasses to galleries that would never consider his bright, tropical colors as serious work.

For Tío Raúl, those experiences working side by side with American black people were good ones. He listened to new music, like gospel and bebop in Harlem, and heard horrible stories about segregation and lynchings in the South. Even though

New York wasn't officially segregated, Raúl learned about the invisible color line at the hotel's front door, gritted his teeth when landlords told him to his face they didn't rent to spiks, and quickly understood that it was his dark skin, not his lack of buying power, which prompted sales clerks at retail stores to follow him and Tía Zenaida around, relentlessly asking if they needed help. By the time Haydée Santamaría came along, Tío Raúl was pretty primed for a battle for justice.

Tía Zenaida reacted differently to their new life. At the hotels where she scrubbed bathrooms and changed soiled linen, she did everything possible to separate herself from the other cleaning women, most of whom were African-American. She ate lunch by herself, refusing to sit at a table with them for fear that she'd be perceived as black herself, and wouldn't accept rides from her co-workers and their husbands, even if they lived in the same little block in Brooklyn, because she didn't want to be seen getting out of a car with black people.

It was Patricia who told us about Caviancito, Tío Raúl's final inspiration to join the front lines of the revolution. Caviancito was a faith healer who had a radio show in Havana. He was eventually banned by Batista because, in his own way, he was riling things up a bit too much. It seems that by healing people with insomnia, blindness and paralysis, Caviancito was giving the populace just a tad too much hope. At one time, Caviancito was so popular he had his own TV show too: Devotees would place a glass of clear water on their TVs as an offering to the spirits.

Patricia says Tío Raúl saw Caviancito quite accidentally, sitting at a Havana diner having a *cafesito*, and that Caviancito told him the revolution would eventually win but that his riches would come from something else—in other words, that Raúl had no business leaving his wife to become a guerrilla. Tío Raúl was instantly offended, became even more radical, and ended up volunteering to drive one of the cars that would eventually attack the Moncada barracks and give Fidel the chance to declare that history would absolve him.

"It was my stupid ego," Tío Raúl says mournfully, "which made me go, and which started the Cuban revolution."

· · · . * · · ·

Back when he would still talk about his exploits, Tío Raúl always said that the attack on the Moncada was not your typical military assault. The rebels drove up to the Moncada in about twenty-some cars, hoping to surprise the one thousand or so sleeping soldiers in the early hours of the day. They figured that because the soldiers had been partying the night before at the big annual *carnaval* in Santiago, they—the rebels—had some advantages by being sober. They also thought that, once word got out about their successful assault, folks would rise up all over the island and Batista would simply step down.

"But it didn't happen that way," Raúl says. "For starters, about half the cars got lost in Santiago and never made it to the Moncada. The other thing is, I was very, very nervous, and when we got to the Moncada, I didn't brake right—this was not my car and I was unfamiliar with it—and I hit a curb by the barracks building. It made a sound—a thud, actually—and it freaked everybody out, particularly Fidel, who was driving one of the other cars, and who fell on his horn by accident, waking up the whole goddamn regiment."

The rest, of course, is well-known: The soldiers slaughtered many of Fidel's partisans, committing the kinds of atrocities that traumatize survivors for life.

"If I hadn't gone, I wouldn't have hit the curb and Fidel wouldn't have honked his horn, and the soldiers would have been taken by surprise—and there would have been no dead, not one person, because we had no intention of killing anybody, just taking over the barracks and the government—and there wouldn't have been a *cause celebre* and maybe, just maybe, the revolution wouldn't have been able to get off the ground in the same way and would have stayed just what it was at first—a beautiful dream, that's all," Tío Raúl moaned.

For Haydée Santamaría, the loss at the Moncada was immeasurable—both her brother and her lover were tortured in the aftermath by Batista's thugs and lost their lives. Tío Raúl swore that, no matter that the revolution eventually triumphed, she was never the same. For him, there was a clear, straight line between the Moncada and Haydée's suicide many years later. "Something went out of her," he said. "The light in her eyes became more of a glaze, it blurred more than illuminated." For Tío Raúl, the need to avenge Haydée's pain and suffering became paramount.

Amazingly, Tío Raúl wasn't captured at the Moncada. Instead, he ran and ran and disappeared into the countryside with a handful of others, surviving by hiding in the cane fields, begging meals from sympathetic and often bemused *campesinos,* and just plain stealing when necessary.

There were times, Tío Raúl told us, when they couldn't move for days for fear of being caught by Batista's soldiers. He said they once spent about a week in a cane field, licking the dew off the stalks at dawn for fresh water, burrowing down at noon, lying flat on their stomachs to avoid the unbearable and relentless tropical sun. They couldn't take their boots off—even for a second—for fear they'd have to run and leave them behind, which was surely a death sentence in the fields, where cane stalks poked through the dirt like razor blades. All the while, they fed off the sugar cane, chewing and sucking, getting high from the rush of so much sweet stuff in their veins.

Patricia says that the heat and suffocation of the cane fields after the Moncada attack are the origins of Tío Raúl's artistic inspiration. She says that, once, delirious from the heat and humidity, his flat pancake-like feet trapped, swollen and blistering in his boots, Tío Raúl imagined his toes had been eaten by worms—had, in fact, turned to worms. He was sure he could see them crawling out between the laces, between the cracking leather and worn soles. He wanted to scream but nothing would come out of his mouth but air. And then, just as he was about to find his voice, a *compañero* silently threw himself on him, covered his mouth with his hand and held him there until the terror passed. Tío Raúl tasted the dirt on the man's hand, felt his breath like steam on his neck, and quietly cried.

Patricia says it was the wild hallucinations while crawling around in the dirt, engaged in hand-to-hand combat with the ghastly, imaginary worms, that prompted Tío Raúl to change his art from the sunny tropical vistas that Zenaida had been hawking to the dark, surrealistic impressionism that first hurled him to fame.

"That much sugar, that much sweat, caused him nightmares for years," Patricia says, always adding that these are not just stories—she has her own memories of her father, walking like a zombie at night through their house, afraid to fall asleep and have to relive the Moncada all over again.

· · · . · · · ·

I don't know the rest of the story too well. I have always been impressed by the bad driving that caused the revolution but I have no handle at all on the chronology of events from there, no matter how often I've heard the tales—first hand from Tío Raúl, second from Patricia, the ever-hostile Manolito, Tía Zenaida, and later, interpreted by my mother, my father and the rest of the relatives.

I know that Tío Raúl got to Costa Rica somehow and that, to raise money to meet Fidel in Mexico after he got out of prison, Tío Raúl wound up making *chancletas* out of old tires and selling them to tourists at the few beach resorts Costa Rica had then. I know that he also made hats from palm fronds, necklaces from seeds and sand pebbles, and *eleguás* from coconuts that he'd carve with his combat knife. He put all of his knowledge to work and let his art save him.

When Tío Raúl finally met up with Fidel again in Mexico two years later, he was more than ready to get in a boat with him and invade Cuba. It's not that he believed Fidel was so great but that he had a sense that his own mission wasn't completed—that he hadn't survived all that, in all those crazy ways, just to stop there. He had to avenge Haydée, contribute to the defeat of Batista (whom he now utterly despised), and prove, at least to himself, that his life had been spared for good reason. But, again, things didn't quite happen the way he planned. When Tío Raúl got to Mexico—prematurely gray, thinner than ever, his skin brown and hard like a macadamia nut—Fidel himself gave him the telegram which read: *Come home immediately. Zenaida in terrible accident. Only a few days left.* They didn't have a phone back in New York so a frantic Tío Raúl called all the neighbors to try to find out what had happened. They told him Zenaida had been hit by a car and was in the intensive care unit of a local hospital, although no one could quite remember the name of the hospital and everybody either misplaced the number or gave him the wrong one.

It was Haydée who, through a bunch of personal connections, got Tío Raúl a plane ticket back to New York to see his dying wife. A Mexican friend loaned him some oversized clean clothes and Tío Raúl, bathed but not shaven, flew back to the U.S. in a state of panic. When he arrived at LaGuardia, he raced through customs because he didn't have any baggage, then flew out of the terminal to grab a cab—an expense anticipated by Haydée who'd made sure he was also given money for that purpose.

But as soon as he started running, Tío Raúl heard voices. They were shrieking female voices calling his name. Frightened, convinced that the whole experience of survival, and what now appeared to be the imminent loss of his wife, had rattled his senses, Tío Raúl ran even faster. He felt his big clothes flapping about him like a loose sail on a boat. People stared at him as if he were insane. He gasped for air and pushed his long, tired limbs faster and faster through the airport—until a huge hand gripped his shoulder and threw him to the ground like a stringless marionette.

When he looked up, scared and winded, my Abuela Olga was standing triumphantly above him. "Raúl Fonseca, *qué carajo* do you think you're doing?" she asked, hands on hips, a sardonic lift of the eyebrows punctuating her words. "Running away, eh?"

"Olga," Tío Raúl said, getting up and dusting off his clothes, "I am so worried."

He tried to hug my grandmother but she pushed him away, still disgusted by what she perceived as an attempt to escape. "That beard—what a disgrace," my grandmother said to him.

He ignored her. "I came right away. How is Zenaida?"

Abuela Olga laughed right in his face. "She's fine," she said, "look for yourself." Then she pointed with her finger down the terminal where they'd just run from and there, among the bobbing sea of travelers, Tío Raúl spied his plumb young wife and my mother, who was just a kid then, waddling toward them.

"But...but..."

"She just wanted you to come home," Abuela told him. "She knew this was the only way. Forgive her, Raúl, and she'll forgive you too."

But Tío Raúl couldn't. Even after he found out that the whole scheme had been my grandmother's idea, he still couldn't forgive Tía Zenaida, whom he felt should have known better and without whose cooperation nothing could have happened. What killed him wasn't just that he was denied an active role in history, or his need for resolution, but that he was lied to, that he was manipulated in such an awful way.

"You were selfish," he told Tía Zenaida, who cried and cried and begged for forgiveness. "You played with my feelings, with my principles, just to satisfy yourself—and for what, eh?"

Abuela, who was *mulata*, told him over and over that they'd been trying to save his life. She explained that Fidel was no good—didn't he see all the Negroes he'd surrounded himself with?—and that the revolution would come to a bad end very soon, everybody knew that.

Tía Zenaida didn't want to argue politics but between Abuela Olga and Tío Raúl, she really had no choice. There was never a moment, a break in the awful screaming between them, to simply say she loved him and missed him and was worried sick about him. His inability to see any of her feelings, his complete focus on Fidel and Cuba, eventually pushed her to join sides with Abuela Olga. In the end, Tía Zenaida became so well primed in anti-Castro rhetoric that Tío Raúl refused to talk to her. Their relationship became a series of silences interrupted with short bursts of machine-gun-like hostility.

· · · . * . · · ·

In spite of the tensions with Tía Zenaida, Tío Raúl stayed in New York, reading the *Times* every day for articles by Herbert Matthews about Fidel and his rebels. He got another cab and a job delivering packages for an architectural firm, and continued to paint. He wanted desperately to be in Cuba, with Haydée, and Fidel and Ché Guevara, whom he had met briefly in Mexico and thought of as the coolest guy he'd ever known. But he felt utterly trapped—in part by Zenaida's fear of abandonment, and in part by his own guilt and shame. How could he ever explain to his guerrilla friends that his wife had lied in such a reckless way? How could he ever show his face to them—whom he considered to be so selfless? What would they think? He spent several years in a state of melancholia, nostalgic for his Cuba, lonely and alienated, boring every passenger he got in his cab with tales of his adventures with Fidel.

Eventually, Zenaida got pregnant and Patricia was born. Any thoughts Tío Raúl may have entertained about leaving evaporated. He was crazy about Patricia (Patricia Haydée, actually—the men in our family seem to like to name their daughters for past loves, consummated or not). She was a fat brown baby, which astounds us because Patricia is now a slender, middle-aged woman who could pass as a New England native.

In the meantime, Tío Raúl and Tía Zenaida continued their war, arguing day in and day out about Fidel and the revolution. He justified having left by claiming he was fighting for ideals and freedom—didn't Tía Zenaida have any ideals? She claimed he was a jerk who got his male ego challenged and went off to prove he was a real man—didn't he realize real men didn't need to prove anything? They argued over every Matthews article—Tío Raúl convinced, because they were published in the *New York Times,* that they had to be true. Tía Zenaida was just as sure that Matthews was an American fool taken for a ride by a gang of wily Cubans.

By the time Manolito was born, Tío Raúl was passing out revolutionary literature in his cab, giving speeches to help raise funds and support for the revolution. Tía Zenaida spent the last few days of her pregnancy laboring over a Spanish/English dictionary and writing letters to the editor of the *New York Times.* She may have been the first in the family—perhaps the first in the world—to publicly label Fidel a communist but the *Times* never published a single one of her missives.

According to Patricia, when the revolution triumphed, Tío Raúl rushed down to Havana just in time to climb on a tank for the victory celebration. There are pictures of him waving a black and red Twenty-Sixth of July flag, dancing arm in arm with other rebels. Because he'd just arrived from New York instead of the mountains, Tío Raúl is the only one with a decent haircut and a neatly trimmed beard. In one picture, you can see his uniform was recently ironed, with a perfect crease down his pants.

Zenaida, of course, stayed in New York, furious, monitoring it all on radio and in the *Times.* She feared that Raúl would move them back to Cuba now, when things were so tense and everything so unstable. As a safeguard to any crazy scheme of his, she packed Patricia and Manolito off to Miami with my grandmother, knowing he'd never move without them, and knowing too that she could buy some time this way to reason with him. Within weeks of the triumph of the revolution, there were already stories of firing squads and fraudulent trials on the island.

When Tío Raúl returned to New York, Patricia says her mother, who'd spent the night before getting a pep talk from Abuela Olga, was all pumped up for her confrontation with him. But when Tío Raúl finally showed up, his clothes tattered and his eyes a blur, she realized immediately something awful must have occurred because he had come back looking like a ghost. Shortly thereafter, he dropped all his Cuban organizations, stopped talking about his days with Fidel or wanting to return to Cuba, and, one day, quit arguing with Zenaida. At first, she couldn't tell he wasn't responding—she was so used to talking over him and then him talking over her, each voice booming over the other until they were both unintelligible. Then she asked him what was wrong. Tío Raúl shrugged his shoulders. "I don't know if you are right," he said, "but I was wrong. I hope not, but I think so."

Patricia, who'd come back to New York with her brother and our grandmother, remembers her father, sitting on the couch and watching the TV news. Her mother asked him to repeat what he'd said because she wasn't sure she'd heard right. "You might think she would have jumped for joy at that point, but she just stared at him, all flat and airless on the couch," she says. "He was dry-eyed, dry-mouthed. You could see the cracked skin on his lips."

Tío Raúl never explained what he was wrong about, never again said another word about his role in the revolution to anyone outside of the family. He cut back on his cab time and sealed himself up in the little studio where he splashed black and white paint on huge canvasses, creating nightmarish swirls. Tía Zenaida had long ago given up on selling his work—it was too ugly, she said, and besides, she was busy with Patricia and Manolito—and she was infuriated with Tío Raúl's absence from the family. She told him that Manolito had asked who his father was, and that Patricia wanted to know why he was always angry (back when she hated Tío Raúl, Patricia would confirm this but now that she's reconciled she claims to have no memory of it).

This went on for a few years. Tío Raúl working and painting, Tía Zenaida raising the kids and complaining. One day, Tío Raúl came home and announced he had a one-person show at a downtown gallery. Abuela Olga laughed in his face again. Tía Zenaida couldn't believe anybody actually liked his paintings, much less thought they could sell them. She worried that the show might hurt more than help—that nothing would sell, that people would make fun of him, that he would die of embarrassment.

Patricia remembers it all as bittersweet. It was a crisp October night. The gallery was a little place in SoHo, well lit and clean, with a huge window showing one of her father's blacker canvasses. She remembers arriving late and seeing a gaggle of men in suits standing outside the gallery, smoking and talking. The opening was almost over and as she, Manolito and her mother went to the door, a man walked out with a canvas all wrapped up in brown paper. They all stopped and watched as the man opened a car trunk and carefully placed the painting inside. Tío Raúl stepped out from the gallery and saw his family but he merely nodded in their direction. He went straight to the man, hugged him and shook his hand many times.

"Raúl Fonseca, it was my destiny to buy your art tonight," said the pot-bellied man, now lighting a huge Cuban cigar. "My uncle assures me that this is a great investment, that you will be one of the great artists of our exile."

Just then the door popped open again, revealing a couple. Between the two of them they balanced an even bigger canvas wrapped in brown paper. They stopped and Tío Raúl turned to them, shaking their hands and making bowing gestures in their direction.

"*Señor* Fonseca, we believe in you," the woman said.

"Her father has never been wrong, you know," the man said, nodding in his wife's direction. "He can foresee the future—and with this painting, so do we."

"You realize we cannot wait for the show to be over to have this piece in our home—it is too powerful!" said the woman.

Tía Zenaida couldn't believe what she was seeing, couldn't believe that Raúl had a patron who had so much faith in him that he had actually talked people into buying the work. She grabbed Raúl's arm.

"My god, how much did we make tonight?" she asked.

"*We?*" he asked, laughing. "*We* made about twenty thousand dollars." Tía Zenaida was sure he was kidding. "Twenty thousand dollars?"

"Yes," he said. "And you know from whom?"

Tío Raúl was laughing hysterically. Patricia says she was frightened when she saw this, that it reminded her of the way people laughed on television shows just before they were taken away by doctors or police. Tío Raúl was laughing so hard, tears were running down his face and he was choking in his effort to get the words out.

"You know who these people are?" he finally managed, wiping his face with a handkerchief plucked from his vest pocket. Tía Zenaida just stared at him. "They're Caviancito's relatives."

"Caviancito—that fortune-telling idiot who talked you into going to fight with Fidel?" Tía Zenaida asked, horrified.

"Well, no, he was trying to talk me *out* of it, remember?"

"Yes, and he did such a good job that you disappeared for years."

Tío Raúl cleared his throat. "Well, remember—the reason he thought I shouldn't go was because he thought I'd be a great artist someday—a rich artist. Well, he told all his friends and relatives about me, he told them that they should buy my work because it would be worth a lot someday. Can you believe that? The whole show sold out—everything!—his uncles and nieces and mistresses all bought my work. And they won't wait—they're just carting the canvases off the wall! The dealer's in a state of shock! Can you believe?"

Patricia said that if she'd heard the story from anybody else, she wouldn't have believed it. But she says she was there for all of it, that she saw the moment when Tío Raúl and Tía Zenaida put their arms around each other tightly, tighter than at any other time, and held each other in silence as they both cried. Patricia says she held Manolito's hand and tried to look away but couldn't. She says they knew it was probably the last time their parents would ever be together.

A year later, they were divorced. Tío Raúl stayed in New York making art and Tía Zenaida and the kids moved to Miami with Abuela Olga. Eventually, Patricia and Manolito left home for college, American-style. After Abuela Olga died, Tía Zenaida moved to Chicago to help us run the laundromat. Not that she needed to work. Tío Raúl made insane amounts of money with his paintings, and long after Patricia and Manolito were grown and out of the house, generous checks continued to arrive for her on a monthly basis.

Neither of them ever re-married. At family gatherings, such as Caridad's wedding, they sit together. Tío Raúl holds out Tía Zenaida's chair for her at the table. When they dance together, he holds her a little bit away but they always gaze at each other.

· · · . · · · ·

Gina always claimed to like the story of Tío Raúl and Tía Zenaida. When we first got together, she'd try to pry a morsel or two more from Tío Raúl or Tía Zenaida about the early days of the revolution, but she eventually gave up. My Tía Zenaida has forgiven Tío Raúl, but not Fidel. She's convinced without Fidel her life would have been very different, that perhaps she and Raúl would have stayed together. Without Fidel, Patricia might not have ever rebelled, and Manolito might have grown up less hostile and more secure about his father's love.

What Gina found was that, like my mother, Tía Zenaida's a master at the counterrevolutionary comeback, the rhetoric about Fidel as a tyrant and all things in Cuba since his arrival being awful. Every time Gina asked Tía Zenaida anything, what she got back was a barrage of anti-communist propaganda that usually left her speechless. On the few occasions when Gina had an opportunity to talk to Tío Raúl, he just shrugged and smiled at her, refusing to trip himself up with those memories again.

I worried then, and understand now, that Gina never quite got the moral of the story about Tío Raúl and Tía Zenaida. The way I see it, it really has nothing to do with Fidel or the revolution, who was right and who was wrong. Whatever his imperfections, whatever her intentions, the message of Tío Raúl and Tía Zenaida is that lies destroy everything, but especially love.

CHAPTER 11

N ATURALLY, GINA'S POLITICS mattered very much—
not just to Gina, but to me too. They determined
everything—what music we listened to, what food
we ate, what clubs we went to, even what clothes we wore. It's
not that I didn't have my own opinions about these things, but
I usually didn't feel as strongly as she did. And although I'm
not political, because it made life easier when we were together, I went along with most of her causes and decisions about
things.

For example, I know Hall & Oates' "Maneater" is just plain
misogynistic, but I can't help but feel like dancing whenever it
comes on the radio. Gina argued that that is precisely the problem—that "Maneater" is so damn effective and subversive
because it seduces with the music then pumps all these women-
hating thoughts through the lyrics into our brains without our
even realizing it.

I explained over and over that the first time I heard
"Maneater" I hardly even spoke English, so the words had no
effect on me whatsoever, and that what I'm responding to is
simply the beat and, perhaps, the memory of Caridad, always
the dancer, teaching Patricia how to move more soulfully. Gina
didn't buy it though; she insisted that language in and of itself is
irrelevant, that it's the message that's being drummed in that
matters, whether it's in Hebrew or Swahili or pig Latin.

Because of Gina's politics, I didn't listen to most rock 'n' roll
during our relationship, put away a lot of old salsa and male-
sung boleros (because they encouraged women to romanticize
instead of working on real relationships) and replaced them
with *Nueva Trova* and *Nueva Canción* (they're okay most of the
time), Lucecita Benítez, Haciendo Punto en Otro Son, and lots
of instrumental jazz, especially by African-Americans. I was just

grateful that Conjunto Céspedes passed her litmus test, and that it was somehow forgivable to listen to Celia Cruz (especially the early *santería* songs). I never asked why, quite frankly, for fear of giving Celia—a Cuban exile—too much analysis and having to take her off the list too.

During my time with Gina, I ate less red meat (I refused to give it up entirely, in spite of her health and political warnings, because it also meant I would eat less Cuban food, which I love and refuse to give up for anything or anyone, including her), no California grapes or lettuce (because of the boycotts), nothing with artificial sweeteners, and no mass-produced eggs. I ate a lot more soy (which I actually like), brown rice (which I think ruins every Cuban rice dish in *Cocina Al Minuto*), tortillas, *plátanos*, and oatmeal (a source of protein, she told me). Mercifully, I was spared *cabrito* except for special occasions, and I eventually developed a taste for *arroz y gandules*.

During that time, I only went to lesbian bars with mixed race clienteles, or on salsa nights, and only wore clothes made with natural fibers—although, whatever their fabric content, absolutely no clothes from Asia which could have been made with child labor.

Gina's politics also mattered to my parents. They didn't say much because the whole situation was so loaded for them, but they were both dismayed. In many ways, particularly for my mother, the concern was practical. Gina often visited prisoners at Menard who'd been involved in what Mami, and a lot of others, I suppose, would label as terrorist activities. Gina's friends were often arrested and sent to prison; at the very least, many of them had contentious relations with the police, who constantly harassed and provoked them. My mother worried about my association with Gina, whether the cops would start looking at me differently in the neighborhood, or that maybe it would affect the laundromat.

"You know," Mami would say, "not all Puerto Ricans have Gina's politics. Some of them are for statehood. A lot of them don't like Fidel."

"*Ay,* Mami, I know," I'd say.

"Not everybody's so...radical, okay?"

"Well, no, but obviously, not everybody's for statehood either," I'd say. "I mean, look at the referendums in Puerto Rico. They always come down for staying a commonwealth, right in the middle between statehood and independence."

My mother would shake her head. "I just don't think they know what they want," she'd say.

But I thought, Maybe they do—maybe they like not having to make a choice. Maybe no choice *is* their choice. Of course, I kept this notion to myself—my mother would have been confused by it, and Gina, I knew, would have been furious.

Like my mother, my father was also wary of Gina's activities but not so much because they were on opposite sides of most issues. Mostly, I think, his concern was less about losing any kind of argument with her than about having to take a stand—if she really pushed him, challenged him in any way, he might have to kick her out of his house or have a meaningful talk with me about the conflict. Naturally, these kinds of things terrify my father. He'd much rather tell stories about himself as a hero and bemoan his lost duct tape fortune.

I'd have thought my cousin Patricia, with her own past revolutionary fervor, would have bonded pretty fast with Gina. But, in fact, of all my relatives she was the one who clearly liked Gina least. It wasn't just competition (as Jimmy, who can't stand either of them, suggested) but that Patricia found Gina's politics confusing.

"She's like a combination Fidelista and lesbian separatist," Patricia would say with a laugh. "And the best part is she's not even out! What a hoot! I mean, all this ecological and feminist posturing has little to do with leftist ideology or Cuba. What does she think about the nuclear plant in Cienfuegos, huh?"

I didn't have an answer. It's not that I wasn't aware of the contradictions between her politics and her closet, the great irony of Gina spouting stuff that would have seemed more at home in a song by a separatist such as Alix Dobkin than in a treatise about Cuba or Puerto Rican liberation. It's just that, plain and simple, I loved her. I was crazy, head-over-heels wild about her. I would have accommodated everything, forgiven anything.

· · · . • . · · ·

It doesn't matter how much time goes by: Some of my memories about my time with Gina remain crystalline. For example, waking up in the mornings wrapped up with her. I remember when the alarm would go off, I'd press up against Gina's back, putting my arms around her so as to cup her breasts in my hands. I remember distinctly that her skin was soft, musky, and rare—I loved the smell of her, whether she was newly showered, still prying her eyes open in the morning, or wet from sweat after exercise.

Waking up with Gina meant I had slept well. It meant I had dreams and could wake up worthy of love, ready for anything. If I could smell Gina on my skin as I headed out the door to start my day, I was in glory. I never, ever, showered in the mornings when I slept with her, only at night, knowing that I'd absorb her, digest her overnight.

Crawling in bed with Gina, feeling her arms envelop me in that snug, warm vise, I felt as if nothing could ever hurt me. I remember the first time we were naked, all tied up like that just for sleeping, how I suddenly realized I had never known how exposed I'd been, how at risk and fragile. I wanted to be with Gina—in Gina, on Gina—all the time. I was sick with love, sick with yearning, up to my neck with it. To me, she was like the purest, blackest earth—that rich, sweet soil in which sugarcane grows. I always imagined her as hills in which I would roll around, happy and dirty, as if I were back in Cuba, or perhaps in Puerto Rico. When I was going through these reveries, I always forgot how sugarcane sucks the earth, makes it barren and dry, how it made my Tío Raúl rich but drove him insane first.

Not sleeping with Gina meant headaches, maybe leg cramps. It meant I'd probably stayed up until two or three in the morning, trying to knock myself out with meaningless TV or cheap novels. Sometimes, when I got insomnia because of Gina's absence, I'd play video games at the laundromat, make huge vats of soup that would last for weeks, or masturbate to sleazy heterosexual stories I found in *Penthouse Letters*. I remember every moment with her, and every anxious moment in between those.

When Gina and I were together, we'd dance merengue on weekends, grinding and twirling so that my knees would crack the next day. I'd be working at the laundromat, hear my bones pop as I bent down to pick up a piece of trash and get this feeling of immense satisfaction. My joints had never snapped like that before, had never felt so useful.

Before I met Gina, I was content. My family gave me a baseline love that let me know I mattered. My cousins provided an irresistible, joyful core to my life. I had friends in the neighborhood. But after I met Gina, I was delirious. I couldn't concentrate, I could barely keep food in my stomach. If she wasn't there to hold me—if I couldn't feel that she was real, and that *we* were real—I was a mess. After Gina, I could never remember my dreams; it was as if suddenly I didn't have dreams, or could only recall snatches of them, tiny scenes that would torment me all day long.

Of course, I could never tell Gina about any of this. I couldn't tell her about my love for her, about the way my veins felt like bursting from just being around her. It's not that she didn't reciprocate me in some way; I understood—from her breathing, from the way her whole body softened just at the sight of me, from the sheer relief I knew she found in my arms when we went to bed at night—that we were connected, that we were in this thing together.

Before Gina, I'd never wanted to tell anyone outside my family I loved them, and that leap was overwhelming for me. Whenever I thought about it, whenever I felt the words like a big fatty ball welling up in my throat, I'd choke. If I said them aloud, what would it mean?

"You gonna marry Gina?" Jimmy asked me one day. His voice dripped with mockery. He knew—in some ways better than anybody else—that I was upside down, shaking in my skin about Gina, and he loved to torture me with it.

"*Juani and Gina sitting in a tree,*" he singsonged while hanging out at the Wash-N-Dry.

I shot him a dirty look. "Shut the fuck up," I whispered between clenched teeth. Jimmy laughed and laughed. I hated the way he assumed he had anything on us.

I tried to be cool. It was important. She was the biggest reason for my silence about my love for her, she was my biggest ache. Because it didn't matter if we were regulars at Tania's or the Red Dog or Paris Dance, dancing until dawn with our pelvises up against each other; it didn't matter that we were together four, five nights a week, breathing heavily on my living room floor, Gina pulling on my hair and writhing across the rug; it didn't matter at all that our friends, and eventually my family, said our names together, Juani and Gina, as if it were one word—*juanigina*—because the bottom line was simple: Gina wasn't out, didn't have any plans to come out, and wasn't in a hurry to even consider it. For Gina, what we had was wonderful, but passing; thrilling, but temporary; an adventure, but only for memory's sake.

I thought a lot about Pauli back then, and about Mike, the old man who had died so happy to have enjoyed her for even a brief moment. But when I mentioned this to Patricia, she looked at me funny.

"Mike was in his eighties," she said. "Pauli was a reminder of something he didn't know he was still capable of—she wasn't the beginning, but an end. For god's sake, Juani, you're only twenty-four, you haven't lost anything yet."

CHAPTER 12

NENA HAD ALREADY MOVED TO MIAMI and Pauli and Rosa had gone back to Mexico to pick up their things when, one night, Gina told me she wasn't very happy with our relationship anymore. We'd been together for about a year then and I'd been looking forward to the beginning of our second, thinking that as we did the same things from one year to the next, we'd develop real routines, maybe even traditions.

In my heart of hearts I know I was afraid—I'd hoped she wouldn't notice the passage of time, that it would quietly consume us, and that once our passion passed, that she wouldn't be able to imagine anything else but what we had. I know I was counting on habit to seal our bond, that I was hoping she'd have as little imagination as me. But it was all I had to hold on to then.

What Gina said was that she was tired of coming over to my family's house and having to put up with my relatives, especially the men, making Puerto Rican jokes all the time, acting like Cubans were god's gift to the world. "You guys run a good laundromat but, you know, so what? It doesn't make you better than the homeless guy outside your door," she told me. She said we were racists and classists and that we only made fun of Puerto Ricans because most of them were darker and poorer than us.

Here's a joke Jimmy told once that really annoyed Gina: What's the difference between a Cuban and a Puerto Rican? A Cuban's a Puerto Rican *with a job*. When he told this one, everybody busted up, even Nena, who immediately looked down at the floor, totally embarrassed. Caridad tittered, unaware that there was much of anything wrong. I remember I was terrified that Gina would finally erupt. But she didn't. She just shook her head in disgust and walked out of the room. I've got to admit I chuckled too. I mean, it was incredibly stupid, but kind of funny. I tried to explain to Gina that it was all meant in fun, but she reminded me that I thought "Maneater" was just for dancing, so that proved where my consciousness was at. I told her it was just a Cuban cultural thing, a generational thing, a Jimmy thing, but none of my words had any weight.

It didn't help matters when, unexpectedly, Patricia took Gina's side by saying that she'd have dumped Ira long ago if he'd let his family treat her the way I let mine treat Gina.

"You assume everybody should adapt to your family's view," said Patricia one night on our way home from dinner just the two of us. "But just because you do doesn't mean everybody else should too. Gina puts up with a lot even before we get to the Puerto Rican jokes, which are idiotic and shouldn't be tolerated, Gina or no Gina."

"I can't change Mami or Papi, Jimmy or Pucho," I said in my own defense.

"No, but you can let them know you think that kind of thing is out of line," Patricia said as we climbed into her VW. "I mean, I do—you don't see them pulling that kind of crap around me."

I had to admit she had a point. Everybody knows Patricia won't tolerate certain racist or otherwise prejudiced behavior and so they do everything possible to avoid the inevitable confrontation if they falter in front of her. Patricia pretty much calls everybody on everything—which often means people think she's humorless and try to avoid her, but which also means she's spared a lot of grief.

I know, for example, that—back when Nena was in charge of the laundromat and Tío Pepe was still alive—whenever he got mad over Nena's strict business practices, he'd accuse her of being a Jew and trying to rip off his profits. But if Patricia was around, Tío Pepe found some other way to say the same thing. Because Patricia's married to Ira, Tío Pepe knew whatever he said would be taken personally—even if what he said was meant in jest, or if he went out of his way to say he wasn't talking about Ira. While he was willing to get down and dirty with Patricia about Fidel, he knew no one would back him if he was offensive to Patricia about Ira, whom everyone more or less liked.

I thought for a minute about Nena, how she shrugged these things off, not because she agreed or disagreed with any of them, but because she was so damn focused on her own escape. I don't think I can remember a time now when Nena wasn't planning her way out of the Wash-N-Dry, to Miami and away from the family. These things may have bothered her back then, but she didn't choose to argue about them. Most of the time, she seemed to just play along.

I thought about Pauli too, how she behaved a lot like Gina, just walking away when the talk got ugly. I knew that ability to detach was part of why we called her the Fortress of Solitude, and why our parents often found her so distant and cold. If we didn't always know Nena's feelings about this kind of thing, Pauli was obvious—and disdainful. We resented it, so we rejected her, little by little.

I didn't have an escape, and I didn't want to be rejected.

"Think about it," Patricia said as she pulled the VW out on the street and headed home. "Don't you think you give people license to disrespect Gina by not saying anything?"

"But Patricia, c'mon," I protested. "What am I gonna say all of a sudden? 'Oh, please, don't offend my girlfriend'? I mean, it's not like anybody's that comfortable with the situation as it is."

There was a cab behind us almost immediately, blinking his brights into our rear view mirror. We slowed down, a little curious about his signal because we didn't seem to be doing anything wrong. He pulled up beside us, but the driver—a smooth-faced Asian man (Indian or Pakistani perhaps?)—frowned when he saw us and kept going.

Patricia sighed. "Juani, you do pretty well walking that weird line between not being in the closet and not being in people's faces, but if you think that it's better to sidestep the nature of your relationship with Gina in order to protect it—you're obviously wrong," she said, taking a sharp turn and jolting us onto a side street. "Gina's telling you you're already in trouble. Don't you get it?"

The more Patricia lectured me, the angrier I got. "Listen," I said, pressing my body against the car door as we sped toward my apartment. "I'm not the one who's saying anything, I'm not doing anything, and I'm not feeling anything racist or classist or whatever else. That's what should matter to Gina: me, not my family. You think I like or agree with everything her friends talk about? No way!"

Patricia spun the VW into the alley next to my house and came to a sudden and dead stop. My head snapped back and forth.

"Do her friends call you names to your face?" she asked me, her own neck ramrod straight.

"No, but, believe me, they say plenty of other things that let me know they don't like me," I said.

"Because you're Cuban?"

"Yeah, sometimes because I'm Cuban—even Gina does it—and sometimes they spew out little homophobic things," I explained. "I let it go, though."

"Why?" Patricia asked.

"Because it's not worth it."

"To whom?"

I popped open the car door and jumped out. I needed air, I needed to breathe. "Why are you doing this to me?" I asked.

Patricia pulled on the emergency brake and climbed out of the car. Its little engine continued to chug in place. She crossed her arms on top of the VW's curved roof. "I'm sorry," she said. "I'm just trying to help but I can see I'm not doing very well."

My chest was puffy and tight. I thought about all the times Gina had just swallowed her tongue around my father and his crazy duct tape stories, how she'd put up with my Tía Zenaida making snide comments about communists, how Pucho's salacious friends hung all over the laundromat staring her up and

125

down every time she came in to see me. And I realized all I'd ever done is roll my eyes, shrug, ask her to ignore the assaults, or whispered something under my breath that only I and, sometimes she, could hear.

"I'm not good at this kind of thing, Patricia," I finally admitted, letting the air out of my lungs. There are so many things I'm not good at.

She smiled indulgently, her chin resting on her arms. "At what?"

"At these kinds of conversations. I'm not good at telling Mami to stop being racist, 'cause it's impossible. Or telling Tía Zenaida not to be anti-communist—that's crazy, it's like her whole reason for living. And I'm not good at telling Jimmy not to make Puerto Rican jokes around Gina because...well, I mean, he'd laugh."

"So?"

I threw my hands in the air and spun my whole body around in frustration. The street was gray and cool and the faint sound of radios and TVs could be heard seeping out of windows. "He'll make me go through hell if I say anything to him, okay?" I said. "He'll go on and on about—"

"About what?"

"Well...that..." I could see it: Jimmy chortling in the laundromat, making faces, grabbing his dick as if it were a southern sheriff's water hose. I cringed. "That...I'm..." I was up against a wall. I felt my lips puckering but I couldn't get any words out of my mouth, as if it had been sewn shut with a thick dissolving stitch that was just now turning into some sort of goo.

"That what?" Patricia demanded, impatient. "That you're...oh god...Juani, no..." My mouth worked to make a sound. "That you're...*pussywhipped?*" Patricia finally spit the word out. She pushed herself away from the VW in disgust. "My god, Juani, what kind of macho game are you playing with him? Who cares what Jimmy thinks? Who cares what anybody but you and Gina think? Juani, c'mon, be a grown up. Get a grip on reality. What's really important here?"

I felt naked. And ridiculous. And I hated Patricia just then. I bit my lower lip, felt it swell like a balloon, pushed my hands in my pockets and stomped off. I couldn't take anymore.

· · · **·** **·** · · · ·

One night—and this was *the* night—several of Gina's friends came over to her place for a little party. It was Gina's mother's saint's day and Gina was making a huge vat of rabbit stew (her mom's favorite). Because the stew had been on the stove for hours, the house had a warm, comforting smell of garlic and onions, basil and tomatoes.

Curiously, we were all talking in Spanish, as if rehearsing for Gina's mom, who preferred her island language to the English that came so much easier to her daughter and her friends. Eventually one of these pals said to me, "You must be Cuban, I can tell by your accent." I nodded. And then she asked, "Are you a good Cuban or a bad Cuban?"

But before I got a chance to say anything, Gina—laughing—said, "*Baaaaaaaad* Cuban!" And they all laughed.

I shrugged and tried to smile. I was sure there was some joke here I wasn't getting, or that was at my expense in a big way, but I was determined to let it roll. I figured it was my penance, and maybe the universe's way of balancing things out. I looked at Gina for some comfort but she wasn't looking back: She was stirring her stew, her head tossed back and laughing, eyebrows arched, mouth wide open and red, very red. I'd seen that expression—and the sweet red of that mouth—so many times in private, just the two of us, that I'd grown to believe it belonged only there, in the space only we created. Seeing her here, now, loose and laughing before strangers (*I* didn't know them) made me shiver down to my boots. Were we still together, connected in any way? Was there anything left between us? Why had she invited me? Why wasn't she looking at me?

"You mean you're a *gusana?*" asked Gina's friend, her face not hiding too well her loathing. Her name was Hilda. The way she was standing, her face seemed to be next to a picture of

Lolita Lebrón, one of the Puerto Rican *independentistas* who had tried to assassinate Harry Truman.

I smiled and shrugged again. I knew I couldn't say anything. "Oh-oh, cat got your tongue?" Hilda teased. She and Gina exchanged a knowing look.

"No," I finally said, "I just don't like that word."

"What word?"

"*Gusana.*"

"Why's that?" she asked, leaning her hip on the kitchen counter. Lolita hovered next to her.

I took a deep breath. "I find it offensive," I said.

Hilda smiled patronizingly. "What would you prefer?"

"Anything but that," I said, trying to avoid whatever trap she might be setting. There was complete silence in the kitchen now, with everybody tuned in to the exchange between her and me. The only thing I could hear was the wooden spoon turning the stew as Gina stirred and a kind of gurgling from the pot.

"Do you like *Cuban-American?*" Hilda asked.

"Sometimes."

Her eyebrow went up. "Really?"

"Sometimes, yes."

"And other times?"

I felt as if I was under a hot light, my face red. My palms itched. I felt my intestines knotting and twisting.

"Cuban, *cubana,* whatever."

Somebody laughed a little but I don't know who. It wasn't a mean laugh, that I could tell. Hilda's eyebrow came down and she smiled, but she wasn't warm at all. Gina was still stirring, still avoiding my eyes. "*Whatever?*" Hilda asked. "Man, that's scary!"

"Hey, she's a woman with flexibility," said Ana, another of Gina's friends. The tension in the kitchen was palpable so I was grateful for her intervention. I looked to thank her but she turned away, gently slapping my shoulder in the process. "What do you want to drink, eh, *cubanita?*"

"A Materva," I said, relieved. Ana smiled up at me, nodding

acknowledgment as she handed me a cold can from the fridge. "¿Y tú?" she asked Hilda, forcing her off her soapbox. Hilda looked around for a way to stay up there a while longer but then the doorbell rang.

"¡Mi mamá!" exclaimed Gina, dropping the wooden spoon onto a paper towel and racing out of the kitchen to get the door.

Her friends scattered, some following behind her; others left to add silverware to the table, stir the stew, and arrange the flowers. I would have thought we were back on track for the evening, to thinking about Gina's mother's saint's day, but for the fact of Hilda, who continued to stand next to Lolita, her hip still up against the kitchen counter, just staring at me and my Materva.

· · · . • . · · ·

When Gina's mother—a wonderful woman, a teacher at a local elementary school—came for the dinner party, she brought a couple of friends with her, all Puerto Rican, but none as seriously into the independence movement as her daughter and her friends, so we got a reprieve from the politics of revolution for a little while at the table. We all praised the stew, which melted on our spoons, and made grunting noises over the bread and the flan we had selected for dessert. Gina sat next to me for the meal and though she didn't say a word about what had happened in the kitchen, she reached under the table and squeezed my thigh, which helped me swallow.

But as soon as Gina's mother left—sometime after the coffee and before the beers—somehow Gina and her friends began reminiscing about their trips to Cuba, about helping on sugar-cane cutting brigades, and hearing Fidel speak at the Plaza of the Revolution for hours on end while they ate ice cream and leaned on each other. They found it all inspirational, a blue-print for what they envisioned for Puerto Rico.

Gina talked about Cuba's colors and how, even being from Puerto Rico, its sister island, she was surprised by how verdant Cuba was, how insistent its landscape.

"You know that line in the Garcia Lorca poem—*te quiero verde?*" Gina asked. "It always sounded so stupid to me until I went to Cuba. It's such a lush place." Then she put her arm around me, kissed my cheek and told me I came from a very beautiful country.

"Have you read Amparo Maure's poems about Cuba?" asked Ana, trying to be helpful again. "She went there in the sixties, at the very beginning of the revolution, and back again after Mariel, and she wrote some beautiful things about the island, and the Cuban people."

Then Ana recited a few lines from memory, which were quite moving indeed. But Hilda was not into poetry or into describing the view. In fact, she wasn't really into talking with her friends, but into lecturing me. At her first opportunity, she started telling me about the importance of the Cuban revolution (as if I, a Cuban, didn't know), and what it meant to Puerto Rican independence, and how throwing off *yanqui* imperialism was the right thing to do. She said that as much as she hates the nationalism of Cuban exiles, she understands that its island counterpart is what has kept the revolution alive, and why Fidel is so strong.

"Say what you will," she said, "Fidel has *tremendos cojones.*"

I chuckled at that. I mean, everybody—even the people who most despise Fidel—agree he's one ballsy character. How else could he have lasted decade after decade? How else could he inspire the kind of intense emotions Cubans have for him? After all, it's not just hate the exiles feel for him, but admiration too. His sheer audacity raises the level and scope of their fury. They see in his outrageousness some measure of their own capacity, of their own ability to survive—him on his island, and they—*us,* because my family's part of it too—here, in the U.S.

"What's so funny?" Hilda asked me.

"Nothing, really," I said.

"Well, *something,* you were laughing," she said. "You weren't laughing at me, were you?"

I shook my head. "God no," I said, exasperated now. "Look,

I was laughing at the idea of Fidel and his *tremendos cojones*—like that's a news flash, okay? I mean, I can be amused sometimes, can't I?"

"You have no respect," Hilda said, getting up with a flourish and standing dramatically by a poster of Frida Kahlo.

"Hey, you're the one who said it," I said. I looked around desperately for help, but no one was making a move in my direction. Gina was leaning back on the couch next to me, staring straight ahead, at nothing, her lips pursed and her eyes hooded.

"It's different coming from me," Hilda said.

"How's that?"

"I'm no *gusana*, okay?"

"Neither am I," I said.

Gina sat up. Everyone's attention shifted to her. She covered her face with her hands.

"You need to explain context to your girlfriend," Hilda sneered at her.

"Hilda, shut up," Gina finally said, removing her hands from her face. "I mean, enough...*por dios.*"

"It's late," Ana said, ever the diplomat. She pulled her jacket from behind a chair and started to work her arms into the sleeves. "I'm going home." Gina nodded without looking up. "Hilda, c'mon, I'll give you a ride."

But Hilda was incredulous. "That's it?" she said. "We're just gonna let it go at that?"

Gina groaned something that sounded like "Aaaaaaar-rrrrgggggghhhh," grit her teeth and threw herself back on the couch. "For christ's sake! For christ's fuckin' sake!" she screamed, stomping the floor, her body twisting in frustration as if she were having a seizure.

Ana ushered Hilda and the others out. I heard the door open and shut, the clatter of so many feet and angry voices down the stairs and then the sound of the downstairs door creaking closed. Gina and I just sat there. On the surface it seemed she'd taken my side, but I knew better. The gulf between us was wider than the ninety miles from Havana to Miami and the air was just as thick with doubt and suspicion.

What was going on here? I looked over at Gina and she was a stranger, her head back on the couch, her jaw tight. I wanted to believe that she was hurt and torn by what had happened—that she was angry at Hilda for insulting me, her lover, but I was afraid Gina might somehow think what had just happened was okay.

And I thought again about Jimmy, about his stupid Puerto Rican jokes, and Pucho laughing, and Nena looking away, and Mami and Papi raising their eyebrows because they thought the joke was funny but knew Gina didn't.

"So I'm a *baaaaaaaad* Cuban?" I asked, trying to keep it light.

Gina shrugged. "It's a bad joke," she admitted. "It's what a lot of people call Cuban exiles."

"Do you agree with Hilda?" I asked. "Do you really think I'm a *gusana?*"

Gina smiled a little, her eyes still closed. "You? You, personally?" she asked. She combed her hair back with her fingers. She was still splayed on the couch, eyes closed. "I don't know, Juani, I really don't."

"What I mean is, do you really think it's so despicable that we're here?" I asked. My lip was trembling. "We wouldn't know each other, we wouldn't be together, if my parents hadn't left Cuba." I was choking a little, holding back tears.

Gina sat up and put her arms around me. "*Mi gusanita,*" she said softly, stroking me. Then she said she understood that the word meant different things to me than to her—that, obviously, I found it pejorative, while she thought it was a vernacular description for exiles, which is what we were. "It never occurred to me that you felt so strongly about it," she said.

"But that's not what I asked," I said, feeling toyed with. "I asked if you really thought my parents' being here was so bad."

Gina sighed. "I wouldn't have left." She paused. "How about you—if you'd been old enough to decide for yourself—would you have left?"

The truth is, I'd never thought about it before. I stared at her, dumbfounded. Who would I have been in Cuba? Who could I still be, in Cuba or here? "I...I don't know," I finally muttered.

"Do you remember anything about your life in Cuba?" she asked.

And images of wooden doors, big and brown and old—like castles doors—came to mind. And smoke billowing from a boxing ring in black and white on my parents' TV, all the neighbors gathered round watching in our house in Havana. And blue uniformed policemen, their pants too tight around the crotch and hips. Hot, hazy days. Hiding in the shadows of thick-leafed trees. Salt spraying off the *malecón*. Big American cars with wings and my father's boxy Lada falling apart, its glass smudged by berries from the overhanging branches crowding the windows anywhere he parked it.

And I realized that I'd left Cuba too young to remember anything but snatches of color and scattered words, like the cutout letters in a ransom note. And what little I could put together had since been forged and painted over by the fervor, malice and nostalgia of others. What did I really know? And who did I believe? Who *could* I believe?

I looked up and there was Fidel on Gina's wall, smiling and smoking and chinning himself.

And I realized, sitting there on Gina's couch, that, among all the dizzying feelings bloating my brain, I was jealous that she and her friends knew so much about my country, and I knew so little, really, not just about Cuba, but about Puerto Rico and everywhere else. I was pissed that, while they'd been to Cuba, I had spent all my time working in a laundromat folding other people's clothes and emptying quarters from the pinball machines in the back. I hated their independence movement, not for political reasons, but because it seemed to give them direction. And hope. Suddenly, I hated that I was just sitting there like a big black hole, like the mouth of one of those big industrial washers into which everybody just throws all their dirty clothes.

Gina said she understood my confusion, because we were so fucked up about the revolution in my family. "My poor little *gusanita*," she said again, and I knew she meant it affectionately. But she really didn't understand how gone I was, so she kissed my cheek and my forehead, and she stroked my arm again with her soft brown hands.

I must not have reacted appropriately—I know I didn't reward her efforts, I was so deep in my own head.

"This is silly," she finally said, annoyed. "I can't believe *I'm* comforting *you*." She took her arms from around me and sighed really deep, like she'd run out of patience with my problem. Then she shoved me a little, it was just a little push with her open palm to my shoulder, and she barely made me move, really. But what I did next, I'm not proud of.

I rocked a bit to the side, just going with her motion, but when I came back up, my fist had somehow rolled into a wrecking ball, the knuckles all pointy and aimed at her face. I don't know why or how but I smashed it into her—she was just sitting next to me, her thigh pressed against my thigh, her sweat and cologne stinging my eyes she was so close—and I felt the bones of her face collapse under my hand. I didn't look at her right away, though, because my hand was tingling. Bits of skin on my knuckles were ripped up like little flaps and blood was beading up underneath. Then Gina screamed—it was like an explosion, the loudest thing—and I looked: Her hands, which were covering her face, were leaking blood through her fingers.

And because I was in shock, and because I didn't know what to do—because I couldn't connect the evidence of my bruised hand with the crime on her face—I said, in a voice deep and calm and flat: "Just shut up."

But Gina kept screaming, *How could you do this to me?* She was shrieking like some kind of animal. Then she looked up at me, her face all black and red and distorted. *I hate you,* she said, and smeared the blood with her hands on my face, getting it all over my eyes and blinding me just long enough so she could sink her spiky nails into my wrists.

We tumbled to the floor and rolled around, knocking over the cocktail table with the ashtray on it, a vase of flowers, a little basket of magazines, and the beer and Materva cans from which we'd been drinking when her friends were over. I had just managed to turn things around and grab her arms when I felt her teeth on my shoulder and I socked her once more, this time in the stomach. She coughed and lowered her mouth automatically, but she was gone now too and didn't realize what she was doing, so when her teeth clamped down again—just as hard, and angrier now—they came down on my breast, which is small and, normally, soft, not very firm at all.

This is the part when I left my body, when I just walked out of it and watched us from across the room, like a ghost or a spirit. And this is what I saw: Gina, like a rabid dog on my breast, even as blood came gushing through my shirt, all of our limbs flailing. It was as if she was gnawing on me, chewing and drooling and absolutely not letting go. All the screaming had dissolved into a high-pitched hum interrupted only by the thud of a fist on muscle, the labored work of our angry lungs, and the crack of an elbow or leg hitting bone.

All of the blood pours savagely from my limbs, all of my limbs are severed, veins sliced open, blood blinding—and here you are, teeth bared, blowing air—I go this way then that, push you away, hit you, bring you to me in a vice-like embrace, feel, again, your muscles stretch underneath my bones, my bones crushing your bones, dark blood congealing blue/black/magenta—my blood like a fountain from my nipples, like a geyser, like rain—and I kiss you, my tongue running inside your bloody mouth, gums, teeth, down to your throat, then we both gasp and choke and spit—and I love you, monstrously and uselessly, but I still love—I will always love you.

CHAPTER 13

I DON'T KNOW PRECISELY HOW we got to the hospital. I've heard that neighbors busted down the door, thinking we were being attacked. I've also been told that Gina's mother came back for some reason, saw the carnage on the living room floor, and, after recovering from the initial horror, called the police and the paramedics to take us apart. Another story says she never called the cops at all, just went screaming out the apartment door, yelling something about how they'd murdered her baby, her hands up in the air, until the neighbors called 911 in a panic.

When I finally opened my eyes, I was on a gurney in the emergency room, my breast all taped up where Gina had ripped my heart out with her teeth. It looked like a glob of white papier-mâché dropped on my chest. And standing there above my head, stroking my hair and telling me everything was going to be all right, was Jimmy, in his hospital janitor uniform, looking genuinely scared. He smiled a little, the smell of cleaning agents on his hands so strong that it cut right through the blood and medicine and everything else on me. The overhead lights were as bright as starbursts, each one exploding in my pounding head.

I closed my eyes—I thought if I closed my eyes I could rewrite the scene, sever the connection, make Jimmy go away. What was he doing there? Why him?

"I thought you were never gonna come out of it," he said. "Man, when I heard about these two chicks in the ER who'd nearly killed each other, I *knew* it was you two!"

I turned my head, I was so ashamed. Every bone ached, every muscle pulled and stung when I made the slightest movement. I was sure I'd vomit if I even tried to sit up. I couldn't believe Gina and I had done this to each other; I couldn't believe I'd caused the end of our world.

I looked up but the damn lights were still there, like minia-
ture suns, pointing into my face and threatening my own
eclipse. I tried to focus on the acoustic tile around them, on the
cool feel of the gurney's metal, on the tip of Jimmy's greasy hair
dangling in his face like a poor version of Elvis Presley. But all I
could really see was that other planet, with Gina and me like
four-legged animals, crawling in slow-motion on the ground
and on each other. The overhead light was a huge fireball hurl-
ing toward us, scorching us so that, in our desperation, we
jumped around as if we were dancing, as if there was something
going on that was joyful and beautiful—when in fact it was all
blackness, all ashes, just me and my papier-maché breast and
Jimmy, gloating over me, his head leaning into the gurney to
see if I was all right, and, finally, blocking the light.

"Is Gina okay?" I asked.

"Oh, yeah, and on her way home," Jimmy said, disgusted,
but I couldn't tell whether it was with her for leaving or with me
for not beating her as badly as she'd done me. "Lots of bruises
and stuff, but all superficial. You must have pulled your
punches, I guess."

"Her nose?"

"Fine, just swollen and bloody. It'll be purple for days," he
chuckled. "You didn't break it, if that's what you think..."

"Did she..." I started to ask but Jimmy finished it for me:
"...Ask about you?" He shook his head. "Not really, Juani, not
really, although I told her what I knew before she took off."

I swallowed hard. My throat tightened and I felt as if I might
suffocate. It hurt like hell that Gina had left while I was still out
of it. I told myself that if the situation had been reversed, no
matter if she'd started it, no matter how angry I was, I'd have
stayed—I'd have waited until she came to and I knew she was
all right.

"Hey, hey," Jimmy said softly, then used his thumb to wipe
a tear from my face. "I'm the one who told her to go home,
okay? You can blame me for that," he said, reading my mind.

I nodded, then closed my eyes. I tried to remember the smell of Gina's hair, the feel of her skin rippling against my back, her arms around me like rope. I tried to hold on to the feeling of her tugging at me, pulling me closer, our bodies like perfect pieces in a puzzle. I knew it would never happen again, and I choked. Jimmy said nothing, just caressed my head and held my hand, patting it with his big rough fingers as if he actually cared.

"Am I gonna go to jail?" I asked, suddenly remembering the paramedics and the blue uniforms, the whirling blue lights and that at some time or another I'd been handcuffed.

Jimmy shook his head. "Naaahhh," he said, "just a little domestic violence, that's what I told the cops—they love cat fights, you know. I gave them a little donation for the policemen's benevolent association—if you know what I mean. And then I talked to Gina and told her that, with how she is about being out and her political work and everything, she sure wouldn't want any publicity—which I promised she'd get if anybody even so much as whispered this to anybody else—so neither she nor the cops are gonna press charges, okay?"

He was so fucking proud of himself: my hero, my savior. I despised him for that.

"Gina went for that?" I asked, covering my eyes with my arm. When I moved it up, my chest stretched. Pain shot through me like electricity. I cringed, grit my teeth.

"Oh yeah," he said, laughing now. "Oh, I know she's real politically pure and everything, but she's got a price, just like everybody else. What a little scandal this would make for her, huh?"

I moaned, in part from physical pain, in part from my predicament. Then just when things didn't seem like they could get worse, I thought of my parents. "I don't know what I'm going to say to Mami and Papi..." I groaned, realizing my wounds were so much worse than Caridad's had ever been, and that make-up wouldn't cover them any better, or be at all convincing on me. My arm started to go numb.

"I got that figured too," Jimmy said, leaning in to whisper conspiratorially. "Gina knows about this too. She agreed."

"Since when are you my state-appointed lawyer?" I asked, slowly and achingly removing my arm from my face. I stared at him. He was so close, and my eyes had adjusted, so I could see the pores on his face. He looked monstrous, like a real Frankenstein, made of pale dead skin and fleshy satin scars I'd never noticed before. They looked like fingernail scratches, tiny little lines as fine as a razor's cut.

Jimmy glanced over his shoulder, stirring the plot. "Okay—you ready?" He was so into the intrigue, the drama of it all. "This is the story—the story is that you two were attacked by an unknown, anonymous assailant. Gina's mom had left the party and so had her friends and they forgot to lock the door downstairs, see? So the unknown, anonymous assailant—who could be anybody, really—just walked in, which is why there are no signs of forcible entry. You thought it was a robbery and clobbered him and then he beat the living daylights out of you, right in the apartment, which explains all the screaming, get it?"

I nodded, biting my lip.

"But here's the best part..."

"There's more?"

"Yeah—listen—you and Gina part ways because—and she liked this part, I could tell—she thinks the whole thing wasn't a robbery but politically motivated, like to teach her a lesson because she's so politically important and everything, and you think it's just too dangerous to be around her, period." He straightened his back, cracked his knuckles above his head and laughed heartily. "God, I'm good, aren't I?"

I smiled almost against my will. He really had thought out almost every angle. But I was still a little confused about something. "Since that story's so good, Jimmy, why bother to tell the cops it was domestic violence? I mean, why spend money when you could get the same results for free?"

He strutted a little. "Yeah, but then you wouldn't owe me half as much, little cousin-in-law. This way I didn't just bail you. This way you'll be careful, okay?" He gave his dick a strong, full-palm yank for emphasis with his big, dead hand.

To my amazement, everyone bought Jimmy's story. As disturbing as it was to think that Gina and I might have been attacked by a complete stranger on a quiet evening in a private home, any other version was more disturbing—perhaps even *too* disturbing.

My father paced around my hospital room, holding up his pants with one hand, loudly proclaiming that if they ever caught the son of a bitch who did this to his daughter, he was going to kill him. He never mentioned Gina or retribution for her wounds. He never expressed an interest in talking to her, in getting clues about who might have done this to us. To hear my father tell it, she didn't exist—the incident was my solitary misfortune, random and sick, something that had happened in an unnamed, unmarked place. My father's eyes watered, his hands trembled and he wondered aloud about where this country was going to. He was properly outraged, threatened letters to the editor, lawsuits and investigations, and finally collapsed into an emotional heap in a hospital chair. Eventually he left, never having said more than a word or two to me, because the whole experience of his baby so badly beaten up was just too much for him.

Of course, I didn't worry about the possibility that my father would actually go through with any of this. He's always relied on me—even more than Nena—to engage the world outside the family. It all started with me helping the adults with language stuff—my English has always been the best in the family; even before the business, I was the one who was always dealing with American authorities. I'd be the one who placed the overseas calls to Cuba, the one who translated insurance forms, the one who talked to the postman. When they wanted to start a business, it was Nena who found out about the Small Business Administration loan (from a commercial on TV) but it was me who wrote away for it. I was about eleven, I guess. So I knew, no matter how loud and angry my father got, he'd do nothing. And if anyone ever said anything about his paralysis, he'd throw his hands in the air and have a little fit about how his good intentions were being diminished.

Of course, my mother was not as dramatic. She sat in the chair next to my hospital bed, shaking her head, jumping up at my every move and asking me if I needed anything. She got me a fresh glass of water every time I reached for the old one, and read to me from the TV guide if I even got near the remote control that snaked onto the bed on a long, stiff plastic cord.

"You realize, Mami, that Jimmy exaggerated the story a little, right?" I asked her, hoping to create some room to maneuver in. I wanted desperately to tell her the truth; I wanted *somebody* to know.

She held up her hand, closed her eyes. "Juani, no," she said in a near whisper. "Don't torture yourself with this. There are some things that are better left unspoken."

There was a terrible silence between us then. I could hear the nurses walking briskly out in the halls, the shuffle of surgical patients taking first steps. I felt cold and pushed the blanket up. And yet, perversely, I was relieved. I looked over at my mother and nodded, because I wanted her to know I appreciated what she was trying to spare me. I thought her acknowledgment might still lead us somehow to the truth, even if it was later, in some undefined future. I nodded at her because I loved the idea that she and I might eventually share this secret—even if it was nightmarish—because, to me, it meant there was a possibility she would comfort me. That everything remained unspoken didn't scare me—that had always been my mother's modus operandi, and I was relieved, yes, happy even.

My mother squirmed in her seat and gave me a resigned, secretive expression. "I'm not going to say I told you so, okay?" she said, focusing on a magazine that had suddenly appeared on her lap.

I stared. "Huh?"

My mother looked around the room as if searching out spies. "Gina," she whispered. "I warned you about her but you didn't listen."

"What are you talking about, Mami?" I leaned forward. Gravity pulled at my breast and its shell of bandages pulled at my skin, like a thousand needles jabbing into me. I couldn't believe this.

"I knew she would get you into trouble," my mother said. "You can't say I didn't warn you. What did you expect, hanging out with people like that?"

"Like what?" I was incredulous.

"You know…" She looked around again, sniffing at the air as if she were a hound dog. "Terrorists…*independentistas*… Juani, you know I thought this was a very bad idea."

My head dropped back, my breast rested against me. "Oh, god, Mami, it's not like that," I said, disappointed. I laughed, disgusted.

"Like what? Like that you almost got killed?" She was angry now, whispering fiercely and holding the magazine in her hand so tightly, it made a crunching sound. "You think this is funny? This is not funny."

I turned to face her. "For god's sake, no, it's not funny," I said, practically shouting. "Of course it's not fucking funny." I didn't hear myself in a normal way anymore, but as a distant sound. I was shouting into a black hole into which all my words disappeared. I struggled up from the bed, holding my breast with my hand. "It's not what you think!" I shouted at my mother, who jumped, startled, from her chair.

She hid behind it unintentionally, for an instant looking like a lion trainer at the circus about to lift it up to keep back the big, bad cats.

"It's not what you think!" I shouted again, but this time weeping, folding into myself and my injured breast, whatever was left of it, as if it were a stillborn chick fallen from a careless nest.

My mother, frightened but with her face nonetheless hard as stone, stood and walked away just as a pair of nurses came running into the room. They surveyed the scene, glancing uneasily from me to her and back again, asked if everything was all right and then followed my mother out of the room.

········

After I was let out of the hospital, I took some time off work, just stayed in my apartment, reading and eating and watching TV, thinking about Gina with every plot twist on the soap operas, every song on the radio, every story I read in the newspaper. I put on more weight than I ever had in my life.

Pauli was still in Mexico with Rosa, getting her things to move back, so I didn't get a chance to talk to her much, other than on the phone. But my situation seemed to energize Caridad. She came right out of her mourning daze, suddenly happy to have me to look after. And Jimmy, playing sympathetic to the hilt, seemed to back off from his edict about keeping us apart. As a result, Caridad came over almost every afternoon during my convalescence. I'd become one of Caridad's *infelizes*. Sometimes she'd bring lunch, sometimes just the paper. We'd watch the soaps together. I'd read while she wrote letters to Rafael, the Peruvian orphan. Sometimes she'd put out food for the cats in my neighborhood, but that only happened a few times because I told her I had no intention of feeding them once I was well and she wasn't around.

"I will drown them, Caridad, I'm not kidding," I threatened. She laughed but stopped the giveaways anyway, just in case.

She, of course, wholly believed Jimmy's story about the beating and was horrified at its implications.

"I just don't want you to be alone," she said, chopping onions one day and inadvertently crying. "I mean, that maniac is still out there, the one who assaulted you. Who knows how he'll react when he knows that you survived? And that you know what he looks like, huh?" She looked at me, wiping her eyes with the back of her hand (and still holding the knife), tears rolling down her face. "I mean, you *do* know what he looks like, right? Like, when the police come to get his description—you know, with the artist and everything—you'll be able to give it to 'em, right?"

I nodded, but said nothing. I was thinking, Yeah, but my *real* assailants are my ex-lover and Jimmy Frankenstein, your fucking husband.

"Once they get that drawing, Juani, we'll put flyers all over the neighborhood so that other women know this maniac is out there, and so they can watch out for you and Gina," she said, chop, chop, chopping again.

But, of course, none of this would ever happen: There was no unknown assailant, just Jimmy's perverse imagination, and even the cops knew that.

. . . .

All the while, the phone rang—family, friends and customers from the laundromat—with get-well wishes and gossip and transparently curious intentions. I wouldn't let Caridad answer. I just let it ring until the machine picked up because I couldn't bear the notion of continuing to confirm Jimmy's lies over and over again.

And, yet, I couldn't bring myself to undo them. I know now that it would have been a lot easier then—all it required was for me to lean over the gurney in the emergency room, shout out for a police officer and tell him he didn't need to take Jimmy's bribe, that I'd deal with whatever they wanted to charge us. I could have told my father, my mother, my brother Pucho (who, like Papi, made obligatory threats about the imaginary assailant), and all of my cousins. But I didn't.

In my own way, I relished the lies, and I was secretly relieved to not be responsible for them. Because Jimmy had invented the whole thing, I knew if anyone ever found out, I could honestly shift the blame to him. I could say I was too dazed, too traumatized to really understand what was going on—and because my family hates him and thinks of me as pretty earnest, I could probably get away with it. And this way, I could be a wholesale victim, both of the incident and of the lies. In the dark, secret parts of my soul, I was actually *grateful* to Jimmy for giving me a way out of confessing to the awful thing I'd done.

"You and Jimmy, you two are so alike," Caridad told me one day when she came to see me.

"*What?*" I was horrified.

"No, no, really," she said, laughing a little. "It's like you're brother and sister. He's like Mr. Protective of you, like you are of me—exactly the same, Juani, I'm not kidding. I mean, he was completely freaked out about you, just nuts. He cried and everything."

"Please, Cari, please," I begged, "no more."

She smiled, lopsided and too sympathetic for comfort. "Really—you two react to things the same way, you know?"

"We're nothing alike, okay?" I said, dead serious. I looked at her hard, so she knew I wasn't kidding.

"Hey, I know you don't like him, okay?" she said. "But it doesn't mean you're not alike. I mean, maybe it's *why* you don't like him. Juani, you talk alike, you even stand alike, okay?"

After that, when I was well enough to go out now and then, it got so that, if Jimmy was leaning against a washing machine at the laundromat while talking to Tía Celia or Tía Zenaida and I found myself in a similar pose, I'd stand up straight or jump up and sit on a dryer (which would only cause whichever aunt to yell at me for setting a bad example for the customers). If his leg was bouncing up a storm so that the chips rattled when we were playing poker with our other cousins, I made sure I was stone still. Everything he said, any little phrase that was particularly his, I never used it. Any song he liked a lot, I didn't play it, I'd turn the dial on the radio so I wouldn't learn the words even by accident.

He's not stupid, so of course he figured something was up.

"You scared of me now?" he asked once, sucking on a toothpick while hanging out at the laundromat.

"No," I lied, "I'm not scared of you." Then I flipped the bird at him.

But Jimmy just laughed and laughed. "You'd love to, wouldn't you?" he said, his grin huge and sure. He grabbed my wrist and brought my hand to his mouth. And though I clenched my fingers immediately into a fist, he caught my middle finger between his teeth anyway. "That's the closest you'll get, babe," he said, "for now." Then he laughed again and strutted out of the laundromat, his hips swinging in that way he has when he knows he's won a round.

CHAPTER 14

A FTER THE "INCIDENT" (as everyone began to call Jimmy's story), even after I went back to work, it wasn't full-time right away. I went back slowly, adding a few hours here and there, trying to ease my way back in. I was afraid of what I'd find at the Wash-N-Dry—afraid that because I'd taken time off, certain things wouldn't be done right, or they'd been ignored, and I figured my desk— Nena's old desk in the back—would be sky high with piles of paperwork.

But the truth is, on that first day I dropped by just to visit, there was nothing for me to do. Everything was in order— detergent and supplies were taken care of, banking and book- keeping was up to date, the Very Fine machine was stocked, and there were even new flyers I'd been meaning to get out to an apartment building that had just rehabbed and had a slew of potential new customers. The flyers had an adorable little draw- ing of the Wash-N-Dry, a before-and-after thing in which a lit- tle cartoon guy went in to the laundromat all dirty and came out all shiny and clean.

Tía Zenaida, thinking I'd be happy that everything was under control, had put her old business skills to work and had everything running at a cool and even pace. "I hadn't done any- thing since I used to sell Raúl's paintings more than thirty years ago," she said proudly, "but they all came back—all my tal- ents—and it made me so happy. See, Juani? We can run the Wash-N-Dry as good as you or Nena."

It was supposed to make me feel good but it didn't. I knew how to run the business because Nena had trained me, but I hadn't trained anybody, and here they didn't need me anyway.

When I told Patricia about it, she laughed, she was so amused. "Well, it's a totally predictable, classic case of disappointment," she said, immediately going into analytic mode, as she always does.

I felt foolish and useless. The bright lights of the laundromat just magnified my aimlessness. If I looked up at them, I got a headache. And no matter what I tried to do to distract myself, I was handicapped by the bandages and pain that continued to assault my breast and arm. I couldn't write for long periods of time, so my journal turned into a silly series of notes. I kept trying to jot down what had *really* happened—I wanted a record of the truth somewhere—but I just couldn't hold a pen and since Nena had moved, I didn't have access to a typewriter. Worse, I couldn't play Lethal Enforcer because it required all the muscles that had been savaged in "the incident."

So I hung out at the Wash-N-Dry like a lost dog, chatting it up with the customers—but not too much because I didn't want to have to talk about what had happened. As soon as anybody alluded to it, I'd lower my eyes and signal that it wasn't a good topic to discuss in front of my family.

"But I wanna hear—from you—how you kicked the guy in the balls and made him run out the place," said one of our Mortal Kombat regulars. I just looked at him, this little skinny runt, his eyes all eager.

"Not now," I said, shaking my head. "You know...my aunts...not cool, okay?"

And he nodded, fast, then rushed off, his hands full of quarters to surrender to our machines.

To kill time, I read the shallow celebrity magazines we put out for customers. I cleaned out the filters on the dryers, because that doesn't require any real strength or mobility. I stared for hours through the window onto Milwaukee Avenue, where life seemed to have gone on without missing a beat. The salesmen were still idled at Polonia Furniture, the white artists on the second floor still splashed their paints and shone their mystery lights on the walls. Traffic came and went in a slow blur. Delivery trucks plucked boxes from behind locked metal doors and dropped them off like presents up and down the street. People huddled at the bus stop, hunching down into their scarves and coats as the weather worsened. Flurries fell and vanished on the shiny, wet sidewalks. I did all this—all this *nothing*—while careful to avoid Jimmy. I just didn't want to see him. I didn't want to be taunted by him—to be reminded that he'd done me such a huge favor, to have to examine and evaluate every little thing to make sure I wasn't mirroring him, or to be made aware of my own cowardice and shame by his mere presence. I hated him. Whenever it got close to when he came home from work at the hospital, I just bolted out of the laundromat—sometimes practically running, my breast in my hand and held against my chest, through the biting cold air of Milwaukee Avenue and back to the warm dark of my apartment a few blocks away.

· · · . ˙ . · · ·

All along, I missed Gina something fierce. It was a worse sickness than any I might have imagined. I fought my impulses every day but, no matter how difficult, I beat them back: I didn't call her, I didn't try to see her, and, most importantly, I didn't seek out information about her. I just didn't want to torture myself more than I had to—and I knew no matter how tormenting it was to avoid her, it would be doubly agonizing to see her, to know what was going on in her life and not be a part of it.

No matter how often her number ran through my head, how many times my fingers danced in the air above the touch-tone pad of my phone, how badly I wished every blinking light on my message machine was her—I didn't call. I didn't dial star sixty-nine, I didn't get caller ID.

When Caridad drove me to the doctor's office (in the Ford Escort she's trying to get rid of now), no matter how close she got to Gina's house—and I swear sometimes she drove right by deliberately, just to see my reaction—I didn't turn, I didn't look, I didn't comment on what she'd done, I didn't even lose my place in conversation. I refused to be tempted, I declined all bait.

"You know, I saw Gina today, she—" Cari would start sometimes but I wouldn't let her finish. I'd make like a zipper with my fingers across my mouth and, if she insisted, walk out of the room. If she followed me, I'd lock myself in the bathroom, turn on the water and start singing. *"Mi prima Cari me quiere gobernar,"* I'd belt out while tapping out a rhythm on my laundry basket. *"Y yo le sigo/ le sigo la corriente/ porque no quiero que diga la gente/ que mi prima Cari me quiere gobernar."*

Caridad would pound on my bathroom door and I'd sing louder and louder; sometimes I'd flush the toilet, anything to drown her out. Then she'd laugh and try to tell me whatever piece of gossip she had heard by screaming over all the noise I was making. Eventually I'd open the door and we'd pretend we'd stopped for a few minutes, then she'd start again, *"Mira, Juani,* according to Gina's friend, Ana, she—" And then I'd plug my ears with my fingers, walk over to my front door while singing (*"Ay que vamos a la playa/ y allá voy/ coje la maleta/ y la cojo..."*), open it and bow in exaggerated fashion for her to leave.

"Okay, okay, okay," she'd say, and finally give in, usually hugging me or kissing my cheek or otherwise letting me know she loved me anyway.

But I was sick, sick, sick—and I knew it. Whenever I heard Gina's name, or footsteps that sounded like her boots, my heart pounded dangerously in my chest. I felt like a huge church bell, swinging and shaking and about to crack and tumble through the termite-riddled rafters at any moment. When I was alone, I'd lie down on the couch and watch the flesh on my stomach tremble. To me, my belly looked like a balloon filled with water. I felt swollen and pale. My mouth was sticky. I was incapable of focusing on anything, and so jumpy I was constantly startled, constantly irritated.

· · · · · · · · ·

"What can we do to get your mind off what's bothering you?" Patricia asked. She'd come over with a stuffed pizza for dinner. She'd set the pizza box on my coffee table and sat herself down on the couch.

After "the incident," I always felt that Patricia, perhaps more than anybody else, had a sense that there was more to the story than Jimmy's version. When she first heard it, she'd interrupted him, looking over at me all bruised and stupefied in the hospital bed, and asked if that was how things had really happened.

"And then the guy grabbed the chair and hit Gina in the back, like on a TV show," Jimmy told her. "And the chair broke up into pieces, so Juani took a leg to defend herself, and, like, sparred with the guy."

I'd nodded silently, slipping lower under the blankets until I almost disappeared. Patricia was so openly skeptical that Jimmy finally told her to go to hell and stomped out of the room.

But, curiously, Patricia didn't ask questions once he'd left. She just stroked my arm and told me a few bad jokes Ira had shared with her and offered to help in whatever way I needed. During my convalescence at home, Patricia would usually come over after she'd finished teaching classes and bring me dinner.

I stared at the big gooey slab of cheese she'd set on a plate for me. "You know, Patricia, I'm *not* Pauli," I said, annoyed.

"Yeah...and what is that supposed to mean?" she asked coolly.

I pointed to the pizza with my whole hand. I thought my point was self-evident, but Patricia looked at me blankly. "And...?"

"I'm not the one who likes stuffed pizza. I only eat it to please Pauli. In my real life, I hate stuffed pizza, okay?"

"Oh, yeah, in your *real life*, of course," Patricia said as she pulled a slice off the big thick wheel of cheese and crust for herself. "I forgot about your *real life*. Imagine that...."

I couldn't believe her. "Excuse me..." I said, "what the fuck is that supposed to mean?"

"I mean I forgot you had a *real life*," Patricia said, still dripping sarcasm, and now melted cheese and tomato sauce too. She grabbed a napkin and dabbed at her mouth and chin. "Wow, this is messy. When you think about it, that's probably why Pauli likes this kind of stuff. It has a certain...hmmm...sensual quality, don't you think?" She wasn't trying to change the subject or make me feel better, I knew that. Pauli was still in Mexico, taking her sweet time coming home, and my resentment spilled onto her too.

"Look, what the fuck are you doing?"

"Eating stuffed pizza, which you just told me you hate. So more for me, right?"

I grabbed the slice she'd cut for me with my bare hands and threw it back in the pizza box. "Please, just go," I said as I closed the cardboard lid.

"Is this your new thing?" Patricia asked. "When you don't like what people say, you ask them to leave? At least Caridad gets a song."

"I just want some respect, okay? I mean, this is *my* house."

She nodded but continued eating. She had no intention of leaving. "Seems fair enough," Patricia said. "Now, can we get back to what you were talking about—about your *real life?*"

I sighed. "I just meant I don't like stuffed pizza and I'd appreciate it if you'd asked me what I like—if you don't know—before bringing food over."

Patricia smirked. "Oh, okay—and what, no 'Thanks for bringing me dinner, Patti, I realize I live totally out of your way and you've probably had a hard day teaching today and I'm just a little itty bitty bit grouchy'?"

I dropped down on the couch next to her. "Okay, I'm sorry," I said, embarrassed. I looked up at her. She was totally forgiving. "You're right, I'm grumpy lately."

"I know," she said with just a tad of exaggeration. Then she handed me my pizza. "You'd better eat this 'cause I'm not going back out for something else. And if you don't want it, tell me, because Ira will gladly eat it."

"No, no," I said, looking to see what part of the thing I could bear in my mouth, "I'll eat it." I felt I had to, just to prove my gratitude.

"So...?" She said, having finished her slice. She sat back on the couch as if she were appraising me.

" 'So...' what?" I asked, filling my mouth with what surely tasted like glue.

"Your so-called real life."

"Oh, come on, can we get off it?" I asked, my mouth stuffed; I could barely talk.

"No, I'm serious," she said. "You're twenty-four years old, you've just had a most traumatizing experience, and you just found out your family—your wonderful, weird family—doesn't need you to run the laundromat. So what are you going to do with yourself?"

I laughed a little. I wanted to say something witty back at her but I couldn't: The thick muck in my mouth wouldn't let me make any kind of intelligible sound. I tried to chew it up fast so I could speak, but the pizza had turned into a big wad of gum—it just got chewier and chewier. And then—as I was sitting there, struggling with this monster in my mouth while we both laughed—I realized exactly what I wanted to do. I grabbed a napkin and pulled the big yellow thing out, spitting and drooling in the process. Patricia was just cracking up, handing me napkin after napkin while I made a disgusting mess.

"Okay, okay—I know what I want," I finally said. I was glowing, I could tell. *It was just so right.* "And you're the perfect person to help with this, Patricia."

"Yeah?" she asked, leaning up. She was excited too, I could tell.

"I want to go to Cuba."

To my surprise, Patricia wasn't thrilled with my decision. Shockingly, she actually sounded somewhat like I'd expect my parents to respond. "Oh, god, Juani, why?" she asked, making a face. "It's nothing like it used to be. In fact, there's nothing there."

I couldn't believe my ears. "Did I just hear you correctly?" I asked incredulously.

Patricia nodded. "I mean, sure, if you want to go, I'll help you with the paperwork and stuff, but I mean, *why?*" she went on. "The revolution's dead, Cuba's just another miserable little Third World country, only a little more romantic than the others because Fidel's so charismatic. What would you do there anyway?"

So I told her—except I left out how my whole inspiration came from the fight with Gina and her friends—how I just wanted to see Cuba with my own eyes, walk the streets of Havana by myself, see where we used to live, talk to people, ask questions.

"I don't know, maybe visit crazy cousin Titi," I said.

Patricia finally smiled. "Yeah, well, that one is special, all right, but probably for different reasons than most of us here think..."

I was hoping she'd say more but she just got a strange, far-away look on her face. When she saw me staring at her, she smiled and shook her head, as if to shake off spirits, or memory.

"You should visit her, why not?" Patricia asked rhetorically. "Of course, you should write her first—let her know you're coming, ask what she needs. I have a friend in my department who's going to Cuba in the next month or so, so he could probably take it for you. That way she'll get it for sure."

"God, what would I say?"

Patricia stood and started cleaning up. "Well, I don't know," she said. "That's up to you."

"I don't even know if my written Spanish is that good," I confessed.

"Well, don't worry about that," she said. "I can fix that for you—if you don't mind me reading the letter."

It was one of those American things you could expect from Patricia: She would, of course, assume the letter was private and confidential—even if it was to a stranger. Of course she'd ask if I minded. Most other cousins would have assumed the opposite, that it was family property, like a bulletin board or magnets on the fridge.

"I don't mind you reading the letter," I said, deciding to take her seriously and not to rib her about her little *americanadas*. I'd always thought it was unfair to kid her about being Americanized when she is, in fact, American-born. Besides, Patricia's always known more about Cuba than all of us put together—our parents included.

"Cool," she said, now wiping the coffee table where I'd made such a mess. "Figure out how much time you want to spend there, then figure out what you want to do when you get back."

"What do you mean, 'When I get back'?"

Patricia stood up straight. "Look, you're not going back to the laundromat—not permanently," she said. "Try to figure out what you want to do...if you can't, at least consider coming down to campus and talking to a career counselor, okay?"

It was another *americanada*, that was clear—but what could I do? I needed her help, to go to Cuba and in so many other ways. And there was no question she was coming from a big warm Cuban heart that loved me tons. I nodded.

"Okay," I said, feeling tiny and grateful. "I'll think about it."

CHAPTER 15

W HEN NENA HEARD ABOUT "THE INCIDENT," she called immediately. It was the first time in our lives something had happened to one of us when we hadn't been together. Nena and I had always been there for each other and this new, and seemingly sudden, separation caused by her move to Miami stirred some dreadful, uneasy feelings in both of us. In spite of the fact that Caridad was around every day, and Patricia stopped by frequently too, I couldn't help feeling abandoned. My main comfort had always been Nena; she'd always known what to do, what to say.

Now with the whole neighborhood buzzing with Jimmy's story about the attack on Gina and me, and the entire family hovering protectively around me, I wished desperately that Nena was home. I wanted to tell her the truth; I'd never kept anything from her in my life. But when I wrapped the cold plastic of the telephone around my face to talk to her, I struggled for words.

"And you really don't have a clue who it was?" Nena asked, surprised. "Wow, you must have been really out of it, sweetie."

"Ah, well, I..." I stammered a little. "He hit me first, I think, and then, ah...that was it."

As soon as I heard what had come out of my mouth, I wanted to die. I had just lied to Nena. Now, to tell her the truth would be a lot more complicated, a lot more humiliating than just explaining about the horrible things that had actually happened that night. Now, I'd have to explain about Jimmy, and about the coward that was living inside of me, the parasite who had made a home in my useless little brain.

"Oh, god, Juani, I am *so* sorry," Nena said on the phone. "I wish I could be there, I really wish I could be there..." As she spoke, Nena cried, her voice breaking now and again. I could tell the guilt was just eating her up, that she was sure that, if she'd been in Chicago instead of Miami, the situation might have been averted in some way—as if that were possible.

"You know, if it would have been the three of us...we probably could have taken him, with the three of us..."

I shrugged, invisible to her. My eyes were misty and I was miserable. My nose was running too and I wiped it on my sleeve. I didn't care about anything. "You wouldn't have been there then, believe me," I said, trying to bring some levity to our conversation.

Nena gasped. She was horrified at the possibility that an intruder could have walked in at an intimate moment, at what greater atrocity could have befallen us if he'd been provoked by such a scene. "You mean, you guys...?"

"No, no, nothing was going on," I said. "We were just cleaning up after the party and stuff but, you know, you would have been gone anyway because I was staying and it was clear and everything."

Nena was silent. Our sniffles filled the line. "I still wish I could have been there. You never know," she said. "And I wish—I *really, really, really* wish—I could be there now."

But she couldn't. Her job was too new to pack up and leave for an extended period of time, and, at least on the surface, it didn't appear to be a situation that demanded her specific attention. After all, I wasn't an invalid, and the rest of the family was around, helping me with what I needed, keeping me company, looking out for me.

"Juani..."

"Yeah?"

"Why don't you come here?" Nena asked. "To Miami...like, for a visit?"

But before I could say yes, before I could even think about it, Nena backed off her invitation. It was as if she'd caught herself, as if, unable to retrieve it, she wanted to make it so unappealing that I wouldn't accept.

"I mean, I'm at work all the time and I...we'd have a lot to talk about," she said hurriedly. "I have a few things to tell you too but...well, hey, it's just stupid stuff about my life and you probably still need space and some time to recover from this horrible thing that's happened—I mean, Juani, I just can't believe it happened right in Gina's apartment, just like that! Do you think—maybe—she's right and it really was some kind of political warning?" She barely paused to take a breath. "You know, here in Miami, Cubans are always shooting each other and blowing each other up because they're not anti-Castro enough. Maybe it's the same for Puerto Ricans with their independence thing, huh?"

"Yeah, I don't know, maybe," I said, baffled. I wanted to accept her invitation, to be with her, to just hang out in the same room as her. For me, Nena's mere presence was often as reassuring as anything she might say. All our lives she'd just intuited my needs, took care of them without much discussion between us at all.

I remember when I first realized I needed to move out of my parents' house. I was nineteen and restless. I'd sat at home for a full year out of high school and I was feeling ridiculous about all the excuses I was coming up with—not lies, just omissions and misrepresentations—so I could stay out and play with my lesbian friends, and so I could sleep over at a lover's house now and then.

Finally, at dinner one night, Nena announced that she thought it'd be good if she and *I* moved out. I still remember our faces—*all* of our faces—including what mine must have looked like: mouth gaping, shocked. Nena hadn't said a word to me—she took the challenge on herself because she knew she had a better chance to get my parents' approval: She's older, she was in school, she's always been tougher. Most Cuban women don't move out of their family's home unless they get married or go off to school. The idea of the two of us sharing an apartment while single and living in the same city as our parents was pure American thinking.

But Nena sold it to Mami and Papi anyway: She explained

that she needed more space, more time alone to study, more opportunity to have classmates over for group work. She made it sound like it was *her* need, not mine, even though I knew better. By the end of her con job, our parents were convinced she was just being considerate to them, knowing they couldn't afford to move to a bigger place that they'd get stuck with later, after we moved out for the right reasons. She was so good, we all walked away from the dinner table sure I was doing her a favor by rooming with her, since I had no apparent reason to leave home other than to keep her company and help with expenses.

Of course, Nena didn't need to move out: In fact, she was better off staying home, saving money. *I* needed my own space desperately, but I would have never had the gall to ask for it myself, or to ask Nena for such a favor. I wasn't even sure I'd known that's what I needed until Nena started talking at the dinner table, pacing herself between bites of rice and *picadillo*. Afterwards, we never talked about it, not directly, but it was totally understood between us that it was her gift to me. That night, as we were getting ready for bed, I came up behind her and hugged her as tight as I could. Later, when she moved to Miami, I kept the apartment and no one dared say a word.

Now—as usual—she'd understood my needs better than me. I *did* need to get away, I *did* need to shake out from "the incident." So why was she backing off?

"Hey, listen...Nena," I said, sniffling still. "Did you mean that invitation? About coming down to visit?"

She paused. What the hell was going on? She sighed. "Yeah, sure," she finally said.

"Is everything okay?" I asked, because if something was wrong on her end, I wanted to know, I wanted to have a chance to be there for her, for once.

Nena laughed. "You know, yeah, everything's fine, finer than I could tell you on the phone," she said, relaxing now. "Look, buy your ticket, come down for a few days, a week, whatever you want. We'll talk when you get here, okay?'

· · · • • · · · ·

So I ended up with a plane ticket to Miami. I packed a small bag with a bathing suit and some books and I trotted over to Tía Celia's, who lives around the corner, before heading to the airport. Because Pauli was still in Mexico and relations with Caridad were somewhat strained because of Jimmy, I was who Tía Celia was relying on for translations and explanations about mail, bills and other things.

Since Tío Pepe died I'd gotten in the habit of dropping by every few days or so and Tía Celia and I had developed a whole routine. I'd walk over for lunch—huge steaming plates of *fufú* with a big slab of meat next to it, or a massive bowl of *caldo gallego,* because everything at Tía Celia's is big and Cuban and delicious but probably bad for you—and we'd sit and chat. At the end of the meal, she'd make me take something from her big bowl full of citrus fruit.

During lunch Tía Celia would ask me about whatever was on her mind—about whether she should switch long-distance companies (AT&T is direct to Cuba, so she kept it), or whether she should invest in a money market fund, or maybe buy a car with the money Tío Pepe left her (not for Caridad but for herself). It's certainly true that I'm not Nena, who really knows about this stuff, or Patricia, who has Ira to guide her, or even Tía Zenaida, who's always done so well and whose English is impeccable. But I think Tía Celia appreciated talking to me because I was there, live and in person unlike Nena, and never in a hurry, the way Patricia and Tía Zenaida always seem.

"I think it's so good you're going to see Nena," Tía Celia said, spearing a big chunk of swordfish out of a pot and dropping it on my plate. "It'll be good for you to rest, and she'll be happy to see you."

"Yeah," I said with a shrug, then immediately got down to the business of eating. I really was looking forward to being with Nena but, even though she'd sounded cheery at the end of our call, I wasn't sure what she had to tell me. I worried she somehow knew I was lying, worried she'd judge me and think less of me.

"*¿Qué te pasa, eh, Juani?*" my Tía Celia asked, pulling up a chair for herself at the kitchen table. She began to peel an orange, the rind dropping on the table like eggshells.

"*Nada,*" I said between mouthfuls. The swordfish was meaty and chewy. I shovelled in a forkful of rice.

Tía Celia shook her head. "So what are you going to do in Miami, eh? Nena plan anything special?" She licked the juice from her fingers, a gesture so sensual it shocked me at first.

"Not that I know of," I said, wiping my mouth with a napkin.

Tía Celia sighed. "I miss Pauli," she said. She sucked in an orange slice. "And I miss Rosa too—I even miss not being able to sleep because of her crying. It's funny what we miss, no?" She smiled sadly, then dropped an orange half-moon in her mouth.

I nodded, fascinated. "When are they coming back?" I took a sip of water from a glass she'd set at the table for me and waded through chunks of lemon floating on top.

Tía Celia shrugged. "*No sé,*" she said. "Maybe next week sometime. It's taking a little longer than Pauli imagined to wrap up her business in Mexico. I guess things aren't always as easy there as they are here." Tía Celia rolled her eyes.

"You think maybe...she's not coming back?"

"Oh no, she's coming back—she *promised.*"

There was no question then that Pauli would reappear. She's the kind who'll get martyred to keep her word. "Maybe what's taking so long is...stuff with Rosa's father?" I asked cautiously. I leaned back in my chair, tilting its front legs off the floor. Lunch had been incredible.

But Tía Celia shook her head again. "Nah, that's not it." She cupped her hands and collected all the rinds, then got up and threw them into the garbage can under the sink. "Whomever *he* is, he's here in Chicago."

I dropped back down to the floor with a thud. "Really?" I was amazed. "What makes you think so?"

Tía Celia smiled slyly. "I just do. Mother's instincts." She washed her hands.

I laughed. "She hasn't said anything, huh?"

Tía Celia smiled again. "Of course not. Who are we talking about here? The Fortress of Solitude, isn't that what you girls call Pauli?" She began to clear off the table. I followed with my plate in hand to the sink. My arm and chest were remarkably pain free.

"Do you and Mami and Tía Zenaida know *everything?*" I asked with a chuckle.

"Almost," she said, winking. "There's some concern about Rosa's citizenship—Pauli wants to make sure she can keep both U.S. and Mexican passports. Also, I think Pauli's trying to figure out something about art school. I guess she took some classes in Mexico and wants to see if she can transfer the credits or something like that." She covered the pots on her stove, which steamed like a witch's cauldron. "And you?"

"What do you mean?"

"Do you know what you're going to do when you get back from Miami?" She asked this with a too casual tone, immediately betraying my family's concern about me. That's when I realized that somewhere, somehow, my mom and my aunts had already turned a corner about my role at the Wash-N-Dry.

There was no point in pretending with Tía Celia, the sweetest of all my aunts. "No, I really don't," I confessed. "Patricia wants me to see a career counselor when I get back. And I will, but frankly, it'll be just to please her."

I thought it wise, at least for the moment, to skip any mention of Cuba until I had secured a visa or a date of departure, something more concrete than just a desire to go and Patricia's promise to help. Not that my family would have political problems with such a trip, but I knew it was the kind of thing that would, at least initially, spin them all into a frenzy of worry. There was already enough anxiety whirling around me. I really didn't want more attention.

"I don't believe that," Tía Celia said. "Of course you're going to see the career counselor for yourself. Everybody has some sense of the future. Otherwise, why would we go on living?"

"Well," I said laughing while scrubbing the few dishes in her sink. "I have enough sense of the future to want to go on living, I just don't know what I want to do when I go on."

"Then maybe you should think about what makes you feel good," Tía Celia continued. "Think about what you want for yourself, then worry about what you need to do to get it."

Since when had my Tía Celia become so wise? I stared at her as she fidgeted around in the kitchen, checking on her food, putting things away, folding this dish towel and that piece of aluminum foil. "Tía?" I said. She looked up at me. I tower over her, as I do over my Tía Zenaida and Mami. Her eyes were eager and wide. "What about you? What's your sense of the future?"

She laughed. "*Ay, Juani...*"

"No, really—I mean, what's yours?" I wiped the sink clean and turned toward her. "Come on, Tía."

We were standing in the kitchen across from each other. Our muscles were suddenly tense, our eye contact direct and challenging. Tía Celia was standing the straightest I'd ever seen her.

"This is it," she said, smiling but stiff, her arm sweeping her kitchen as if it were a show room on a TV game show. "My sense of the future was always to live without pain, without humiliation; to have Pauli here, with her own child, so she'd understand what it's like to be a mother; and Caridad...well, my vision isn't complete yet."

Tía Celia turned, grabbed a pear from her fruit bowl and walked off into another room. I stood there, as stunned as I'd ever been, my body against the sink. Tía Celia's vision of the future had obviously *never* included Tío Pepe. I shuddered.

· · · . · · · ·

"It's him again," Tía Celia said, looking out the window at the cab that had pulled up, ready to take me to O'Hare. She bit into her pear with a loud crunch.

"What do you mean?" I asked. I pulled the blinds apart with my fingers, like she'd done, and looked outside. A yellow taxi hugged the curb in front of the house, its driver a nervous young man who paced on the sidewalk. He was handsome, Asian or Middle Eastern. He looked awfully familiar but I couldn't place him.

"Every time I call a cab, I get him," Tía Celia said, amused, her mouth full.

I laughed. "Maybe you tip too well," I said. "Or maybe he knows you're a beautiful widow and he has a mad crush on you."

Tía Celia waved me away, her face all scrunched up. "*Ay, Juani, por dios,* you're so disrespectful," she said, but she was enjoying my teasing, I could tell.

I grabbed my bag, gave my Tía Celia a tight squeeze and a flurry of kisses, and trotted out to meet the cab. But as soon as the driver saw me, I swear all the air went out of him. His shoulders fell, his eyes misted and dropped. He was clearly disappointed.

I gave him directions and climbed in the back while he circled around to the driver's seat. As he settled in, punching mysterious buttons into the computer set-up that connected him to the cab office, I couldn't help but notice his big round black eyes and the long strands of jet black hair that fell on his sad, ageless face. I glanced over at the name on his cab permit: Ali Ahuja.

I decided to take a chance. "Excuse me," I said to him. "Do you know my cousin, Pauli Gonzáles?"

His head spun around to me, his eyes dancing. "Pauli, yes," he said excitedly, nodding over and over. He has a very slight accent. With his face so close, his coloring so clear, I began to understand why Ali had seemed so familiar: He was the cabbie that had followed Patricia and me that night she was lecturing me about how the family had been treating Gina; he was the one blinking his lights behind us.

"Look," I said. "I think you're scaring my aunt. She says you come every time she calls a cab."

"Yes, yes," he said, nodding wildly. "I'm trying to talk to Pauli. I *need* to talk to Pauli." He was clutching at his chest, as if his heart were held in place by his fingers.

"Yes, but she's not here—she's in Mexico."

"In Mexico?" For a moment, he seemed confused, as if he didn't understand. "In Mexico?" He jerked, as if somebody had just hit him. "And...and her baby...?"

I pretended I didn't know what he was talking about. "Pauli lives there," I said, lying a little, "in Mexico."

Ali turned around but I could see his face glistening in the rear view mirror. I wanted to reach over the front seat and squeeze his shoulder but I held back. He sighed.

"Okay," he said, pulling himself together. His shoulders straightened, his neck stiffened. "O'Hare, right?"

I nodded into the mirror, where we were making eye contact now.

"Are you from India?" I asked as the cab melted into traffic. I already knew I didn't need to test this guy's DNA, just his "impossibility."

"Yes, yes," he nodded again. "And you are from Cuba, yes?"

"Yes," I said.

"Like Pauli," he said, satisfied with himself.

"Well, no, not like Pauli," I said. "I was born in Cuba, Pauli was born here."

He nodded.

"And you are Moslem, Hindu, what?" I knew I was being impertinent but his answer could be vital. Just how "impossible" was he?

"Hindu," he said, smiling with gleaming white teeth into the rearview mirror. He really was beautiful, almost too much so.

"I'm going to Miami, to visit my sister," I said, hoping to cut him off.

I remember reading an article about Hindu attitudes toward female babies and I began to wonder if Ali would be disappointed knowing Pauli's baby was a girl. I was curious as hell, bursting with questions for him, but I also knew I was out of my league here. I could only go so far before I might fuck things up with Pauli, whom I knew would be unforgiving if I did the wrong thing.

I took a book out of my bag and pretended I was instantly absorbed into its pages. Ali tried to keep the conversation going once or twice, but I didn't respond. I counted on his confusion, and a bit on the formality of his culture, to keep him from pushing me. As I sunk back in the seat, I realized I was going to have more to discuss with Nena than I'd ever imagined.

CHAPTER 16

THE RIDE FROM THE AIRPORT WITH NENA was terrific. It was so wonderful just to be with her, to feel her close by. Nena looked great too: brown and firm, her eyes bright and her hair a luscious, wavy black. When I saw her at the airport, I was momentarily taken aback: She was so beautiful. Could we really be from the same gene pool?

We rushed out to her new red Mazda Navajo truck that I would have never imagined my sister driving. We dashed from the air-conditioned terminal through the humid tunnel of cars and vans spewing exhaust to her big truck sitting in a fire lane, a ticket flapping under the wipers. She grabbed it and cavalierly threw it into the back seat, where it joined what appeared to be a collection of tickets. I was struck by what an unlikely act that was for her, so free and optimistic. Then Nena sealed us in with a touch of a button, immediately cranked on the AC and strapped on a pair of mean-looking sunglasses. With a flick of her hand, she had bouncy reggae coming from the speakers. As she drove along, she sang with the music, perky and alive. This was my sister?

Within seconds we were on the long, curling freeway, speeding toward her place. While Nena chatted it up with me about how happy she was to see me, and how I didn't look bad at all considering the circumstances, I stared out through the green-tinted glass at the tall palmettos, the huge American cars honking and cutting each other off, and the unending landscape of new apartment buildings and shiny strip malls. Everything was so bright, images came through bursts of white. I'd forgotten my sunglasses and squinting so much was giving me a headache.

"God, isn't anything old in Miami?" I asked as we passed yet one more new glaring glass-surfaced building.

"No, there aren't even old Jewish retirees in Miami Beach anymore," she said. "It's all *Miami Vice,* European models and Gloria Estefan's restaurant."

Everyone talks about the flatness of the Midwest, but Miami makes Chicago look like the rolling hills of San Francisco. Miami is an arid pancake with splashes of neon, even in daylight. And because of the swamps underneath, there's not much height to the construction, so the city has a kind of stunted look to it.

"Welcome to Havana, U.S.A," Nena joked.

"No way, no way!" I protested. "Hey, I've seen photos—there's no way Havana's this ugly!" And I've heard, I thought to myself, not just from Patricia, but from Gina and her friends: Cuba's green and lush and majestic, no matter how badly it may be crumbling. *Te quiero verde,* I remembered.

This looked like as good a time as any to tell her—about my proposed trip to Cuba, about what actually happened between Gina and me. I was thinking at the very least it was a good set-up, it would create context and make it easier to explain later. But just as I was getting my story together, just as I was rehearsing it in my head, Nena pulled abruptly off the road.

"Listen," she said, suddenly so serious it was frightening. She kept her sunglasses on, making eye contact nearly impossible. "We've got to talk." The engine was still running. The air was blowing ice cold. I felt myself shiver.

"Okay," I said. But this wasn't how I wanted to do it. I'd hoped it would be more casual, even if it was in the car, but not in this hermetically-sealed silence stopped dead at the side of the freeway. I glanced over my shoulder, afraid a state trooper might drive up and ask if there was trouble. I was convinced there were warrants out for me somewhere, somehow.

"Anything wrong?" Nena asked. I shook my head. She took her glasses off. "Okay, listen, I mean...you probably know..."

"Know what?" I was jumpy again, sweat on my upper lip. I felt the way, I'm sure, bombing fugitives from the sixties must feel when, even after a lifetime of peaceful underground exile with good deeds and community work in the peace and hunger movements, they're finally caught. Even if all that turns out to be worthless and they draw a twenty-year sentence, at least they can be themselves, sign their real names to letters, make phone calls, and beg for forgiveness. It had only been a month or so for me but it already weighed in as a lifetime. I was ready to give up, relieved to surrender.

Nena looked at me. "Give me a chance, okay?" She took a deep breath, then bit her nail.

It was then I realized Nena was far more nervous than I was. She didn't know my secret, didn't even suspect it. As I stared at her, I realized Nena's eyes were red, tears brimming. Whatever the secret was, it was hers.

"Nena, what's going on?" I was scared. I reached over to touch her, to hold her, but she started laughing.

"God, Juani, you really don't know, do you?"

"Know what? Know what?"

She pulled me to her, laughing into my shoulder and wiping her tears with her wrists. "I'm in love! I'm in love! I'm in love!" she shouted, pulling away, her face flushed. "And it's incredible!"

I know I had a huge grin on my face. I was happy for her, of course. "When did this happen? Who is he?" I asked. "What's his name? Does he love you too?" I had so many questions— Nena in love! This was big news, *huge* news! Nena had dated, she'd had quite a few admirers, but she'd never been seriously interested in anybody, much less in love.

"His name is Bernie, Bernie Beck," she said, "and, yes, he loves me too, he loves me very much."

"He's Jewish," I said, registering the name. "Well, Patricia and Ira will get a kick out of that. You guys can start a support group for Cubans and Jews who love each other."

She was supposed to laugh but Nena got a little quiet instead. "Yeah, something like that," she said, then stopped, but it felt unfinished, like a pause instead of a period. "Bernie's *half* Jewish…"

"Yeah?"

Nena sighed. "Listen, Juani, he's a great guy," she said. The air got heavy again. I was getting cold, really cold.

"Of course, if you love him, he must be," I said, but I had no idea where we were going now.

"Yeah, I'm crazy about him," she said.

Traffic was whipping by. I was sure we were begging for trouble just sitting on the shoulder of the freeway. If not the cops, then a carjacker, a rapist, something awful for sure. "Nena, I want to hear all about him—what he does, how you met, everything," I said. "But can we go somewhere? Anywhere, really—your place, a coffee shop, a park, whatever. I want to be able to savor this a little, okay?"

But Nena was still. She stared out to the freeway blurred by the traffic and heat and reached across the seat to touch my thigh. "He's black," she said.

I couldn't help it, I laughed. "So?"

Nena turned back to me, grinning. "And he's gorgeous," she said, pulling the car into gear.

"Mami's gonna die," I said as we dove into traffic, both of us laughing all the while.

· · · , · · · · ·

As it turned out, Bernie was amazing. The son of a Jewish literature professor at NYU and a black Puerto Rican poet I recognized—Amparo Maure, who wrote *Plena Voz,* a classic of modern *independentista* literature. He was a handsome, chocolate-colored man with an easy smile and dreds down to his waist.

"You really know my mother's work?" he asked, surprised and pleased when Nena introduced us.

I spouted back a few lines I'd learned from Gina and her friends. Bernie was impressed: He clapped his hands and hugged me close. His body was warm and he smelled naturally sweet. "I love you already," he said, all smiles, laughing it up.

His mother, it turned out, is a lesbian. His parents divorced long ago but they're friendly, like Tío Raúl and Tía Zenaida (I remember thinking, It must be a New York thing...) so he was pretty unfazed about me. But, as much as Gina and her *independentista* pals yakked up Amparo Maure, they'd never mentioned a word to me about her sexuality.

"Yeah, well, the *independentista* movement doesn't do well with lesbian and gay issues," Bernie said over a dinner he'd cooked in my honor: pumpkin tortellini in a white cream sauce with nutmeg, cold shrimp in some sort of spicy mango chutney. "They're in solidarity with everybody but gay people. They're like Spartacists—they're not *anti*-gay per se, they just think homosexuality's a product of a capitalist society. As soon as the revolution comes, men will stop being narcissistic, which will put an end to male homosexuality. And they'll stop being sexist, which will dampen lesbian ardor, since, obviously, women only turn to women 'cause men are dogs, right?"

Bernie laughed. He had a great laugh, deep and robust, and he squinted his eyes when he smiled. He and Nena were constantly giggling, gazing at each other, and touching. I'd never seen her like this in my life. It was wild to watch my normally tense and serious sister so playful and happy, as carefree as a co-ed during the first few days of school.

Apparently, they met days after Nena moved to Miami. Bernie was a bicycle messenger running a package to her office and he stopped dead in his tracks when he saw her. It was love at first sight, they both say. Within a week, they were living together in an old warehouse off Biscayne Boulevard. Bernie and some friends had converted it into a fairly livable loft. Although it wasn't air-conditioned, the concrete and the breeze off the bay kept it pretty cool. There they'd set up house, a rehearsal space for Bernie's band (Garvey Way, the tape Nena had popped on in the car; they play everything from reggae to souk, salsa to soca), and a bank of computers from which Bernie and his pal George run the messenger service. That explained the half dozen bicycles which hung from hooks in the ceiling. Both he and George still pedal now and again, Bernie explained, because they cover emergencies, it keeps them in shape, and helps them stay on top of what clients think as well as what the messengers actually have to put up with.

"It was total luck he ran the delivery that day we met," Nena said, laughing.

"Nah, not luck," said Bernie, beaming at her, "fate—it was fate." He reached across the table and squeezed her hand.

Watching them together, I was really happy for Nena. But their unabashed love only underscored the emptiness in my own life. I felt ugly and envious. And miserably alone.

· · · **.** **.** · · ·

I stayed with Nena and Bernie for a few days before I decided to go down to Key West. It was sweet to be around them, but suffocating. Besides, I wasn't getting any time with Nena. There didn't seem to be even five minutes to say anything about Gina, or to tell her I'd met Ali and what I was thinking about him and Pauli. Bernie was always around, working with his partner George or at the computer, rehearsing with his band, or cooking for us. The guy couldn't seem to stop chopping and blending, sautéing and blackening. It's not that I didn't trust him, but I just didn't know him that well—and I wasn't used to Nena having a lover. I wasn't used to not having her all to myself whenever I wanted.

I borrowed Nena's truck and sped down south, to the one place in the U.S. where, on a clear night, you can see Havana. In Key West, I rented a room at a gay guesthouse where I was one of only two women in the entire place. The rest of the clientele were sinewy red-skinned men from up north who wore tiny Speedos to show off their equipment. The guesthouse used pink napkins, pink towels, pink curtains—they played up the faggy stuff just for fun. I hung out by the pool, drank *mojitos* (the Cuban influence was still very intense), played dominos at the pier, went to Hemingway's house, and checked out the places where José Martí used to talk to Cuban cigar workers back in the 1800s.

Even though I'd brought a bathing suit, I couldn't get it together to go to the beach; it seemed too much like pleasure and I was sure I didn't deserve any of that yet. Besides, I was convinced I still looked like an accident victim, no matter how much Bernie and Nena had assured me to the contrary, so my attitude was to keep my body covered. Even by the pool, I stayed in my clothes, ordering drinks from the bar and reading, writing in my journal now that my arm didn't seem to pull on my chest muscles so much anymore.

In the last month, my journal had become a nightmare. Not writing about "the incident" right away had been a terrible mistake. Now, every time I began to jot down my story, it got confused with Jimmy's mess. I'd be right at the place where I hit Gina when suddenly, I'd look down at the page in horror: *And then the guy grabbed the chair and hit Gina in the back, like on a TV show. And the chair broke into pieces, so I grabbed a leg to defend myself and sparred with the guy.* But I knew that wasn't what happened! *Or was it?*

I'd flip through the pages and find this: *I kicked the guy in the balls and made him run out of the place.* But none of that was true, none of it. So what was it doing in my notes? How had it made its way into my journal?

One night I strolled down to the pier, hoping the few clouds of the previous nights had lifted and I might get a glimpse of the lights in Havana. I thought the view would free my head. I'd bought a pair of binoculars but I knew I didn't really need them if the skies were clear. This night was spectacular: a swash of stars seemed to create a bridge between the Keys and Cuba, and the sky was a deep blue velvet. I closed my eyes, breathed deep and held the salty air in my lungs. I'd bought an ice cream cone and it was melting right through my fingers.

"Waiting for somebody?" the other woman at the guesthouse asked, out of nowhere, while I was staring off the pier at what I was sure was the halo over Havana.

"Huh?"

"You know, a *balsa* or something?" She was trying to be

funny but I wasn't amused. I remembered all those times my cousin Titi had tried to leave and had never made it very far off the shore. I tried to project myself into her place, to consider the impact of those ninety miles and the possibility of washing up here, in this crazy queer town that has so little do with the rest of the world. I turned around and tried to find Miami in the opposite direction, but the sky was mysteriously black and starless to the north, with a toxic haze over what might be the city.

"There used to be a railroad that connected the Keys to Miami but it got destroyed by a hurricane," the woman said, apparently reading my mind. She wasn't going away, regardless of the fact that I was ignoring her. "Now there's a highway," she said, turning her attention away from me and to the jugglers and hustlers who flock to the pier.

"Yes," I said, realizing just how small she was, how like a child who I could just hold in my arms. I assumed she was trying to pick me up, and I considered it for a minute.

"*No hay mal que por bien no venga,*" she said, turning in my direction again. Her accent in Spanish was Colombian or Venezuelan. While I thought about it, she repeated what she said in English, in case I didn't understand: "There's no bad that's not good in the long run." She dropped some coins into a hat a mime had put out on the ground for just that purpose. The guy, dressed in green—including green face make-up—looked like a giant sprout and was pretending he was trapped in a box.

"Why do you say that?" I asked, licking the ice cream dripping around and between my fingers.

"You don't really look like you came here to have fun," she said, "but more to get away."

I laughed. "What are you, telepathic?"

Now it was her turn to laugh. "Well, no, not exactly," she said. "But I'll do a Tarot reading for you for ten bucks if you'd like."

When she said that, I laughed aloud. So she wasn't after my

body after all, but my money and soul. I thought about my mother and the *babalao* who told her she'd marry my father and have beautiful white-skinned children, and how now Nena was in love with Bernie, whom she no doubt would marry, and with whom she'd have children, darker than Rosa, with curly *mulato* hair and lips like rose petals; and I thought about my Tío Raúl and his encounter with Caviancito, how he'd ignored his advice and met his destiny anyway.

"What good would a reading do me?" I asked, but I was smiling.

She shrugged. "It's different for each person," she said. "You know, for some people, it confirms their plans, their ambitions. For others, it helps them stay away from dangers. I suppose, if you don't believe, it's worthless."

I tossed the remainder of my cone into a trash can and wiped my hands on my shorts. I hadn't realized we'd been walking together.

"You know," I said, "I actually do believe in those sorts of things—Tarot, shells, tea leaves, the works. But I think I'd rather not know my future. I think I'd rather be surprised. But thanks anyway."

Then I stepped off the sidewalk and crossed the street to a little stationery and book shop, where I bought a copy of *Penthouse Letters*. I needed to get my journal right, and to write that letter to Titi, but first, I needed to wipe myself out, I needed to put my head down and stop thinking.

· · · **.** · · · ·

"Hey Bernie," I said in his direction when I got back to Miami. I'd just walked in the door and he was sitting at his computers, his head bent intently into the screen. Nena was at work.

"Hey Juani," he said, smiling but barely looking up, his fingers working furiously on the board. I guessed he was tracking couriers for his business or doing some other mysterious technological work.

I didn't want to bother him, so I quietly set my bag down on the floor, and plopped down on the couch. I liked Nena and Bernie's loft but I didn't think one big open room was for me. It didn't matter how large it was or who I lived with—even Nena—I'd want to close a door sometimes. I watched Bernie, his shoulders curving toward the screen, all his muscles tight. The phones were curiously quiet. There was no music on. Bernie's arm arched on the desk, moving his mouse in a circle. He was so at home. It struck me, in fact, that this was much more his home than Nena's—his business was here, his rehearsal space. I knew that big bed in the corner hadn't come with her. The art was too African, too Third World, to be Nena's—the elongated bodies of the wooden sculptures by the door, the multi-colored handwoven *kentes* on the walls. There were a handful of surfboards, phallic and thick, leaning against one wall. For an instant, they looked like an installation.

I was tired but I knew I couldn't sleep with Bernie working in the same room, no matter how far away from me he was. It would just feel like he was watching, even if he never even glanced my way. I figured I'd try to work. I took out the notebook on which I'd scribbled a few notes to Titi. Nothing was coming to me. What, after all, do you say to someone you've never met? Someone who, you've been told all your life, is nuts? Someone whom you suspect is a lesbian, like you? I didn't want to make assumptions but I also wanted to make a connection.

I'd come to the realization that, if I went to Cuba, I wanted to stay with Titi, or at a hotel. My cousin Tomás Joaquín, whom I love, is just too much of a gossip. Whatever I did on the island would be reported back to my family in more detail than I'd ever care for. (I suspect Patricia knows that, which is why she didn't recommend writing to him, much less staying with him.) I was starting some new scratches when Bernie let out a yelp on his computer, shot up from his seat and hit the refrigerator for a carton of orange juice, which he guzzled straight.

"Want some?" he offered me.

"Nah, thanks," I said.

He nodded and wandered back to his computer. "Okay, level twenty," he said, settling back in.

"Hey, you're not working!" I exclaimed, slapping down my notebook. "And here I'm trying to be quiet and everything."

He laughed. "Well, so was I!" he grinned. "You play Mario?"

"Hey, man, I play anything if you teach me," I said, leaping over to his side of the loft and settling into his partner George's chair.

Bernie turned on a second computer. He had loaded it with a slew of games I'd never even heard of. When I told him I liked Lethal Enforcer and Mortal Kombat, he found a killer kickboxing game with stunning graphics and some nasty sounds. Bernie stacked six CDs into the deck and we took off on our respective screen rampages with a soundtrack that spanned the globe: Guillermo Portabales, Angelique Kidjo, Khaled, Sheila Chandra, some weird klezmer compilation, and The Beatles.

For at least a few hours, I was in heaven.

CHAPTER 17

"**W**HY DO YOU WANT TO TORTURE your father with this?" my mother asked me on the phone. She was back home in Chicago, but I knew the distance between us was much greater than actual miles would ever indicate.

Still in Miami, in that vast, modern loft where Nena was living, I couldn't take my eyes off Bernie's computer screen: *Natural adhesives come from a variety of animal and vegetable sources. Synthetic adhesives are compounded from simple chemicals,* read the text.

"Mami, please, if you won't ask him, then let me, *por favor,*" I begged.

I'd been trying for more than an hour to get her to let me talk to my father about his duct tape formula. I don't know what had come over me—why it suddenly became so fucking important—but I was obsessed: I had to know the truth about this stupid thing and the human cost seemed irrelevant.

But my mother refused to put Papi on the phone the minute she found out what I wanted. And her refusal seemed to fuel my insistence. I kept calling back but she was as quietly adamant as the guards at Buckingham Palace. She wouldn't take the phone off the hook, and I wouldn't give up, so we just kept playing the same game: The phone would ring, she'd pick up, I'd implore, she'd say no and eventually hang up. There was no yelling on her end, no emotion. Then I'd re-dial and we'd start all over again.

But I was starting to get sick of it, so I got a little threatening: "Listen, Mami, if you won't ask him now, I'll just ask him when I get home—I'm gonna ask him, no matter what, okay?"

Mami stayed silent. I could hear distant traffic on the phone, as if she were sitting by an open window. There was a TV too, or a radio, something broadcasting the news or some kind of informational program.

Nena and Bernie sat nearby on the couch with worried looks. They were letting me play this out, dangerous as it was. Nena rattled her fingers on an end table, got up and began pacing. I could see her in my peripheral vision, shaking her head. Bernie looked nervous and guilty, occasionally glancing up at Nena but avoiding her eyes when she looked back.

"Just ask him this, just ask him if the base for his duct tape was a natural or synthetic adhesive," I told my mother. "And if it was natural, if it was animal or vegetable, okay?"

"What does it matter?" she asked. "His invention was the concept, not the specific product."

I kept reading: *A major type of natural adhesive is animal glue. The animal glues are made from collagen, a protein found in skin, bone, and sinew. Since ancient times animal glue has been used in woodworking and now it is also used in making books, sandpaper, and certain gummed tapes.* I wanted to know what my father really knew about duct tape, I wanted to test him, I wanted him to fail that test, and to nail him. I wanted to throw myself on the floor and kick and scream and cry.

"I don't know if it was animal or vegetable, I tell you," my mother finally barked into the phone. She was so frustrated with me, I thought she might cry. But she was still trying to keep her voice even; she couldn't afford for my father, sitting in the next room reading the newspaper, to have a clue about what was going on. His ignorance was her bliss. So she'd pause, breathe, then answer.

"Juani, *por favor*," Mami pleaded.

I read on: *Both natural and synthetic rubber are used as adhesives in pressure-sensitive tapes, such as masking and cellophane tapes.*

"But I thought you carried the duct tape formula to the boat," I said, my voice so mean now I barely recognized it myself. It was a low growl, robotic but desperate. I could feel my face twisting as I spoke; I was sure I looked like my own version of Jimmy.

Nena's head snapped around when she heard me. She wasn't so much worried as angry now: Her look was hard, unforgiving. Bernie sat on the couch, slumped and miserable. He covered his face with one of his hands and stared at the floor.

"I lost the formula, remember?" Mami said, breathing hard, exasperated.

"And you didn't read it? It didn't occur to you to read that stupid piece of paper, just in case something happened?" I badgered.

"It was your father's formula, Juani, don't you understand? I had nothing to do with it."

I was slowly dying from the venom coursing through my veins, doubled over in Bernie's chair now, my legs shaking. "If it was so fucking important, if it was so goddamn vital, how could neither of you think to memorize it, or to have a duplicate copy?" I yelled into the phone.

"It was too difficult to memorize," Mami said in a terse whisper. "It's a *chemical* formula."

"Well, how come Papi never tried to duplicate it?"

"Juani, the *yanquis* stole it—do you understand?—there was nothing to duplicate, it was already for sale at the supermarket when we got here," my mother said. She'd surrendered. She was crying now. I could hear the sniffling, I could picture her shoulders sloping, shaking. "And we had no proof of anything. We couldn't sue—there was nothing. Do you understand? How many times do you have to hear the story to understand? There was nothing!"

But I was on an evil, evil quest. "You're lying," I said, hearing the words like bullets piercing my mother. She gasped then folded, sobbed. But I didn't stop: "You expect me to believe the Americans stole the formula and put it on the market between the time we left Cuba and the time we arrived here? What was that, Mami, a couple of days? Is that what you expect me to believe? You're lying, you're both lying!"

I started screaming the same thing over and over into the phone, my own tears coming down hot and salty. I was up, stomping and pacing, my face red, my body acrid from sweat. I was going under with some hideous fever, lights flashing in my eyes from imaginary strobes.

Then I felt Nena's strong arms around me, restraining, not comforting, and the jerky way she took the phone from my hand, now frozen into a claw-like shape. As soon as I sensed her grip on me, the way she lifted my whole weight off the floor, even if it was for just an instant—less than a second, a moment utterly immeasurable—I fell into the abyss. Nena let go and I collapsed on the floor.

"Mami, I'm sorry," Nena said into the phone. Her voice sounded cold and alien. "Juani's out of control," I heard her say. "I don't know what's wrong, but I'm sorry, I'm so, so sorry." I heard Mami's fuzzy response, then Nena set the receiver down.

"What the fuck are you doing?" she demanded. Her eyes were red; she was furious. Her whole body leaned forward as if she were a wrestler, ready to take me. Her arms hung just a few inches away from her body.

"I...I don't know," I tried to say, but I was wailing now. I was a pile of human debris on the floor, shaking from the pain and havoc I'd wreaked.

Nena took a deep breath, bent down and cradled me. "*Ay, Juani...*" She was finally crying too.

I put my arms around her and felt her, flushed and damp, up against me. She was all softness, which surprised me. Bernie got up from the couch, came over and hovered above us for a minute or so, but he was too freaked out to do anything other than his own cautious pacing. I saw him pull on his lower lip with his fingers, sort of plucking at the skin there, then he turned around and walked away.

"What...I mean, did Mami say anything else?" I asked as I slobbered on Nena's shoulder.

"No...no, but she'll talk to me later," she said, patting me on the shoulder and head as if I were a baby needing to belch or vomit. "She was too upset. She was kind of out of it, mumbling something about the duct tape and milk."

I couldn't believe it! Had she really just said that?

I pulled away and leapt to my feet, maniacally searching out the keyboard and scrolling down the computer screen. Nena stood by, stunned and helpless. There it was: *Casein glue, made from milk, is from an animal source but it is not a true animal glue.* I slammed my fist on Bernie's desk.

"What? What?" Nena asked nervously. She was at a complete loss. She looked as if she wasn't sure whether to call the mental health authorities or the cops, hit me, or just cry until she fell asleep and perhaps hope to wake up from this hideous nightmare.

I dropped into the chair in front of the keyboards. "I just don't know who or what to believe," I said, "ever."

. . . .

It had all begun innocently enough. After hours of video games on Bernie's machine, I asked him what he used the computer for. Maybe we could use one at the laundromat. I'd been thinking there might be ways of being more efficient that I just didn't know about. Later, when I got back to Chicago and told Patricia the story, she accused me of wanting to introduce a computer to the business because it would scare Mami and my aunts—and make me indispensable again, at least for a while. I got mad when she said this but now, with some time to think about it, I realize she may have been right.

At my request, Bernie walked me through some of his basic set-ups on the computer and I began to understand how we might be able to use one at the Wash-N-Dry for inventory and cash flow purposes, but I also knew pretty instantly that our business was so simple, we really didn't need one. It would make me indispensable to have one all right, but it would also trap me. Papi would never consider learning it—he was such a figurehead manager anyway—and my mother and aunts would feel compelled to pretend they were intimidated by it, regardless of their true feelings. The only one who might not care if it became obvious she knew more than my father was Tía

Zenaida, and I wasn't sure how ready I was for that kind of competition. She'd certainly done a good job of making me feel useless since "the incident."

"Sometimes, the computer's just fun, though," Bernie said with a grin.

"Yeah, the games are cool," I said.

"Well, yeah, but also, you can learn all kinds of weird stuff," he said, punching up some music charts. "See? I can find out the Top Ten in Brazil, in Puerto Rico, in South Africa—all in, like, a minute."

I peeked at the screen. "Yeah, that's neat," I said, "for you, being a musician and all."

"Oh, but you can find out all kinds of other things too," he said, his fingers flying again. Up on the screen came a quick paragraph on his mother: *Maure, Amparo (Amparo Angelos, born 1944), Puerto Rican poet, performer, and author of candid autobiographical works, born in Ponce, Puerto Rico; encouraged to write by older brother, Jaime, an anti-statehood Puerto Rican legislator who was later killed in a terrorist shoot out. New York University, 1968; poetry,* Plena Voz *(1970), an anti-statehood history of Puerto Rico in verse, and* La Papaya *(1974),* Mujeres y Niños *(1976);* Godless Children *(1986), her first English language book;* Move It *(1990).*

"Wow," I said, actually impressed. "I didn't know any of that, other than *Plena Voz.*"

Bernie laughed. "This is from one of the on line encyclopedias," he said. "They pretty much tell you what they want you to know. Like, they don't mention any of her feminist activities, or that she runs the only press in the world exclusively publishing Puerto Rican lesbians. And, of course, everything's 'anti-statehood,' like that's the only way you can read her work. I mean, that's part of the fun with this stuff, I guess—reading between the lines."

I had an idea. "Hey, call up Tío Raúl," I said.

Bernie played on the keys. And there it was: *Fonseca, Raúl (born 1930). Raúl Fonseca created his trademark pieces by using only black and white paint. Raúl Sigfredo Fonseca Torres was born in Matanzas, Cuba, and came to the United States in 1960, an exile from Fidel Castro's revolution. He studied under Thomas Bentram, whose realistic style of painting he later rejected. During his early years, he drove taxicabs and did maintenance work in New York City. Fonseca's early paintings rely on the use of bright colors and reflect the influence of his upbringing in the tropics. After encountering his first northern winter, he began to paint exclusively in black and white. His first one-man show was in 1962. Since then, Fonseca has held shows of new works nearly every year, including exhibitions in Venice, Milan, and Paris. In his later works, faces and shapes are recognizable behind the mass of shadows. Among his best-known works are* Gusano Ghosts, Winter Rhythms, La Cafetera/Christmas Morning *and* Blue Boots. Havana Mist, *which the artist sold for fifteen hundred dollars when he painted it in 1962, was purchased by the National Gallery of Art for more than two million dollars in 1986.*

I couldn't believe it. "That's not right," I said. "Tío Raúl isn't an exile. He was here long before the revolution. Heck, he went *back* after the revolution."

"See? It's what I was telling you," Bernie said. "You have to read between the lines."

"And it wasn't the winters here that changed his style, it was being in Cuba and Costa Rica and almost dying a couple of times," I continued, aghast.

"Yep," Bernie said, like this was just the way things were supposed to be.

Then the real light bulb went off: "Bernie," I said, "let's look up *duct tape.*" I don't know why this occurred to me—clearly everything was unreliable. The whole world was one big liar's club. What the hell was I thinking? But Bernie just giggled and made the right strokes. A run of lines popped up on the screen.

"Oh, great, *alt.sex.duct-tape.hamster,*" Bernie said, laughing heartily.

I glanced over his shoulder. "Here's something," I said, using my finger to point at an entry about adhesives in the tropics. From there on, I was a goner: *Natural gums are the solidified juice, or sap, of certain plants. Many gums are soluble in water, swell up in water, or form a mucilage in water but do not dissolve in alcohol or ether. The word* gum, *however, is sometimes applied to resins or mixtures of gums and resins.* And there was Papi dancing in my head: stirring his stinking buckets, Cheo and Felo and Cuco churning stalks of god-knows-what in those silly hand-held machines used to make *guarapo,* and Mami standing at the door to the patio, her hands on her hips, eyes in shadows, doubtful and disgusted.

I closed my eyes. *A number of different gums have industrial uses. They go into adhesives, sizing (glazing) for silk and cotton fabrics, calico printing, and candy. Medically they are soothing to mucous membranes and are also used to suspend insoluble substances.* And there he was again: Papi, glossy with sweat, standing in our patio in Havana, gulping down a cool drink Mami brought out on a tray for him, talking about plant gums, complex compounds, neutral salts, potassium, magnesium, acidic polysaccharides and Cuban tree frogs, their tiny, sticky feet like suckers to help them up and down plant stems.

And it was as if I were at the beginning all over again, the beginning of all my doubts, the beginning of my very existence. *Because how could I remember any of this?* I was just a kid when the whole duct tape episode occurred—a five, six year old, running around between the buckets of bubbling mystery soup, between the legs of Felo and Cuco and Cheo as they rolled the *cinta magnética* into messy balls that we—me and my little friends from the neighborhood—would later throw against the wall in a game to see if they would stick.

"Who invented duct tape?" I asked Bernie.

He looked at me askance. "Well, I guess it depends who you believe," he said, but he was uneasy now. I could feel myself glazing over; I knew he saw something was wrong.

I made him punch in Papi's name but there was nothing, absolutely nothing.

"Juani, this doesn't mean shit," he said. "Remember my mom's bio, Raúl's bio."

"So you believe my father invented duct tape?" I asked him. "Are you gonna tell me that, huh? Seriously? I mean, Bernie, *we* don't believe he invented duct tape, okay?"

"Okay," he said with a shrug, "then what are we doing? Why are we trying to look him up?"

"Because," I said, gritting my teeth, muscles spasming all over my chest and arm, "...you never know. With my family, you just fuckin' never know."

CHAPTER 18

THE DAY AFTER MY HORRIBLE OUTBURST, I woke up on the couch, where I'd been sleeping during my visit, and found Nena bent over the newspaper at the kitchen table. A *café con leche* steamed near her hand. She was still in her nightgown, her face weary, eyes puffy. Bernie was nowhere in sight and the loft was so quiet I could hear the birds outside. The place felt cool and still.

"*Buenos días,*" Nena said, looking over as I tossed my legs down to the floor. I grunted something back, scratched my calves and stretched but everything hurt. My breast pulled, causing that blunt pain I'd become so familiar with since "the incident."

"You want some coffee?" Nena asked, not waiting for an answer. She pushed her chair back, got up and poured me a cup. As she walked over to the couch, she made a scratchy, shuffling sound with her slippers on the floor. "Here," she said, handing me my *cafesito.*

"*Gracias,*" I muttered back, my head down, refusing eye contact. Had yesterday really happened? Was that really me yelling and screaming at Mami on the phone? Crying in Nena's arms?

"How are you feeling?" she asked, dropping into the chair opposite the couch.

I nodded, eyes still down. I gulped down some coffee, which was strong and black and bitter. My head hurt. "Where's Bernie?" I asked.

"Running some errands," Nena said. "I thought maybe you and I should talk, you know, by ourselves."

I cupped my *cafesito* in both hands. I'd drank it all, leaving just a few grounds at the bottom of the porcelain cup. "Didn't Mami tell us you could read the future in the coffee dregs?" I asked, glancing up for an instant.

I could see Nena nodding somewhere through the hair hanging in my face. "Yeah," she said.

Then I looked down at us, as if I were perched on one of the loft's beams: We were like survivors in the hushed morning light of a battlefield—limbs worn and tired, skin pale.

"Do you want to tell me what really happened with you and Gina?" Nena asked. "What's going on with you, huh?"

I shook my head. "Nothing," I said, but I wasn't even trying to be convincing.

Nena leaned up, her elbows poised on her thighs like Jimmy staring at his clothes whirling in the washing machine. "Well, something's gotta be up," she said. "Something's wrong, I can tell, something's really wrong."

I didn't say anything, didn't move.

"Have you talked to anybody else?" she asked.

I shook my head, then dropped back, my remains slumped on the couch.

"If you don't want to talk to me, fine, but you should talk to somebody, Juani," she said. "Keeping stuff like that inside isn't good for you."

I snickered at that: I mean, really, what moral room did she have to say anything to me about keeping secrets?

Nena stared at me. "What?" she asked, surprised by my change in attitude.

"So why didn't you tell me about you and Bernie?" I asked, smirking.

She rolled her eyes and sat back on the chair. "Please," she said, disgusted.

"No, really," I insisted. I put the *cafesito* down and crossed my arms on my chest. My breast twinged with pain when my hand unexpectedly fell on it.

"For starters, I thought you knew," she said.

I let out a sarcastic little laugh. "Oh, really?"

"Yeah, really."

"How the hell would I know?"

"Well, because Bernie's father is a friend of Ira's from New

York and I'm pretty sure Patricia knows, so I thought, since you two talk so much these days, that you at least suspected something," she said.

"Small world," I said. I picked at my lip, like Bernie had done the day before.

"Are you upset because I didn't tell you?" Nena asked.

I shrugged. "I don't care, really," I said, though it was obvious I cared very much. "I was just surprised, that's all. I thought we told each other everything."

"Probably not *everything*," Nena said, trying on a little smile.

"Everything important," I said.

She nodded.

"Bernie seems kind of important."

Nena's smile became easier. She looked over at me like maybe we were back to being our old selves. "He *is* important, very important," she said. "I think he's the most important thing that's ever happened to me."

I didn't need to hear this. I knew it already. "So why didn't you tell me about him?" I pressed.

Nena sighed, slouched. The light was coming in through the warehouse windows in strong shafts of shimmering yellow. Bernie's surfboards sat darkly, in contrast to everything, like a black fortress in the corner. My headache kept pounding. When I closed and opened my eyes, I could see starbursts, just like at the hospital when I was still on the gurney.

"I was going to tell you," she said, gathering her legs under her body on the chair, pulling down her nightgown. "There was never any question of that. But I needed time, Juani—it's my first real relationship, the first time I've ever really been in love. I mean, I'm twenty-seven and a little behind everybody else in this way—even you, my little sister—and I'm still getting to know who I am when I'm in love and intimate with a man."

And with that, we finally relaxed a little, the two of us, wearied but real for what was probably the first time during my visit. Nena told me about her and Bernie, little things and big things, but mostly how she was, at first, afraid of having a relationship with him because he was so different from us, from her, and so unlike anything she'd ever imagined for herself.

"I couldn't figure out what he saw in me, either," she said. "I mean, I know I'm attractive—that's not it—but I'm not very exciting, and he is—he's been all over, met everyone, read everything. Done everything too—traveled, surfed, skied, gotten high, meditated with swamis. I've just been sitting in that laundromat, you know?"

And, of course, I knew, because that was me too: waiting and waiting there, whirling in a space as small and suffocating as the inside of one of those dryers.

"And there's Mami," Nena continued. "I was so incredibly attracted to Bernie from the first minute I saw him, and yet, even though I know her whole thing about skin color is bullshit, it kept haunting me. You see, I know I would never give Bernie up because she won't approve, but I also know that my being with him is going to torture her, even though her reasons are totally fucked up. And I'm my mother's daughter, I don't want to hurt her." She paused and looked my way. "I wasn't keeping the secret from you as much as from her. I just don't want to fight with her, not now, not while everything is so wonderful with Bernie. Later—if we break up, then it won't matter that I never told her."

"You're already planning on breaking up?" I asked, stunned.

"No, no," Nena said, dropping her legs back to the floor and squirming her feet into her slippers. "But I'm being realistic. I'm just giving us some time, and I'm giving *me* some time."

"You could have told me."

Nena shook her head. "No, I couldn't," she said. "You'd go to lunch at Tía Celia's with some shit-eating grin on your face and give away that you knew *something*, even if you didn't tell the actual story. And then they'd be all over both you and me, and one of us—probably me—would crack and tell, and everything that I was hoping to avoid would happen."

She got up and went shuffling into the kitchen area. I sauntered over to the CD player and popped on some Pérez Prado.

The hyper-happy sound filled the room. Trumpets struggled against saxes, saxes against trombones. "*Unnngh!*" grunted Prado. I couldn't take it. I turned it off and flipped on some Beny Moré, with his smooth as brandy voice, singing, "*Viiii-idaaa...*" Now I could see dancers in the open space. I could see myself effortlessly moving, stepping this way, then that, propelled by an inner ecstasy—turning smoothly, going down—suspended for a moment in the arch of a lover's arms, then returning to earth again, graceful, sweet.

God, I thought, would I ever feel that way again?

I walked over to the kitchen and dropped down at the table while Nena, in what seemed like an imitation of Bernie, or maybe Caridad or even Tía Celia, sliced and chopped some fruit into a bowl.

· · · , · · · · ·

"Pauli said the same thing," I said.

Nena placed the bowl of fruit on the table. There was banana and apple, kiwi and strawberries, tangerine slices and green grapes, and bits of *mamey* scooped out of the shell with a spoon which made them look like little ice cream balls. I thought of Tía Celia and the way she gorges on fruit now that Tío Pepe's gone.

"What do you mean?" Nena asked, placing a couple of smaller bowls in front of us. She folded a napkin and tossed it to me, then handed me a spoon.

"Pauli said the same thing you did, about why she wasn't gonna tell me stuff."

Nena smiled. "What wasn't she gonna tell you?" she asked, avoiding my invitation to talk about why they didn't trust me to keep secrets.

"Who Rosa's father is," I said, deciding to go along with her for now.

"Oh," Nena said, and the way she said it made me think she knew—and I looked up but Nena had just set me up, that's all. She was grinning. "I was just kidding," she said, and it was obvious. "I don't know who Rosa's father is, honest." She laughed a little.

"Oh I know you don't know," I said, *mamey* oozing out of my mouth. I grabbed the napkin from my lap and wiped my face. "But *I* know."

"Really?" Nena's eyes widened. "Who? Who is it?" she asked, excited. "And how do you know?"

I wagged my finger from side to side. "Uh uh," I said, "I'm only gonna tell you *if you tell me something I don't know!*"

Nena laughed. "This is bribery, extortion, blackmail!" she shouted, but she was hooked, she was into it—she was definitely going to spill the beans about somebody. "All right, what do you want to know?"

"Heck, Nena, you're the one supplying the *what*—I don't know what I don't know," I said. We were feeling good now, connected. I was pain free.

"All right, *who?*"

"Ah, let's see..." I pondered. I leaned up on the table, my bowl of fruit emptied. "Caridad?"

"Nah, there's really nothing about Caridad I know that you don't."

"Honest?"

Nena nodded. "Yeah, really, and I think we both have the same questions about her anyway."

"Why the fuck she ever married Jimmy, you mean?"

Nena nodded again. "Exactly," she said. "And why she puts up with him, and why she lets him beat her...all that."

I could tell by the look on her face that just thinking about it made her immensely sad. I knew this was another opportunity to tell her the truth about me, about the ugly things I shared with Jimmy, but I just sat there, played with my lip and rolled the end of my napkin. Maybe I could keep *some* secrets after all.

Nena got up and poured some milk into a little pot then put it over a flame. *Café con leche* was coming. "Somebody else," she said. I was relieved.

"Patricia?" I offered.

Nena wrinkled her face. "Let me think..."

"Tía Zenaida? Titi?"

"Oh, I know," Nena said, her eyes bright again. "Patricia and Titi—consider it a two-for-one special."

"Patricia *and* Titi?" I asked, surprised. "I didn't even think they got along."

"Well, I think that's what you're supposed to think," Nena said as she poured us a couple of *café con leches*, "but, once upon a time, things were pretty *intense* between them."

"You mean...?" I sat back, aghast. Titi I'd guessed, but Patricia? Hadn't she always been married to Ira?

"Well, I don't think anything ever happened," Nena said, "but there was tremendous sexual tension between them when they first met and—"

"Patricia?" I asked, still in shock. "But she's straight as an arrow!"

Nena shook her head. "God, no," she said. "I mean, she loves Ira and is totally faithful and wouldn't have it any other way, but I've picked up that Patricia was pretty sexually active in college, until Ira came along."

"Yeah, but with women?" I couldn't believe it: Patricia? The same cousin Patricia I knew and argued with and never picked up the slightest vibe from? "Nena, my radar for these things is pretty good and I gotta tell you, she just doesn't register!"

"Well, no—I don't think she's very sexual at all anymore, even with Ira," Nena said, "but according to Manolito—"

"Manolito?" Nena had always been closer to Manolito than the rest of us, but Patricia never confided in her brother, so what would he know?

"Yeah, yeah, yeah," Nena said. "Look, are you gonna let me finish or are you gonna keep interrupting?"

I agreed to shut up and sit still. And Nena told me how Patricia, on her first visit to Cuba, fell pretty hard for Titi and wanted desperately to be with her. But she'd already married Ira, who hadn't a clue, and Titi wasn't interested in being anybody's mistress, nor was she interested in *pagando los platos rotos* of their relationship: Patricia, after all, could come and go from Cuba and never be harassed, but Titi would have to stay and endure the loneliness and isolation of their arrangement, so she refused.

"How does Manolito know all this?" I asked. "And why do you believe him?"

Nena shrugged. "I just do, he's not a liar."

I guffawed. "Nena, *everybody* in our family's a liar," I said. "Mami and Papi make up stuff about the duct tape fortune, Caridad lies about Jimmy, Jimmy lies about everything, Patricia lies about Titi, god knows Tío Raúl and Pauli both have tons of secrets, and hey, you're lying about Bernie. Everybody's dancing around the truth. I mean, how do you wander through it all? How do you tell Bernie about our family? What do you say?"

"Well, I just tell Bernie what's true for me, and I let him know I have doubts, and that there are varying stories," Nena said. "For example, if I were gonna tell him about Titi and Patricia, I'd tell him Manolito's story and then maybe your story and then my story—what I believe—and by the end, there's a new story—Bernie's."

I shook my head. "Very relative," I said. "It must take forever to tell all the stories."

"Hey, we're into communicating, okay?" she said with a chuckle. "It's sort of like singing 'Guantanamera'—everybody gets a chance to make up their own verse."

"Memory mambo," I said, one hand in the air, the other on my waist as if I were dancing, "one step forward, two steps back—*unnngh!*"

Nena waved me off. "So, your turn: Tell me about Rosa's father."

I leaned back on the chair, tilting its front legs off the floor, just like I always do at Tía Celia's. "His name is Ali Ahuja," I began. "And he's a cab driver."

As the morning wore on, I told Nena how I met him, and how I'd put together that he must be the one. She asked questions and added her two bits. While chatting, we did the dishes and wiped down the table, threw out the garbage and made up the couch. We were so relaxed, I was so happy that we were able to talk again like before. Then, as I was grabbing some fresh clothes in order to shower and change before Bernie got home, Nena intercepted me on the way to the bathroom. She put her hand on my arm.

"So, are you gonna tell me what really happened with you and Gina?" she asked.

I stared right at her big brown liquid eyes, so loving and open. And I took my own hand and put it over hers, sat her back down on the couch, took a deep breath and started talking.

"Well," I said, "Gina and I were sitting on the couch, exhausted from a long, late dinner party celebrating her mother's saint's day. Everybody had left already. Then we both heard this noise, like a footstep on the stairs on the way up to her apartment. And I think we both got kind of tense but we didn't really pay any more attention to it. I know I closed my eyes, I was so tired. And then, the next thing we know, there's this raving lunatic in the apartment, and he's heaving this chair at us..."

As I spoke, I put my whole body into it, ducking the imaginary chair, slicing away with a chair leg at the phantom assailant.

All the while, I watched Nena. Of course, she believed every word I said. And the more I spun my tale, my impossible version of events, the more I realized what was happening: Nena wasn't listening to the story at all, she wasn't concerned with its logic or coherence. Nena was listening to *me*, her sister, whom she trusted completely. And though I should have been comforted by her faith in me, I was sickened instead. Her utter confidence in the fact that I couldn't lie betrayed how little she knew me, how far we'd already drifted from each other.

CHAPTER 19

"STOP WASTING MY TIME WITH THIS STUFF," Jimmy says, bunching the letter from his cousin Vicky into a ball and tossing it overhead with both hands into the garbage a few feet away.

Caridad and I both watch the balled-up airmail envelope as it lands softly on top of used paper towels, empty detergent boxes and sticky pop cans. Cari sighs and looks down at the laundromat floor. Then she walks over to the garbage, reaches in and wordlessly picks the ball out of the heap. She irons it out on one of the counters, using the palm of her hand. Jimmy watches, satisfied. No one speaks.

Then the phone rings. I reach over the counter and pick it up. It's Tía Celia. "Pauli and Rosa are coming home!" she says excitedly. "They're coming home! They're coming home!"

Caridad takes the phone from me, all nerves and smiles all of a sudden. Jimmy hands her a cigarette, which she accepts without glancing up at him. When she reaches for it, I see the fresh scratches on her hands from the night before. Was it just last night that I went over there to comfort her? She pulls her hair down in front of her face with a quick, monkey-like gesture. Then she's off, smoking and chattering with her mother, their voices squeaky and high-pitched.

"Let me guess," says Jimmy, leaning like a thug on the counter, "they need a chauffeur, right? Somebody to pick them up at the airport, right?" He's beefy and tough.

I shrug. "Hey, if you don't wanna do it, I will," I volunteer. "I've missed Pauli and Rosa, I'd love to pick them up."

Jimmy scoffs. "In what car, huh?" He finishes flattening the airmail envelope Cari rescued, folds it and stuffs it in his pocket.

"Well, either in your car—"

"Forget it."

"—or in Patricia's car—"

"Oh, yeah, like Celia and you and Caridad and Pauli and Rosa are all gonna fit into that *cucaracha*." He laughs.

"—or I could just spring for a cab." As I say it I realize I have to be careful. It can't be Ali's cab, not yet anyway.

Jimmy makes a face, like he's impressed or something. "Oh, Miss Money Bags here... What? You filed for Crime Victim's Assistance money? Shouldn't I be getting a cut?"

"Eat me, Jimmy."

Caridad's still puffing on her cigarette, her body tense, arms wrapped tightly around herself. She's still talking a mile a minute to her mother.

"You wish," Jimmy says, smug again, his eyes hooded again.

"Like you'd know how," I say, taking a little of his attitude for myself.

But he surprises me. "You can teach me," he says, "I hear that's what dykes do best." He makes a gesture with his hand like he's going to scratch himself but just sort of pats his cock instead. "And I'll teach you what I do best," he says, his voice hoarse. His dick is growing again, without regard to the fact that his wife is just a few feet away. But this time, Jimmy's self-conscious.

"I gotta go buy a Little Lotto ticket," he says, his voice still husky. Then he walks out of the laundromat but it's not his usual swing.

· · · , · · · ·

This time, I don't go home and get off, I don't shiver, I don't get a fever at all. Instead, as I watch Jimmy awkwardly exit the Wash-N-Dry, I feel my hands go clammy, my heart speeds up. This is different, every bit of it.

Eventually, Caridad gets off the phone. Her expression is bored, arrogant. She lights another cigarette.

"You're not supposed to be smoking in here, you know," I say, barely looking in her direction.

She shrugs. "What's your problem?"

"What's *my* problem?" I ask back. "What's *my* problem?" I'm incredulous—how does her mind work? How do her cerebral connections hook up? "Cari, don't you have a clue what just happened here?"

She pinches the end of her cigarette to extinguish it, as if the fire means nothing, as if it could never get through her thick skin and burn. She tosses the butt in her vest pocket. I imagine the hideous, penetrating smell of nicotine all over her.

"Look, we know what my problem is," she says, looking at me hard. "What's yours, huh? I mean, what are you doing here, hanging around? It's like, every time something goes wrong, you're there"—she illustrates by putting both hands up, palms open— "a witness to the crime but with no blood on your hands."

"Excuse me," I say between gritted teeth, "but if I remember correctly, you called me last night, isn't that right? I mean, if I was at the scene of the crime last night, it's 'cause *you* decided I was 911, remember?"

"So?"

"So how about taking some responsibility here?"

"*Me* taking some responsibility?" Caridad's face is a mess of muscles twitching. "How about *you*, huh?"

I can't believe this. I feel my chest filling up, my throat tightening and my eyes finally bursting with tears. "What the fuck is going on? Why are you doing this to me?"

Cari's hands tremble as she reaches back into her pocket for the butt. "You're going too far, Juani," she says. "You're getting too involved in everybody's business. You gotta let go."

"Cari, *you* called me!" My fists open and shut, open and shut. "Caridad, you *always* call me. What do you expect me to do, huh?"

"Yeah, yeah, I know, but just 'cause I call you—just 'cause anybody calls you—doesn't mean you gotta run." She's quaking like a house about to splinter before the swirling, massive force of a tornado. Her hands shake as she brings the just extinguished butt back up to her lips. As she searches in her pockets for a lighter, she realizes she just put this cigarette out at my request. She hates me, as she so often does the morning after I've held her hand through a hideous night. She shakes her head, like a dog after an unexpected shower. "I gotta go," she says.

I try to stop her. I put my hand out and wrap my fingers around her wrist but she jerks herself away, practically running out of the laundromat.

· · · . · · · · ·

Patricia's office is stifling.

"But I thought you said Jimmy doesn't cheat," she says, horrified. "Wouldn't this constitute cheating?" But she doesn't wait for my answer. "This is disgusting, that's what this is. You know that, don't you?"

I nod. I'm standing in her office looking over some forms a career counselor on campus wants me to fill out. We had a quick interview and from the three words I said she determined I could be a writer, a business manager, or a dental assistant. She gave me these questionnaires to fill out to get a better sense of my skills and desires. Then I made the mistake of strolling over to Patricia's, because she'd said she wanted to know how things went with the counselor. And then I compounded the mistake by telling her about the interaction with Jimmy this morning.

"He's a pig, a fucking pig," Patricia's saying. She's totally upset, totally riled up about this. "I think you should tell Caridad, that's what I think."

I laugh aloud. "Oh, right," I say, "right—now *there's* a smart move." There's no way I'm telling Patricia what Caridad said to me this morning—I couldn't bear the psychoanalysis. And I feel too naked, too disturbed.

"I'm not kidding, Juani, I think you should tell her," she insists.

"Like she's gonna believe me?" I protest. I get up and I'm flapping the counselor's papers around, like Jimmy did with his cousin Vicky's letter. "Patricia—*Caridad was right there the whole time!* Do you think she's gonna believe she missed the whole thing? C'mon, get real!"

I wish Patricia could tell that Caridad's not listening to anything except the voices in her own twisted brain; why can't anybody else see that?

Patricia shakes her head. "Well, weren't you just saying she's starting to get it? Didn't you tell me that after the fight with Jimmy last night she was talking about how she had a better understanding of their dynamic?"

I roll my eyes. I'm always amazed she didn't go into psychology instead of political science. "I didn't say that," I say. "I said she said she didn't know why she always forgives him. That's what I said."

"Same thing," she says, rifling through her desk. Unlike Nena's and mine, which is always perfectly neat and clean, Patricia's desk is a perpetual landfill. Stacked full of books and papers, it isn't unusual to occasionally unearth a dead candy bar or a crushed paper cup. It's in total contrast with her cool, patrician air.

"Caridad needs to know," she says.

"Patti—Caridad already knows everything she *needs* to know, okay?"

Why Caridad stays, why she still loves Jimmy—these are mysteries. When I think about them sometimes, I get jealous. Why is everything Jimmy does forgivable? How does Cari always wind up in his corner again? If they can do that, why can't Gina and I find some way to talk again, to start again, to forgive each other? Why do I have to suffer?

Patricia stops the excavation of her desk long enough to give me an exasperated look. "Why are you always protecting him?"

"Who?"

"Jimmy."

"Oh, *please.*" Why can't she tell I hate him right now?

"I'm serious—you're not telling Caridad because you're protecting him. Why? I don't know, I really don't know. It's pathetic, and dangerous, and sick, that's what it is," she says, tackling the task at hand again.

"Look," I say, "I gotta go." Patricia would never understand, that's clear. I'm protecting myself.

I'm tired, suffocating in her tiny office. Patricia doesn't rate a window, although she does have a supply closet jammed with books and file folders bursting with papers. There used to be posters of Fidel and Ché on her walls but now there are placards from Tío Raúl's shows in Mexico City and Paris.

There are also family pictures tacked to bulletin boards, balanced precariously on bookshelves and on her desk: Tío Raúl riding a horse on the pampas in Argentina, Manolito and his family, an old black and white of the four of them from their New York days (in it, Tía Zenaida's plump and radiant). There are photo-booth strips of Patricia, Nena and me; a few of the three of us and Pauli. There's Patricia and Ira looking tan and fit back in their college days, his hair long and curly. There's one—a fading Polaroid in a frame—of Patricia and Titi holding hands while sitting at the *malecón*. Funny how I've seen that photo a hundred times before and never gave it a second thought. Now I look at it and realize their fingers are tangled in a scattered, urgent way. Their faces are a little tense, a little too close.

"What's the hurry?" Patricia asks. She's wearing her reading glasses, which are barely holding onto the tip of her nose.

"Pauli and Rosa are coming home tonight," I say.

Patricia doesn't even blink. "You picking them up?"

"No."

She looks up. "Is there a family something I've not been invited to, a welcome home party or reception?"

"No, no, no," I say. "Jimmy and Caridad are picking them up."

"So my question stands: What's your hurry?" She stops everything, waiting for my reply.

"Fine, Patricia, here's the deal, okay?" I say. I lean up on her desk, talking as if I were a TV lawyer giving a final argument.

"They're all coming back to Tía Celia's, okay? And I thought I'd go over and hang out because I want to see Pauli and Rosa—I've missed them, unlike some people—"

She shakes her head and leans back in her chair.

"—and I figured, since it's Tía Celia's night at the Wash-N-Dry, I'd make myself available and make it easier for her to ask me to take her shift, all right?"

"I think if Tía Celia was going to ask you to take her shift, she would have done so by now, don't you think?"

"No, I don't."

Patricia dives into her desk again, throwing papers every which way. "I don't think you give her enough credit," she says. "She obviously doesn't need you to take her shift."

"It's Pauli and Rosa's first night back—and they just called this morning, so it's not like anybody's had time to plan."

"Tía Celia's had time to ask you if she wanted to ask you," Patricia insists. "Whew...finally," she says, dusting off a piece of paper.

"Look, can I go now?" I ask, frustrated as only Patricia can make me. I'm antsy, shifting from foot to foot.

"Yeah, of course," Patricia says, as if this whole conversation has been my idea. "But a couple of things first."

"What?" I'm gritting my teeth. My fists are wrecking balls.

"Don't forget the letter to Titi."

"Don't worry—I won't." I glance over at the photo of the two of them. Now that I know, it's so *obvious*.

She looks at me suspiciously. "What does that mean?"

"Christ, *nothing!*" I exclaim. I push my arms out, all tense. "Patricia, you're driving me nuts. Now, what else? What? What? What?"

"We're a little testy today," she says.

"Is that it?" I sigh. I'm dying here.

"My colleague leaves for Cuba in four days—that means you have three days to write the letter and get it to me if you want him to take it to Titi, okay?"

"Fine." I start to turn.

"And one more thing."

I glance back. Patricia's holding out the piece of paper she dug out from her desk.

"What's that?" I ask.

"E-mail for you."

"E-mail? What do you mean e-mail? For me? I don't have an e-mail address. Who's it from?"

"Bernie Beck," Patricia says, opening a book on her desk and pretending to be casual. There's a little smile on her face just dying to get out.

"Bernie Beck?"

"Yeah, he sent it to Ira to give to you." She looks up, past her glasses. Her eyes are twinkling. Christ, she knows about Nena and Bernie. "I guess he knew how to find you."

"Yeah," I say, "I guess so." I take the paper, nod at her and walk out of the room. I offer no explanations. I figure, nobody else does, why should I?

. . . .

I wait until I'm on the train headed home before I check out Bernie's e-mail. It's still before the afternoon rush hour, so the train's not too crowded. I park myself in a window seat and swing my legs onto the empty space next to me. Even though it's cold out, the sun, coming in through the glass, is warm on my neck and head.

I unfold the paper and read: "Subj: casein glue." I remember, Yeah—casein glue, the adhesive made from milk that Mami mentioned to Nena the night of my outburst.

I read on: "From: BBeckBB, To: HippyBoy." I realize this must be Ira's screen name—what a hoot! I go on: "IRA: PLEASE PASS THIS ON TO JUANI CASAS—THANK YOU!!!!! Since it seemed to interest you, a note about casein glue: it's what they used in making redwood and/or balsa surfboards, starting in the thirties and through the fifties."

Why is Bernie sending me this information? I wonder. So what if casein glue was around in the thirties? That doesn't mean it was being used on adhesive tape then.

I read on: "Did you know those old boards were not shaped from solid slabs? To make them strong, they took several ten- or twelve-foot four-by-fours and glued them together length-wise, sometimes with one-inch spruce in between. Redwood on the outside for strong rails, alternating with balsa for lightness as you went towards the middle. God, I would love to find a wooden board in a barn somewhere!"

I'm thinking, Why is he telling me this?

"I once investigated this stuff while still living in California, as I was planning to build myself a retro log. Apparently casein glue is hard to find nowadays. The other thing is tools, you have to have a drawknife, can't use power tools."

Then it hits me: I know what he's trying to tell me—that this is definitive proof Papi didn't invent duct tape, but I don't need it. I've always known Papi was a fraud, I've always known the whole duct tape story's a fantasy.

"I remembered all this after you left, and ended up asking George about it. George used to build those kinds of boards. He said he used 'powdered' casein glue. He didn't clarify what you mixed it with, if it was water or something else. BTW, wood boards are making a big comeback, but usually for collec-tors only, since they run about twenty-five hundred to three thousand dollars…"

As I read this, some guy comes up and nods at my feet on the seat next to me, so I drop them down to the floor and straighten up. I close my eyes and feel the sun now on my face. The guy next to me is shifting his legs and papers, getting com-fortable. I hear him tear something and open my eyes. He's bal-ancing a cup of coffee between his knees and he's pouring a pair of sugar packets into it, the little white sacks pinched between his fingers.

Powdered casein glue?

Didn't Papi used to haul huge sacks of a mystery powder between his buckets of goo in our patio in Havana? Just as I'm conjuring the scene, I think—No, wait, casein glue's been around since the thirties, my father wasn't even born then!

I let my head relax against the glass. The sun's too bright for my eyes now.

Why do I want so bad to believe?

CHAPTER 20

A T TÍA CELIA'S, THERE'S A FEAST for Pauli and Rosa. Tía has outdone herself: *ropa vieja, maduros,* rice and creamy black beans, *arroz con leche,* hot Cuban bread, and Chilean red wine for everybody. Everything smells of garlic and sweet onions; everything's warm. The salad is fresh and massive, with little mandarin orange slices and a tangy, lemony dressing. I swear Tía Celia's doing this just to keep Tío Pepe away. Not even his ghost could get near it without having an allergic reaction.

Pauli looks fantastic. She's tanned and fit and her eyes are sparkling once more. Before she left for Mexico again, she'd seemed depressed and gangly but now she moves with her usual grace, her long arms reaching across the table for food or encasing each of us in tight, hearty hugs.

"I'm so glad to be home," she says, walking around her mother's house, touching the Spanish lace draped on Tía Celia's furniture, the framed photos on the wall. It's as if she's reclaiming them.

"I have some things that are coming via DHL—some textiles and paintings," she says to no one in particular. "Maybe we could find room somewhere—although, god, I like everything here just the way it is." She's so open, there's nothing about her now that would suggest the Fortress of Solitude.

"We'll find room, of course," says Tía Celia, delighted. Every time she walks by Rosa on her way to or from the kitchen, she leans down and kisses her or squeezes her little body. Rosa giggles. She's a happy baby—laughing and grabbing at everything, sitting upright in our arms, drooling all over each of us in turn. She's too excited for sleep so Pauli's not even trying to get her to bed yet.

I'm sitting at the dining room table, stuffing myself as usual at Tía Celia's, and drinking a Very Fine. Cari's here too but she's not eating.

"How about this one?" she says while pointing to a classified ad. She's got the paper all spread out on the table, bumping right up against Tía Celia's buffet. She's got long sleeves on to hide last night's bruises from her mother and sister. *"GEO '92 Metro LSI Convertible Auto, AC & New Top. Exceptional $6,995 dealer 800-PRICE-12."*

Since Tía Celia and Pauli won't let her smoke in the house now that Rosa's here, Cari fingers a cigarette now and then. She brings it up to her nose for a quick, meaningless fix.

"Sounds cool," I say. But she's not talking to me. It's clear that this morning's events have erased me from her screen.

"Jimmy, what do you think?" she calls out to him. He's in the living room, his face in a huge pile of food, watching the Bears on *Monday Night Football.*

"I think a dealer's gonna charge you more for less," he answers. His voice seems to come out of the wall. "Try just a person who's trying to sell a car—you might get a better deal that way."

I know what this is: This is payback, the unspoken apology. After he beats the hell out of Caridad, Jimmy usually gives her something, or gives in to something, depending on what she wants and how badly their fight went. It's his form of repentance—it's his way of never having to really say he's sorry. Unfortunately, Caridad knows this pattern a bit too well and she's learned to work it. Instead of leaving the bastard, she's going to get a car out of him this time.

"How about this one then: *GEO '89 Metro. This Week's Special, $1,995, AUTOBARN, 312-372-7900?*" she asks. She's practically pushing the cigarette up her nose. Pauli and I look at each other; this is so inane, neither one of us can believe it.

"That's a dealer, Cari, try an individual," Jimmy says again.

His patience is exaggerated, patronizing. But he's pretty sedate right now. When they got back from O'Hare, he checked his losing Little Lotto number by phone then plopped down in front of the TV. The Bears rarely do well on Monday nights, but he's out there grunting with every play. He didn't even say hello to me when I came in. Pauli says he barely said a word to her either, just acted real shy and bounced Rosa around in his arms a little bit at the airport gate.

"But, Jimmy, look how cheap it is," Caridad says, not looking up from the paper.

Behind Cari's back, Pauli points out her scratches by pantomiming clawing on her own hands. I turn away, say nothing, but I can sense Tía Celia's anger and disgust. Her gestures are sharp all of a sudden. She grabs her empty plate a little angrily, swipes the silverware off the table in one movement before heading for the kitchen. Cari continues reading the ads, ignoring us, ignoring the food, yelling from one room to another.

"Okay, how about this one: *GEO '93 Metro LSI Convertible, White, Auto, A/C, Full Power. Only 15,000 miles, $7,745?*"

"Caridad, if you're going to be yelling at Jimmy in the living room, why don't you just go in there and talk to him at a normal volume?" Tía Celia asks as she steps back into the dining room. Her eyes are like gleaming steel.

"What's the big deal?" Cari asks. "I want to be in here." She's distracted, consumed with her ads. She's also irritable, crazed for nicotine.

"Cari, just go in the living room—don't yell, okay?" Pauli says, backing up her mother. "We want to talk too. And to put Rosa to bed at a reasonable hour."

"Uh...okay," Cari says, gathering up the newspaper and going into the living room. As she walks, she pats her pockets for a lighter—it's clear she's going to step out for a smoke. I think, What a relief, maybe she'll calm down some.

Tía Celia shakes her head sadly, takes Rosa from Pauli's arms, and disappears into the kitchen again.

"God, what the fuck is going on?" asks Pauli, taking a seat next to me at the dining-room table. She pulls her legs up under her, like Nena did during our big talk in Miami.

I shrug. "Same ol' thing," I say.

"No, not same ol' thing," says Pauli. "Since when does Caridad talk back to Mami?"

"Huh?"

"That 'What's the big deal?'—what's that about?" Pauli asks, whispering.

I shrug again. "I don't know," I say. "Misplaced anger."

Pauli laughs, slaps my shoulder. "Whoa—that psychobabble sounds like Patricia," she says. "You've been hanging around her too much! It's rubbing off!"

I smile at her but it's weak. I've got a headache, my temples feel tight.

"Tell me what's going on with you now," Pauli says, genuinely interested.

"Nothing," I say. I don't want to discuss the career counselor and I can't say anything about what happened with Jimmy and Caridad at the laundromat while they're in the next room.

"C'mon, really," she insists, her hand on my arm, just like Nena. "Do you ever hear from Gina?"

I shake my head. It's so strange to have Pauli ask about her like this—as if Gina might simply pick up the phone or drop by, as if we could just stroll down the street and run into each other and decide to have a cup of coffee together.

Pauli squeezes my arm. "I guess...I guess I just couldn't believe that you'd decide not to see her," Pauli says. She's so serious, her forehead's wrinkled. "When Cari told me you cut her off because you didn't like the idea of being a target of that kind of political violence, well, honestly, it just didn't sound like you—especially because, Juani, I mean, I *know* how much you loved her..."

She stares at me so hard and so close, I can barely meet her gaze.

"It's a lot of different stuff," I say, pulling my arm away. "It wasn't just the attack. We had problems before that." (I tell myself there's a lot of truth to this.)

Pauli nods. "Still..."

"And you?"

"Me?"

"What are you gonna do now?"

"Go to art school, raise Rosa." She's smiling and it's real—she's absolutely glowing. "I've got some money from Papi's insurance and my own savings. I actually made good money in Mexico. With some financial aid, I can pay my tuition and help out here."

I think back to Tía Celia's vision of the future, how she imagined Pauli and Rosa living with her. And now here they are, in her house, under her roof. I remember too that Tía said her business with Caridad is still unfinished.

I look around the room, searching for spies the way my mother does when she wants to talk confidentially. "I gotta admit, Pauli, you seem really different than when you left," I say in a low voice. "What happened?"

She laughs. "I worked some things out in my head, that's all." She's still smiling, amused. Whatever's going on with her, she's not going to share it with me.

"And Rosa's father?" I ask, but Pauli laughs, gets up, and vanishes into the kitchen with her mother and her daughter, leaving me alone.

There's chattering in there, baby gurgles and the sounds of pots and pans being moved; in the living room, the TV announcers blare, Caridad's squeaky voice bounces above them and Jimmy snorts. Here, where I am, there's a strange, constant humming.

. . . .

All night long, I keep waiting for Tía Celia to say something to me about her shift at the Wash-N-Dry. I look at my watch so often that Pauli teases me.

"You got a big date or something?" she asks at one point, eyes twinkling with mischief.

I blush, inexplicably. "No, no, no..."

Pauli laughs. "Okay, okay—you'll tell me when you're ready to."

"No, really, I'm just gonna go home," I say, but she's not convinced. "I'm just tired, that's all."

I don't want to tell her I obviously misread the schedule—I mean, it's way past nine o'clock and Tía Celia's still puttering and playing with Rosa. I'm embarrassed to let Pauli see I'm so scattered. In a way I'm glad it all worked out this way, though. I got to spend time with Pauli and Rosa and so did Tía Celia. Nobody missed anything. And the fact is that I'm still exhausted from my visit with Nena in Miami. I'm still sifting through everything that happened there, still trying to figure out how I'm going to face my parents, and especially my mother, whom I've managed to put off since I got back.

"Hey..." It's Caridad, Jimmy's empty plate in hand. "Whatcha' doin' just sitting there?" she asks.

Her cheeks are pink; obviously the cold air bit at her while she sucked on her cigarette outside. It's the first time she's talked directly to me all night.

"Aw, nothing," I say, getting up from the dining-room table, grabbing Jimmy's plate from her and dropping it on mine. "Just thinking, I guess."

As I walk into the kitchen, Tía Celia and Pauli tiptoe out with a sleepy Rosa on Tía Celia's shoulder. Caridad turns away from me and follows them down the hall to Pauli and Rosa's bedroom. I think, It's just as well. We don't really have anything to say to each other anymore.

I toss the plate in the kitchen sink, which is frothing with suds, and pick a piece of *maduro* off a pan waiting its turn to be dunked in the steaming, cleansing water. I drop the *maduro* in my mouth and savor its singed sweetness. I'm just pulling the trash out from under the sink when Pauli walks back in.

"Hey, will you stay?" she asks. "I think everybody's leaving and then we can talk, you know, just the two of us."

I look at my watch: It's about a quarter to ten. "For a little while, I guess, yeah," I say.

"C'mon," says Pauli, "I'll make you a *cafesito*."

"Okay, okay," I say, wrapping up the garbage.

211

Tía Celia re-appears, her arms stretching into her coat as she walks. "You sure you'll take care of everything?" she asks Pauli, surveying the dirty dishes and pots, the food that's still to be put away.

"Absolutely," Pauli says, helping her with her coat and kissing her cheek. .

I'm confused. "Tía, where are you going?" I point to my watch. "It's almost ten o'clock."

Tía Celia leans my way and kisses me good-bye. "The laundromat, to help close."

"The laundromat?" I think, What the hell's going on?

"Zenaida took my shift for me tonight so I could be with Pauli—"

I hadn't misread the schedule after all!

"—on the condition I help her close out."

"Well, that's ridiculous," I say, reaching out to unbutton Tía Celia's coat. "You stay here, I'll go." She resists, but in a friendly way. Nonetheless, I start for the living room, where my jacket's draped across the couch.

"No, Juani, c'mon, I thought we were gonna talk," Pauli says.

"But I'm happy to help Tía Zenaida," I say, "and that way Tía Celia can hang out with you and Rosa longer."

Tía Celia waves me away. "Rosa's in bed," she says. "Now you stay here, talk to Pauli. You two haven't had any time to talk. You know, they live here now—I can talk to them whenever I want." She winks at me and wanders out of the room.

"So you'll stay?" Pauli asks.

"Sure," I say, "of course."

But I can hardly hear my own words: Now the room's like a mass of bees, humming and buzzing. I can't believe nobody even consults me anymore. It's as if I don't even exist.

· · · . · . · · ·

They're supposed to leave together—Tía Celia, Caridad and Jimmy—so Cari and Jimmy, who live just upstairs from the laundromat, can accompany Tía Celia the block or so to the Wash-N-Dry. Tía and Cari are ready, all buttoned up and wrapped in scarves, but Jimmy's having a hard time. He's got his coat in his hands but he's not paying attention—his eyes are glued to the television set, where the Bears have unexpectedly gotten into field-goal position to go into overtime. The announcers are all excited, hooting and screaming. Jimmy's body leans over at an angle. When the Bears miraculously kick the ball through the posts, he jerks, pumps the air with his fist, and yelps.

"Okay, they won, we can leave now," Cari says. She's impatient and Tía's already by the door, her hand on the knob.

Jimmy laughs and explains it's a tie, it's overtime, and the game's going to keep going. "It'll be just a few minutes," he says, smiling broadly and relaxed. "Really, honest," he says, "let's just wait a few minutes."

Tía Celia protests. "Zenaida's waiting," she says. "Look, you two stay, I'll walk over alone. I do it all the time."

Jimmy objects, insisting it'll be quick. As he talks, his eyes dart back and forth between Tía Celia and the TV. The Bears have the ball. But Cari's exasperated—she says the Bears always lose and he doesn't have to stay to find *that* out. She tells him football's so stupid anyway. Tía Celia, Pauli and I all watch, amazed at her audacity, but Jimmy's too into the game to be concerned. He makes a face as the Bears go to second down already.

"Look, I can't wait, it's Zenaida," says Tía Celia. "She's doing me a favor. I can't do this to her." She turns the knob and starts out. "I've got to go."

"Well, then, I'll go with you," Cari says, practically daring Jimmy, but he really doesn't care. Pauli and I look at each other, a little surprised.

"Cool, cool," he says, relieved, dropping his coat on the arm of the chair and throwing himself back down. He glances up at Pauli and me for a second: "Cool with you guys if I stay for a few?"

Pauli speaks for both of us. "Yeah, fine." But I'm not so sure.

Tía Celia darts out, saying *buenas noches* over her shoulder, and Cari follows. Jimmy sits in the bluish TV light intent on the game, his monstrous face aglow, leaning up, his elbows on his thighs, foot tapping restlessly, vein vibrating.

"Jimmy Frankenstein," Pauli whispers to me with a giggle and pulls on my sleeve to follow her into the kitchen, where she starts the process of making us a pair of *cafesitos*. I look back to make sure Jimmy didn't hear—to make sure we don't have a problem—but he's lost in the game. The Bears punt, it's miserable, and he groans loudly.

Pauli unscrews the *cafetera*, snaps her fingers against the hardened old coffee, which crumbles into the fresh new trash bag I've put under the sink, and washes out each individual mechanical part as she talks. "Listen, how's your time these days?" she asks as her hands work under the faucet.

"It's okay," I say. "Why?"

"Well, I've got this huge list of things to do—everything from 'finish portfolio' to 'get a haircut'—and I thought some things— like 'buy new jeans, get a gym membership'—might be fun to do with someone else," she says, spooning Bustelo into the now clean *cafetera*. "With you, actually."

"Yeah, okay," I say. "I've probably got a few things I need to do myself. I could get Jimmy's car—"

"No, no, no," Pauli says, resting the *cafetera* over a flame. "I don't want to owe any favors. I was thinking we'd just take the train, hang out, hang loose, be pals."

I shake my head a little and laugh. "It's not a big deal, Pauli," I say. "He lends me the car all the time." Or *most* of the time, I think to myself.

"Yeah," she says, not convinced, "and what do you have to do for it?"

I check out the kitchen door, making sure there's no movement in our direction from Jimmy. I know he can't hear us— the TV's on loud enough and there's plenty going on here to blur Pauli's words, but I'm uncomfortable anyway.

"Nothing," I finally say. But the truth is that my mind has spun back to that first time I met Jimmy, when he was sitting in the same living room he's in now, leaning back, massaging his huge dick.

"*Something,*" says Pauli, dropping her voice down to a whisper now. "Jimmy Frankenstein's not the type that does favors for free. He'll collect at some point, mark my words."

I don't say anything. *What can I say?*

As I reach across Tía Celia's counter and start rolling the edge of a paper towel, I realize I don't have much to say about anything lately. I can't talk to Nena, to my mother, to Patricia, to Cari, and now, apparently, to Pauli. Strangely enough, sometimes Jimmy's the only person with whom I have real conversations—tense and offensive as they are.

I wish I hadn't stayed. I wish I were on my way to my apartment, walking out in the crisp, cold air, taking long strides, feeling my body free out on the streets. My breast and arm have hardly hurt today—I'm practically back to normal. I want to go shoot hoops, dance at the Red Dog, play Lethal Enforcer, make love with a beautiful woman whose body is slick, pungent and dark.

I'm brought out of my head when Pauli pours us our *cafesitos*. The stuff is black, intoxicating. She's leaning against the counter and talking about the color pink—she knows from her nightly visualization exercises that it's the best, most calming color, and so she wants to give that serenity to Rosa by painting their room pink, but she doesn't want to fall into the trap of gender-stereotyping.

I sip the cafesito, trying hard to pay attention. In my head, I'm singing: "*Ay Mamá Iné'/ ay Mamá Iné'/ todo' lo' negros tomamos café.*" I probably haven't heard that song since I was a kid being rocked to sleep. I know I'm not interested in discussing the color pink, I'm not even sure how interested I am in discussing anything at all right now. I'm tired and horny.

Then we both hear a noise—although Pauli keeps talking, not missing a beat, I see her eyes jump to the back door and scan the window for shadows behind the little lace curtain Tía Celia has there. There are footsteps in the backyard. A dog barks nearby. Pauli and I both tense up but we pretend it's not important. I look out in the direction of the living room, considering for a moment the absolute worst—that Jimmy might be stalking us, might be out there, circling the house, his body bent over, hiding something heinous in his hands, waiting for just the right moment to pounce...

"Hey!" It's Jimmy, out of his chair, in the kitchen doorway with the remote between his fingers. I'm ashamed to admit I immediately look down at his crotch but it's flat, calm. I don't know if he notices because he's clearly preoccupied with something else. "Did you hear something?" His face is strained and for a second I consider he heard us talking about him, but his attention is directed outside.

"Yeah, but it's probably a cat," says Pauli. "Cari left some food for them. You know her..." I chuckle.

But Jimmy's not buying it. And I realize he's seriously worried—the game's not over, there's not even a commercial break. I can hear the announcers barking out a play on the TV.

There's a knock on the door. It's sharp and urgent and repetitive, as though the doorbell were an inconvenience. Jimmy turns on his heels, snaps the TV off with the remote and goes to the door. "Expecting anybody?" he asks Pauli and she shakes her head. I peek at my watch: It's almost ten-thirty. This is no casual call.

"It's some guy," Jimmy says, looking through the peephole. We're right behind him, our *cafesitos* idling back in the kitchen. "He looks pretty *impossible*," he says sarcastically, turning quickly back to Pauli.

"I'm not expecting anybody," she says, but her voice is trembling. I reach my hand to hers, squeeze it.

The knocking continues, hard and rapid. A voice calls Pauli's name. "I know you're in there," he says. He has a slight, unrecognizable accent. "Pauli, please..." The voice fades.

"Let me get rid of him," Jimmy says, waving us away.

He takes a deep breath, puffs his chest out. His vein is quivering. We step back a bit but not much. Jimmy opens the door. The brisk air rushes in, the smell of new snow fills the room. Pauli gasps. The man at the door is dark-skinned and young. He's shielding his eyes from the light above the door with his arm.

"Pauli...?" he pleads.

Jimmy and I glance at each other, unsure what to do. And this is what I mean: Our communication is instant, silent, totally natural.

Pauli's arms quickly fold across her chest. The man at the door brings his own arm down slowly, revealing his beautiful face. It's Ali Ahuja.

. . . .

As if on cue, Rosa wails from the bedroom—it's a long, yearning sound, like blood calling to blood. Pauli loses all her color.

Ali's head snaps in Rosa's direction, his mouth drops open. "Is that...?"

Pauli drops her arms and squeezes my hand hard. As she steps forward, blocking Ali (who has made no move to come in the house), I bolt for the bedroom, gather Rosa in my arms and rock her in hopes she'll calm down.

Through the walls and wails, I hear Ali—he's nervous but very controlled. I can't make out his words but he sounds like he's trying to explain something, to reason. Pauli responds now and again, her voice also muffled, but maintaining a cool, business-like tone.

In spite of my efforts to soothe her, Rosa continues to sob. My shoulder is soaked through from her tears and spit. I stroke her little head, her long black curls. I kiss the soft, brown skin of her face and shoulders. I whisper reassurances she can't possibly understand, trying to sound calm and strong, hoping to scare away whatever has upset her so suddenly and dramatically. She's warm against me, her heart like a drum.

"*Mamá la negrita/ se le salen los pie' la cunita/ y la negra mese/ ya no sabe que hace'*," I whisper-sing to Rosa.

217

Through the walls, through the constant humming in my head, I hear rustling sounds at the front door, then the door itself shutting softly. I hear footsteps down the hall—nervous, hard steps—and a towering black shadow drapes itself over the door. Instinctively, I turn my body, protecting Rosa with my shoulder. She quiets down immediately.

"Juani?" It's Jimmy.

"Where's Pauli?" I ask.

He's a wreck, his eyes flying all over the place—to me, to Rosa, around the dark bedroom and out the window between the drapes. "She went with that guy," Jimmy says. "They're outside, look." I see the sweat shining on his upper lip.

When he pulls the drapes over a bit, I see Pauli, her arms stretched tight across her chest, leaning against Ali's cab on the curb. She's got my jacket thrown over her shoulders. They don't seem to be talking, just standing there. Ali paces a little, rubs his chin.

"She wouldn't let him in," Jimmy says. He's holding the drapes apart. I'm standing right under the crook of his arm with Rosa. I can smell his sweat. "I mean, I can understand that but what the fuck's she doing out there talking to him?"

"He's Rosa's father," I say. And as soon as I utter the words, I realize I've betrayed Pauli. Telling Nena is one thing, telling Jimmy is quite another. I bite my lips. There's nothing I can do now to undo it. My eyes start to water and I'm secretly relieved it's so dark in here.

Jimmy's stunned. "You're shitting me!" He pulls the drapes over a little more. "I thought it was somebody in Mexico." His hand grabs at his crotch, pulls on it.

I shake my head. Rosa takes a deep breath.

"How do you know?" Jimmy asks.

"It's a long story," I say, rocking Rosa gently in my arms. She smells sweet, like violet water.

"You think he's gonna cause trouble?" Jimmy asks, his forehead all crunched up. His hand is still on his cock.

"I don't know," I say. "I know very little about him."

When Rosa's body finally goes limp, I put her back down in her crib. I signal quiet to Jimmy and we tiptoe out of the room. In the hallway, he sighs. "Man, this is weird," he says. I nod. In the light I can see he doesn't have an erection, regardless of all his fidgeting in Pauli and Rosa's room. "So what do we do now?" he asks. "I don't know," I say. "I'm gonna hang out, make sure somebody's here for Rosa while Pauli's out there. In any case, Pauli will want to talk after Ali leaves."

Jimmy nods. "Yeah," he says. "You know, I'm gonna call Cari, tell her to keep Celia busy. I don't think it'd be good if she came home while Pauli's out there talking to that guy."

He goes off to the kitchen. I hear him dial and whisper to Caridad. I trot out to the living room where I part Tía Celia's blinds with my fingers and check up on Pauli and Ali. Now they're both leaning against the cab, their heads turned toward each other. Pauli's still got her arms crossed but I can tell from the angle of her shoulders that she's more relaxed. I'm thinking this might work out after all.

· · · , · · · · ·

It's snowing while Pauli and Ali negotiate. Now and then Jimmy or I peek out through the blinds and check up on them. Neither one has lost their temper, neither one seems inclined toward harsh, quick moves. Their silhouettes fall on the freshly fallen snow, sometimes creating long shadows that remind me of Bernie's African sculptures.

I've emptied the *cafetera* but I'm so tired I can barely keep my eyes open. I keep thinking I should be worried about Pauli and Ali, hoping that kind of nervous energy will keep me alert and awake, but I'm struggling. My lids are dropping, my head's still humming.

Jimmy, on the other hand, hasn't needed caffeine the whole time. He's pacing back and forth between the living room and the kitchen, scratching his head, scratching his balls, eyeballing the two of them out in the front yard.

Now and then, Rosa cries out and I get up from the couch or the chair or wherever the hell I'm sitting and go sing to her: "*Tú drume negrita.../ que yo voy a comprar nueva cunita/ que tendrá ca'cabel...*" I rock her and stroke her, kiss her and hold her. I listen to the insistence of her breathing and watch until I'm sure she's asleep again.

It's been about an hour now that Pauli and Ali have been out there. I'm getting worried Tía Celia's going to be coming home any minute, no matter how Cari tries to keep her at the Wash-N-Dry or at her place. Caridad's not that imaginative; I can't see her being successful for very long.

Rosa starts again, a long siren-like sound that lifts me off the couch and sends me flying into her room. "*...Si tú drume yo te traigo un mamey muy colora'o...*" I keep thinking I should just stretch out here, on Pauli's bed, but I'm afraid I won't hear Pauli—I won't know when she comes back in, or if something happens.

After Rosa falls asleep again, I wander back out to the living room. I'm stiff and slow as I walk. Jimmy's turned the TV on but with no sound—he's reading the closed captions running along the bottom of the image. Both his hands are at his crotch but they're spread out, as if he's covering it instead of stroking it. He looks up at me and shakes his head.

"You look like hell," he whispers.

I sit down on the couch. I decide to ignore him. "It's so strange, it's like Rosa knows what's going on or something," I say.

"At least one of us does," he says, then he turns his attention back to the TV.

I drop my head back, stare off at the ceiling. With the overhead light turned off, Tía Celia's flat white ceiling looks like an empty canvass. I imagine Pauli painting a mural up there—Pauli upside down like Michelangelo. She splashes pink paint, soothing and smooth, little Rosa handing her brushes like an assistant. They are joyful and beautiful, dancing about until all the white is covered over, then the pink turns to yellow, and finally to black. When I hear Rosa calling again, another voice answers—it's deep and hoarse. It's not mine, but that's okay.

· · · _· · _· · · ·

As I try to wake up, I realize I've seen that strange face on Rosa before. She's falling through my arms. I'm struggling to open my eyes but they feel glued shut. My lids push up, but it's as if I've been asleep so long that spiders have spun webs between my eyelashes. Rosa's falling through my arms like a slippery fish. I'm standing right there the whole time, watching her descend, not moving. There's a hideous drone, a vacuum, a fluttering and crash like a bird ramming into the grill of a high-speed automobile.

I open my eyes and the scene is clear, as clear as anything I've ever witnessed in my life: Jimmy's sitting in the chair in front of the television set, its ghostly light casting shadows on his gruesome face. There are no sounds at all. His head is back, ecstatic, lips red and shiny. One hand is on the back of Rosa's puny head, pushing her down; the other is on his cock, inflamed and purplish, its glossy tip disappearing into her tiny, tiny mouth.

I leap across the room, yank Rosa up from his lap so hard I'm afraid I've dislocated bones. He tumbles, his cock bopping up and down, spewing semen all over the carpet. I scream and yell, all of our limbs flailing.

CHAPTER 21

THERE IS AN EXPLOSION OF SOUND: chains rattling, wood crackling as if in a fire. Ali and Pauli burst through the door, adrenalin running like the Mississippi. Chairs topple, lamps crash to the floor, the room spins and thrashes like a runaway locomotive. Ali, his face twisted and white, pounces on Jimmy, whose cock is a flattened balloon dangling out of his zipper. Pauli stands in a corner, cringing and whimpering, holding Rosa so tightly to her that her tiny body seems to disappear like a baby kangaroo into her mother's pouch. Rosa is dazed and droopy and I am paralyzed.

It doesn't matter that Jimmy is thicker, more muscular, stronger in every way than Ali. It doesn't matter that Jimmy's arms are free and Ali's harnessed by a long coat, his neck encircled by a scarf that could easily become a noose, that Jimmy has been in a million fights in his life and Ali so clearly in only a few. What fuels Ali makes up for everything. He's pink-eyed, fierce, suddenly throwing Jimmy about the room as if he were nothing more than an empty, airless peanut shell.

When Ali hurls Jimmy against the wall, he seems momentarily suspended. Tía Celia's family pictures topple in slow motion, then shatter. The glass shards are stalagmites, the photographs a gasoline rainbow running all over the floor.

Ali rampages; he hurls his legs against Jimmy, who's howling and spitting, rolling around on the glass on the floor. The splinters in his skin shine like tiny icicles, then drown in blood. Ali has a shadow, an oily elephantine musth that propels him. He kicks between Jimmy's legs, kicks again and again, and geysers of red seem to spray the room.

· · · · · · · ·

After the explosion, there's a lull. In the distance, there's a clock ticking. I don't know how Rosa was taken from my arms. I don't know how I wound up on the floor, my sleeve torn, my face wet from sweat. I'm trembling and weak.

Ali holds Jimmy down by the neck. He's on all fours but barely, coughing and spitting up blood. His crotch and buttocks are magenta. His cock has vanished. Jimmy wobbles. Some of his teeth are missing and his mouth is suddenly full of bubbles and black craters. The teeth themselves look yellow and canine, scattered on the floor.

"Juani..." Jimmy pleads, his eyes practically rolling back in his head.

When Caridad and Tía Celia hurry back from the Wash-N-Dry—their eyes wide, their breaths cold clouds that cover their faces—Ali jerks Jimmy up. Caridad screams, then leaps, beating her fists on Ali's back and shoulders, but Ali's not letting go. Pauli, who's been shivering in a corner, finally loses control, yelling at Caridad—who's a fire alarm, an air-raid siren—about what Jimmy has done to Rosa. Tía Celia immediately takes Rosa from Pauli. As if knowing she's finally safe, Rosa instantly begins to cry and wail.

Everything is happening too fast. Pauli and Caridad are all over the place, their nails like knives digging into each other's skin. Caridad demands to know who Ali is and what's happened to Jimmy, Pauli shrieks hysterically. Rosa screams while a stone-faced Tía Celia runs her hand all over her as if to heal her. And I'm just here, on the floor, worthless.

"Juani..." Jimmy says, his tongue thick. At first no one hears him. There's so much noise, so many limbs are flying that we're a blur, a giant smear. Then he swallows and says it again: "Juani..."

Caridad is the first to notice. She turns her head, fast, and Pauli follows her gaze down to Jimmy's face. Ali is holding him by the collar as if he were a rabid dog.

"Juani..." he says again.

It takes Ali an instant to realize something's happening but by the time he looks down at his captured prey, all other eyes are on me, including Tía Celia's.

"Juani..." Jimmy says. "Tell them...tell them what really happened..."

His voice is so low, such a whisper, I'm not sure anybody hears it—I'm not sure *I* hear it—I'm not sure I didn't just imagine him, his lips cracked, words trickling out. I'm thinking, Maybe it's all in my head, in my head. I close my eyes and open them again but there's Jimmy: "Juani, please..." he pleads.

I close my eyes again, hard like a bank vault, but when I open them again—and this time it's all swirling water and salt— Jimmy's eyes are red too—*everything's red*—he's crawling toward me until Ali yanks him back.

"Juani...tell them what really happened...god, please...help me..." He's breathing hard now, his fingers curling under his palms.

Ali makes Jimmy heel, paying no notice to his pathetic requests. But Pauli and Caridad are both staring at me, their faces twisted, pained and horrified. I turn toward Tía Celia but she's not paying attention to me anymore. She's checking Rosa instead, gripping her arm and shoulder as if she were putting whatever bones might have been dislocated back in place.

I look at Jimmy. "C'mon..." he says. "Please...tell them what happened..." He's begging me, his mouth melting into the most awful grimace.

But what really happened? *What really happened?*

"Juani?" It's Pauli and she's so frightened, so vulnerable and raw. Her hand pushes her hair away from her face. She bites her lip. She starts to lean down to me—slowly, very slowly, everything's very, very slow—and she reaches a trembling hand over to Ali for balance. It's such a natural gesture, I have to force myself to remember there's no relationship between them, no love, no connection except for one moment, that impossible moment that produced Rosa.

"Juani, what happened?" Pauli asks, both hands now resting

on my legs, soothing me, holding me. Caridad stands next to her as if she were holding her breath.

I don't know why but I look over at Jimmy again. And what I see now is so different. There, through his blood-spattered face, his swollen mouth and engorged eyes, there's a smirk emerging.

"Yeah, Juani, tell them," he says, leaning back on his heels. "Tell them what happened." He nods, as if he were giving me permission.

"I..." I start to speak but I stumble. Caridad nervously hands me a tissue from her coat pocket and I wipe my mouth and nose. I start again but I can't—there's too much inside me. I feel my face dissolving, my shoulders shaking. I'm crying.

"Juani, it's okay," Pauli whispers. "Just tell us..."

But Jimmy's impatient. "You stupid bitch..." he says, gritting what's left of his dog-teeth. "You stupid bitch..." His eyes are inflamed.

I feel everybody turn to him. He's still on all fours, still at Ali's mercy, but his rage is building, his muscles pumping.

"What the...?" It's Pauli.

I don't realize at first that I'm crawling backwards, inching away from Jimmy, totally terrified. Pauli grabs my legs.

"It's okay, Juani, it's okay," she says.

Then Jimmy detonates. "I helped you, you stupid bitch, I helped you!" he shouts in my direction. He lunges toward me, his face demonic, but Ali throws himself around his neck and Pauli hurls her body between us.

I don't know where my energy comes from but when Jimmy's huge hands reach over to me—he wants to kill me, I know—I jump up and kick him in the face. There's a thud and a squish. Caridad gasps and drops down to help him, as if she were Mary Magdalene and he were on the way to a crucifixion. But Jimmy's a bull, a herd of buffaloes: In his effort to get to me, he grabs Caridad by the hair and throws her down to the floor. She screams and flails. Jimmy grunts and tries to crawl over her. Ali and Pauli hang off him like puppets and I feel his breath and his fury. But I'm faster—I'm faster than him, faster than all of them.

I push myself off—I feel my legs extend like a hurdler, my hips leading, my head back—and I'm out of there, out of that furnace of all their passions and tempers, out of that sucking spiral to hell, out of their circle of darkness and fire. As I run, run out to Milwaukee Avenue, I feel fresh, clean snow on my face.

· · · · · · · · ·

I don't know how long I'm walking. It's gray and black out. It's the middle of the night. The street lights are fuzzy, like faraway suns. The snow is unspoiled, twinkling like in the movies. I'm coatless but I'm not cold. All the stores along Milwaukee Avenue are closed, their burglar bars drawn. There's no one at the bus stops. There's a jazzy piano playing somewhere, people laughing and drinking. Traffic is slow, only an occasional taxi pulls up to a late-night bar here and there to take the moneyed revelers home; they're from other neighborhoods, here for the cheap thrills.

I pass a homeless man covered in canvas bags—bags for rice and barley and wheat. He is black and big and even the hat he wears is made of this burlap, this scratchy stitch. He is sitting on the floor in the vestibule of a closed store. The windows display religious figures—Christ on the cross, angels, various virgins. There are Saint Christophers, *Santa Bárbaras,* products of our imaginations, all of them. The man is quietly eating a banana. When he finishes he puts the peel in a plastic bag he has dangling from his waist by a rope. Everything smells of urine.

I lean against one of the windows and my stomach wrenches. What comes out of me is green and red and white and drops from my mouth like lava, steaming on the sidewalk. I'm sweating, even in the cold. My torn sleeve flaps up and I wipe my mouth with it. I stink.

I raise my eyes and realize I'm no longer in front of that

religious goods store or before that big homeless man but somewhere else entirely. The windows are brightly lit. There's a
blurry rainbow shadow, my reflection on the pane. Inside, the
overhead lights are on. When I put my hand to the glass, I can
feel vibrations: fax machines, computers, telephones. They're
not on but there's a hum, a steady hum. I try to focus, to read
the signs on the windows and doors. The letters are rather big
and I have to step back a bit to decipher them: *Migdalia Colón
For Congress.*

I can hardly believe it. I cup my hands to contain the glare and
look inside. There, alone at the main desk, her head bent, her
shoulders leaning intently into her paperwork, is Gina. Migdalia
Colón is her new Rudy Canto, the new hope for the neighborhood, her new ride through the belly of the beast. And Gina,
workaholic that she is, is here now, in the wee hours, still putting
together tomorrow's schedule, still writing the speech that needs
to be delivered first thing in the morning, still editing the new
brochure, still doing whatever needs to be done for the cause.

I take great comfort in seeing her here: I interpret it to mean
there's nobody else yet, nobody else to rub her feet while she
writes, nobody else to work the tightness out of her muscles
from a long hard day, nobody else to lie next to in bed while
reading the latest poll figures. There's nobody for her to go
home to; my heart aches from this knowledge.

Gina doesn't see me at first, doesn't register me at all. She's
scribbling and twirling her hair absent-mindedly (a habit I recognize as meaning there's a deadline of some sort approaching).
I tap on the glass but she doesn't hear me. I tap a bit harder.
She looks up sleepily, doesn't recognize me (and I think, What
must I look like that Gina, who has touched every inch of my
face and body, cannot tell who I am now?) and goes back to her
writing. I tap again and she looks up once more. She squints
and waves absent-mindedly, then re-focuses on her work. I
move over to the door and turn the knob but it's locked so I rat-
tle it a bit. Gina looks up yet again, squinting so hard her face is
all scrunched up. Then she gets up, grabs a dry donut from

what's left at the food table in the campaign office, and comes toward the door.

I realize immediately what's happened. And I know that if she sees my face before she opens the door to hand me that donut, that lock will remain shut, and I'll be left out here in the cold. So the closer she steps to the door, the farther back I move, out of the light and into the dark. I turn my body a bit so that my face is obscured.

The lock clicks, the door creaks open and I hear Gina's voice, at first far away, inside, behind the door as she's opening it, and then outside, inches from me, leaning into me with her eyes narrowed from effort, her nostrils flaring as if sniffing for clues. "My god, don't you have a coat?" she asks, half in, half out of the office. She still doesn't know who I am.

What I do next, I do quickly: I grab her arms and push back, back into the campaign office, where it's warm and the lights are shining. She's off guard and falls backward; she stays up because my arm wraps around her and keeps her from dropping; I smell her hair, her skin, feel her in my arms as if we were dancing a tango and dipping for pleasure.

She drops the donut somewhere, pulls away, gasps, stumbles, brings her hands to her mouth and starts to shake. "Oh my god," she exclaims. I close the campaign-office door behind me, lean my back to it. Now we're face to face, except that she keeps stepping back, away from me.

"What...what happened to you?" she asks, her dim eyes racing from my head to my toes, surveying the damage. "Juani, you aren't supposed to come in here...you can't come in here..."

She reaches for the telephone but her hands are shaking so badly she can barely hold the receiver.

"*Ay*, Gina, who're you gonna call, huh?" I ask. I realize I must sound like Jimmy, that pig. I don't move from the door. I don't want to scare her but mostly I just don't want to move. I am suddenly so tired. "What will the cops think this time, huh?"

She blinks, as if she doesn't know what I'm talking about, but she puts the phone down, clumsily; it rattles on the cradle before settling. "What do you want?" she asks. Her voice is a little firmer now. I can tell she's trying to get herself together, to come off like she's not scared, like she's in complete control.

I sigh. *What do I want?* I want to know what happened, I want to know how I could feel so much, and how she could feel so much, and how we could wind up here, with so many fax machines, typewriters and computers humming between and around us like an electric fence.

"Listen..." she says from across the room, her arms crossed on her chest.

I notice her nose is a little different, a little crooked, and I realize that, in spite of what Jimmy said, I must have broken it. Or has it always been that way? Could it be that I never noticed before? Could I have missed something that obvious?

"...You've got to go," Gina says. "I mean, I'm working, you're not supposed to be here, and I swear, if you get near me, I'll call the cops—I really don't care."

I close my eyes, I nod. I feel the cold coming in through the slit of the door behind me. "Don't worry," I say. "I'm not going to hurt you—"

She guffaws. I open my eyes. "Uh huh," she says, trying to be cocky but she's not convincing. She's too caught up in her own fears to pull off the attitude she wants.

"I'm not going to stay, don't worry," I say.

"No, you're not," she says, "and I'm not worried about it either." But she is; I can tell. "What do you want, Juani?" she asks. But this time she's using my name, and that means something.

"I want to know what happened," I say, and I close my eyes again. All I see is darkness.

"What happened?" she asks, confused. "What do you mean, 'What happened'?"

"What happened—between us?"

I hear Gina tap her foot impatiently, I can imagine her looking away as if she can't believe I'd ask anything so inane.

"We were attacked at my house by an unknown assailant," she says in a monotone. "He was after me because of my community organizing. You scared him away with the leg of a chair. Then you got scared of other possible political violence and I couldn't promise that it wouldn't ever happen again, so we stopped seeing each other."

I laugh and open my eyes again. "Wow—that's quite a story," I say. "I notice it's got your own little revisions."

She stares at me and says nothing.

This isn't what I want. "That's not what I meant—that's not what I meant by 'what happened between us'," I say, finally leaving my post at the door. I step up but she flinches and so I slowly sit on a desk near the door. "I meant *between us.*"

"I don't know what you mean..." she says, not a question, not a statement, but something in between. She's confused.

She's beautiful, that is important to say.

"*Between us,*" I say again. "One minute we were in love, the next minute, we weren't."

"What kind of amnesia are you suffering from?" she asks, and she's angry now. She's forgotten she's scared and she's walked right up to me. "Don't you remember? You beat the shit out of me."

"That's how you remember it?" I ask, holding my breast with my palm.

"That," she says, nodding at my chest with her chin, "was self-defense." She crosses her arms again, but this time it's defiance, not a sense of protection, that motivates her.

"What I mean," I say, standing right up to her, "is this: How could that happen? How could we do that to each other?"

"You tell me," she says sadly, "you tell me." She walks away from me, but this time it's not fear. Her shoulders are slumped, her hands are limp. She throws herself in a chair, exhausted, vanquished. "Tell me. Please."

She's not pleading, but I can tell she longs for explanation as much as I do. My chest hurts but it's not a physical injury.

Does she hurt?

"I miss you," I say.

She shakes her head. "Juani, don't..." She looks away, out the window to the falling snow.

But I can't stop now. "I loved you very much," I say. "I still love you..."

She shakes her head again. My own eyes are filled with tears, my face is hot, but I swear I see something falling from her face—a tear too perhaps?

We are silent for the longest time. We stand there, in the hum of the machines, peering at spider webs in the corners, at paper clips on the floor, at pieces of donut strewn by the door. We say nothing.

Then the phone rings. To my surprise, Gina answers it. "Migdalia Colón for Congress," she says in her most professional voice. It's nearly four o'clock in the morning. There's no way anybody's volunteering at this hour.

"Yeah, I was just leaving," she says, "don't worry...no, honest, I'll be home soon." There's a pause. "No, nothing's wrong...really." And another one. "Yeah...me too, okay, see you soon."

Before she's hung up the phone, I'm at the door, turning the knob. As soon as I open it, the cold slaps me—it's as if there's been a temperature drop of about twenty degrees since I came inside.

"Juani," Gina calls out behind me. I don't want to turn around but I feel her hand on my shoulder, so I obey that yearning my skin has for her touch. "I'm sorry," she says.

I don't want to know who that was, so I don't ask. I don't want to know what it means, or when it started, whether it's a woman or a man, because I can guess most of those answers and none of them really matter anyway. What I want to know is something else entirely.

I turn to her. I look her right in the eye. She's looking right back, open and scared, but not of ordinary dangers. "Did you...did you ever love me?" I ask.

Her eyes widen. "Did I ever love you?" she asks, her mouth like a rose, red and fragile. "I...well..." She struggles, she shifts her weight and puts her hands in her pockets, all without taking her eyes off me. "Yes, of course I loved you...I'm sure I still do."

And so, for an instant, I imagine forgiveness—I imagine a waterfall, silver and cold, in a lush garden, a serene Eden. I think, *Te quiero verde.*

We hug, we wrap our arms around each other and it's real. I feel her heart beat next to mine—pounding, really—and I bury my nose in her hair and feel everything from her shoulders to her waist with my open palms.

"Gina..." I whisper, because I'm not sure I can talk other than in a whisper, "I'm sorry, I..."

"Me too," she says, holding me back, sniffling.

I breathe her in, getting a lungful. "Maybe...I mean, we still love each other..."

But she reads my mind and doesn't let me finish. She pulls away and she is stronger than me by far. "No," she says, shaking her head, "no—we can be sorry but I can't forget what happened, I can't—trust is permanently broken for me."

"But time," I beg, struggling to keep my arms around her but losing the battle fast.

"No," she says, "no." And before I realize it, she has me out the door, shivering in the dark. "Good-bye, Juani," she says, and the door closes, the lights go out at the campaign office, and all the machines go dead.

CHAPTER 22

THIS IS ALWAYS MY PROBLEM: These overwhelming feelings, this contained madness; to accept, for example, what just happened with Gina, but without accepting it. What I mean is this: to accept *enough*, to accept so as to make everyday existence bearable, to be able to run into her at the train station (without either of us hesitating) in front of the entire neighborhood if necessary, and to say hello, to perhaps exchange a few words about whatever campaign she's working on, to smile, to mean every moment of it. And then to *not* accept—how could I accept this madness? To accept it, I think, is to lose hope. I don't mean hope about us, but about *me*.

I'm stuck here, in a booth in a coffee shop with a window looking out to Milwaukee Avenue. I'm stuck mostly because I can't muster enough energy to move. My legs are free. My arms are free. I just can't seem to lift my butt off the cracked vinyl seat, to lift my hand higher than necessary to bring some coffee to my mouth.

I can turn my head. I turn it one way and I see the sunrise, sort of, behind the buildings on the other side of the street. I don't really see the sun, of course—it's cold and pale and cloudy, but there's a swash of color at one point, however dim, and that's my sunrise.

About an hour later, groups of people walk by the window to the train station. They're bundled up. They carry back packs and briefcases and artists' portfolios and they're all walking very fast even though I can see in their faces that they're really still back in their beds, still sleepily piecing together fragments of dreams and the previous night's TV offerings. They walk swiftly, think slowly.

When I turn my head the other way, I survey the coffee-shop

counter, where middle-aged white men read the newspaper, drink their own cups of coffee and push a fork around a plate of greasy eggs and bacon. I imagine these guys read meters, hang drywall, perhaps move beds and dressers for Polonia Furniture. Some read the *Tribune,* others the *Sun-Times,* a few read the *Zgoda,* with its gray pages and crowded headlines. It smells of burnt meat in here.

I borrow a pen from a waitress—a sassy, older Polish woman with fried-dyed red hair, legs like toothpicks and a fast and furious demeanor. I'm scribbling on a stack of white napkins I liberated from the dispenser. I litter a bunch of dots across a napkin I've spread out on my table and try to connect them, one to the other, across, around, in loops. A fly buzzes near the window—I hear it, but I can't see it. It's that hum.

What's important now is to maintain lucidity, to not give in, to not betray myself.

I try to remember what happened back at Tía Celia's, with Jimmy and Rosa, but I don't want to. One part of me says, *Yes, connect the dots;* another part asks, *What dots?* Whatever I doodle on the napkins smears the minute I move it onto this little puddle of water in the middle of the table. The napkin sucks up the liquid and the dots, the lines, all the connections, vanish.

· · · · · · · · · ·

What really happened?

My own authentic memory: I hurt Gina, she hurt me. I don't know who hurt whom first—I know I hit her first—but I don't know when we first hurt each other, or whether that particular detail matters. It is possible—it is entirely possible—that I need to see it in this way and that need dictates what I remember.

Another memory: Jimmy's penis sliding around Rosa's lips. That's undeniable. It's the same penis that got me wet before, that made me jerk myself loose countless times.

I don't want to remember any part of this.

· · · · · · · · · ·

When Patricia slides into the seat across from me, I'm not surprised. I wasn't expecting her—not here, not now—but I've got to admit I'm comforted by her presence.

"Hi," she says. It's the shortest greeting I've ever heard from her; it's the smallest sound she's ever made.

"Hi," I say back.

She is very pale. Even under the red sparkle of her cheeks from the cold outside, she is pale; the red, in fact, just underscores it.

"Whatcha' doin'?" she says, sounding more like Caridad or Pauli, not at all like herself, whose English is always more clipped, perfect, not so slangy and open-mouthed. Patricia is trying too hard to be casual. I can tell she's relieved to see me.

"I'm writing a letter to Titi," I say, pushing the napkins with all the blurred dots at her.

Patricia looks at them, confused, but struggling desperately to find my meaning. "Yeah?" she asks.

"Yes," I say. I lean back in the booth. "These are, well, rough drafts."

Patricia relaxes, sighs, even laughs a little. "I see," she says, taking one of the wet napkins in her hands and holding it up as if she were actually trying to decipher it.

"Yeah," I say, pointing to a place on the napkin in her hands. "This is the part where I was trying to explain why I want to go to Cuba."

"And why is that?"

"For belonging," I say. "To get away," I admit.

Patricia nods. "Well, you'll belong in *some* ways, not others," she says. "And when you get back, everything will still be here, pretty much just like you left it. I learned that lesson myself with my trips to Cuba."

I ignore her. "How's Rosa?" I ask. The fly continues to hum somewhere around the booth's window.

"Fine, actually," she says. The waitress rushes up to us and Patricia orders a cup of coffee. "A little shaken up but she seems okay for now—there wasn't any *physical* harm, and we all

235

just pray she's such a baby she won't remember any of this lurid episode. It's hard to tell." Patricia swallows. "It'll be a long time—years—before we'll really know with Rosa."

I sit up. "So you believe me? ...About what happened?"

Patricia reaches over the table to take my hand. I'm ready to be soothed. "Juani, you didn't tell anybody anything, remember?" she says. "You ran out. Tía Celia called me. I've been looking for you all night. Everybody was very worried."

"I didn't...? Then how...?"

"Pauli and Ali saw the whole thing, remember?"

I think back, hard. I can see them crashing through the door, frantic.

"They heard you scream," Patricia says. "But they saw it—they got there in time to see it."

"Then why were they all over me? Why were they questioning me like that?" I'm annoyed, irritable. I always end up uncomfortable around Patricia.

She raises an eyebrow. "I...I don't know," she says. "Confirmation, probably. Everything seems like it was kind of nutty, from what I hear. And, besides, Caridad and Tía Celia didn't see anything...my guess is, you were the objective witness."

"Objective!" Even I find that ridiculous.

Patricia's coffee arrives and she sucks it up as if it were a shot of whisky. Her hand trembles a bit. I don't think I've ever seen my cousin Patricia betray any kind of nervousness before.

"And...Cari?"

The fly escapes from somewhere on the window, makes a flourish in the air and throws itself at my face. I swat at it and it falls in the puddle on the table, its wings shivering. It's a good-sized fly, with shimmers of blue, out of season today.

Patricia shakes her head solemnly. "A mess," she says, "but standing by her man."

I'm absolutely horrified. I feel my jaw go slack, the blood drain from my body.

"I know, I know," Patricia says. "It's unbelievable, but in a way, it's not. You know Cari. Anyway, I'm sure she'll come around, but it's a matter of time. It's just going to take a while to sink in, that's all." Patricia squeezes my hand. "You okay?" she asks.

"No...I'm...I don't know what I am," I say. I feel airless, numb.

"I think everything will actually be okay, Juani," she says. "It'll be a while, but we'll get through this. I really believe it. So does Tía Celia."

And I think, Yes, she would—Tía Celia has her vision of the future. I reach over to the wet napkin we'd been pretending was my letter to Titi. I point to one of the few dots still discernible. "This is the part where I tell Titi about what really happened with Gina," I say.

Patricia just stares at me, but it's kind. I put the napkin down. "Do you already know?" I ask, my voice so tiny and weak. The fly, seemingly lifeless, floats on the skin of the water on the table.

"I know what you and Gina said happened couldn't have happened, but that's all I know," Patricia confesses.

"Instinct or rumor?"

"Instinct," she says.

"You're good," I say.

"So are you," she says.

She smiles. It's a knowing, intimate smile. It occurs to me that I love my cousin Patricia very much, more than I would have ever imagined.

"We have a lot to talk about, I guess."

She nods. She pulls a few bills from her purse and pays the restaurant. "Want to wait here while I pull the car around? It's pretty cold out there."

I shake my head. "Nah, I'll just walk with you." I think, That's warmth enough.

As we get up to leave, I flick my finger at the fly, freeing it from the puddle of water. It crawls a bit, then takes off, making an aimless loop in the air, then smashes itself against the window pane.

It's quiet now.

Glossary

abuela	grandmother.
aquí	here.
americanada	an American thing or mannerism, usually relates to behavior or attitude rather than objects; usually pejorative.
arroz con leche	rice pudding.
arroz y gandules	Puerto Rican-style rice and beans.
"Ay"	oh.
"Ay Mamá Iné'/ ay Mamá Iné'/ todo' lo' negros tomamos café."	"Oh Mama Inéz/ Oh Mama Inéz/ all us black folks drink coffee"; from an old Afro-Cuban folk song, "Mama Inéz," popularized by Bola de Nieve.
"Ay que vamos a la playa/ y allá voy/ coje la maleta/ y la cojo..."	lyrics to an old Cuban song, "María Cristina": "Oh, we're going to the beach/ I'm coming/ grab the suitcase/ and I've got it."
babalao	a Cuban shaman, usually associated with *santería*.
balsa	raft.
barbudos	the bearded ones; a name used to describe Fidel Castro's early followers.
bodega	grocery store, usually Cuban- or Latino-owned, very ma and pa style; never a supermarket, which is a *supermercado*.
bohío	a Cuban peasant's thatched hut
boliche	Cuban-style stuffed beef.
buenos días	good morning.

buenas noches	good night, or good evening.
Bustelo	a very popular Cuban-American coffee brand; a very rich, dark roast espresso.
cabrito	goat.
café con leche	Cuban coffee and steamed milk with lots of sugar.
cafesito	a Cuban coffee, usually served espresso-style in a demitasse.
cafetera	coffeemaker; Cubans and many other Latinos use the stove-top coffeemakers, usually used for French espresso, that go directly on the burners.
caldo gallego	Galician-style white bean stew, usually made with different kinds of sausages.
campesinos	peasants, rural people.
carajo	hell, but stronger, more profane.
carnaval	carnival.
cha-cha-chá	a popular Cuban dance in the 1950s that became a North American sensation.
chancletas	informal, often cheap, sandals, more for hanging around the house or the beach than for street use; zories, thongs, slippers.
chivato	tattle-tale, informer—often reserved for Cubans who betray anti-revolutionary activities to the communist government.
"cinta pata, cinta maricona"	"fag tape"; both *pata* (or *pato*) and *maricona* (or *maricon*) are pejoratives for gay men and lesbians; the latter is more polite, the former is vicious.

claro   of course; clear.

Cocina Al Minuto   the quintessential Cuban cookbook, both on the island and in exile.

comemierda   jerk, asshole, but much stronger and more profane; literally, "one who eats shit."

compañero(a)   literally, "companion"; used by the early rebels as a mutual address; may also mean "lover," depending on context.

coño   all-purpose Cuban curse word; absolutely profane; may be used in a variety of combinations to provide different meanings; so strong, sometimes only the second syllable, " 'ño," is necessary (in this way, it translates as something akin to "wow," yet retains its profanity); literally means "cunt."

corazón   literally, "heart"; used mostly as a term of endearment, like "honey."

cubana(o)   Cuban.

cubanita(o)   little Cuban; either affectionate or pejorative, depending on context.

cucaracha   cockroach.

descara'os   Cuban slang, from *descarados*, meaning shameless ones; pejorative.

eleguá   one of the deities in *santería;* a god who opens and closes doors, creating opportunities; the messenger of the gods. Also refers to the figures or icons representing the god, usually made of wood, shells and other natural items, shaped into a head. May be placed behind doors or on altars.

"en confianza"   in confidence, or confidentially.

"Es que..."	"It's that..."
"Ese tipo es un comemierda."	"That guy's an asshole."
felicidades	congratulations.
flan	a custard made throughout Latin America, with regional variations.
fufú	green plantains, boiled and mashed, served with bacon or some other spicy meat; a holdover from slave days in Cuba.
gracias	thank you.
guarapo	sugarcane juice.
guayabera	a four-pocket shirt, which can be either casual or formal, worn in the tropics, almost exclusively by men.
gusana(o)	a pejorative used to refer to Cubans exiled from the revolutionary government; literally means "worms" but actually refers to the shape of the duffel bags used by the first wave of refugees, who left by planes or ferries.
independentista	an independentist, or freedom fighter; one who supports independence from colonial powers in one's country.
kente	handwoven, hand-colored African textiles.
La Habana	Havana; what Cubans call the capital.
lavanderia	laundromat.
"los infelizes"	"the unhappy, or unlucky, ones."
maduro(s)	fried ripe plantain.
malanga	a root used widely in Cuban cuisine; it's steamed, fried, or boiled; also

known as taro in Polynesian and other Asian cuisines.

malecón the dramatic, crumbling seawall in Havana.

mambo a dance popularized in Cuba and the U.S. in the 1950s and early 1960s.

"Mamá la negrita/ se le salen los pie' la cunita/ y la negra mese/ ya no sabe que hace'" "Ay mama, the little baby/ her feet stick out of the crib/ and mother cradles her/ she doesn't know what to do"; from an old Afro-Cuban folksong, "Drume Negrita," popularized by Bola de Nieve.

mamey a red, juicy Cuban fruit; very sweet.

Marielito sometimes pejorative, sometimes affectionate, depends on context; refers to those exiles who came to the U.S. through the port of Mariel in 1980, in a mass exodus used by the Cuban government for propaganda purposes—official Cuban broadcasts referred to those who left as "social scum," which often stuck in the U.S. Many of those who came through Mariel were young, single men. Many were dark-skinned and/or gay. Marielitos as a whole have prospered and proven most of their detractors—including earlier Cuban exiles—wrong.

marrano pejorative given to Spanish Jews during the Inquisition, the term endures to describe their descendants; literally means "pig." The more appropriate Hebrew term is "anousim" meaning "the coerced ones."

José Martí commonly referred to as the Apostle of the nation, he was the Cuban-born son of Spaniards who helped plan and lead, with Antonio Maceo, the Cuban War of Independence against Spain in the late nineteenth century. A writer of essays, newspaper articles and classic children's stories, he was also a poet whose work probably anticipated modernism. He spent much of his adult life in exile, mostly in the U.S., and died within the first few days of the actual war. Today, he is praised and claimed by both the Cuban revolutionaries and by Cubans in exile.

Materva a brand name for a non-alcoholic beverage bottled in Miami and very popular among Cuban-Americans. It's made from maté, an herb particularly celebrated in Argentina (for tea), and very fizzy.

"Me da tanta lastimá." "I feel so badly."

merengue an extraordinarily fast-paced dance music from the Dominican Republic, very popular in U.S. Latino enclaves.

"Mi gusanita" "My little worm"; affectionate, vernacular; see *gusana*.

"¡Mi mamá!" "My mother!"

"Mi prima Cari me quiere gobernar.../ Y yo le sigo, le sigo la corriente/ porque no quiero que diga la gente/ que mi prima Cari me quiere gobernar." a take-off on an old Cuban song called "María Cristina," in which the words are: "María Cristina wants to run my life/ and I go along, along with it/ because I don't want people talking/ about how María Cristina runs my life." Here, Juani inserts *mi prima Cari* (my cousin Cari) in place of María Cristina.

milicianos literally, "members of a militia"; Fidel Castro's uniformed soldiers and guards.

mira	look.
mojito	a delicious Cuban drink made with rum, lime juice and mint.
Moncada	the military barracks attacked by Fidel Castro and his followers on July 26, 1953—the official beginning of the Cuban Revolution.
moros y cristianos	a black beans and rice dish; literally means "Moors and Christians," and harkens back to the Moorish invasions of Spain.
nada	nothing.
negrita(o)	term of affection, especially among Cubans and other Caribbean Latinos; literally means "little black one."
"No sé"	"I don't know."
Nueva Canción/ Nueva Trova	twin musical genres, the first generically Latin American, the second specifically Cuban, essentially folk-based, often including indigenous or Afro-Latin rhythms and instruments; lyrically and politically progressive, often using the work of well-known poets or a similar, highly imagistic style.
pagando los platos rotos	vernacular, to have to deal with the consequences; literally, "to pay for the broken dishes."
pasitas	diminutive of pasas; literally means "raisins"; refers to curly, kinky hair usually associated with African ancestry.
picadillo	spicy, Cuban-style ground beef.
plátanos	plantains.
por dios	by god; an exclamation.

por favor	please.
primo(a)	cousin.
prima(o) hermana(o)	first cousin; literally, "cousin sibling."
puertorriqueñismo	Puerto Rican-ness; Puerto Rican nationalism.
qué	what?
qué carajo	what the hell?
"¿Qué pasa?"	"What's up?"
"¿Qué te pasa?"	"What's the matter with you?"
raza	the people; our people; more typical of Mexicans than Cubans or other Caribbean Latinos, but widely used.
rock nacional	Mexican style rock 'n' roll, particularly as popularized in the 1980s and 1990s.
ropa vieja	shredded spiced beef, Cuban-style.
rumba	the archetypal Cuban dance rhythm, the perfect balance of African and Iberian musical influences; the roots of salsa.
Santa Bárbara	the Christianized figure of *Changó*, one of the most powerful deities in *santería*. Santa Bárbara is usually white-skinned, red-haired, fierce, and on horseback.
Haydée Santamaría	a historical figure; one of the original rebels fighting with Fidel Castro. She lost her brother and lover at the Moncada and later married Armando Hart, Cuba's longtime minister of culture. She served in various posts in the revolutionary government. She eventually committed suicide.

santería	a religion which combines Christian and African beliefs and iconography; extremely popular in Latin America, especially in the Caribbean.
Santiago de Cuba	a city on the eastern coast of Cuba; the island's original capital.
"Si tú drume yo te traigo un mamey muy colora'o..."	"If you sleep I'll bring you a very red mamey..."; again, from "Drume Negrita."
"Te quiero verde."	from a poem by Federico Garcia Lorca; literally, "I love you green."
telenovela	a Spanish-language soap opera; unlike North American soap operas, which go on for generations, Spanish-language soaps are finite.
tía	aunt.
tío	uncle.
tortilleras	slang for "lesbians"; literally means "tortilla-makers."
"tremendos cojones"	vernacular; literally, "tremendous balls."
tres leches	an unbelievably heavy, rich, sweet dessert made with three different kinds of milk. Originally from Nicaragua, but widely served among Cuban exiles since the influx of Nicaraguans into Miami after the 1979 Sandinista revolution and the subsequent "contra" wars.
"Tú drume negrita.../ que yo voy a comprar nueva cunita/ que tendrá ca cabel..."	"You sleep, little girl/ I'm going to buy a new crib/ which will have bells..."; again, from "Drume Negrita."

"un indio"	literally, "an Indian," but the reference here is particular to the indigenous people of the Americas, specifically Latin America, rather than American Indians of the northern hemisphere.
usted	formal second person; Cubans rarely use it, especially among family.
Vanidades	a monthly women's magazine published in Miami and distributed all over the Spanish-speaking world. It covers fashion, gossip, news, medicine, science, and politics. Its glossy covers rival anything by *Glamour* or *Mirabella.*
Varadero	a beach resort outside of Havana, probably one of the most spectacular beaches in the world; a favorite of North American businesspersons and tourists prior to the Cuban revolution, now mostly visited by Canadians, Europeans and other Latin Americans.
"Viiiiiidaaa..."	"Liiiiiifffe..."; the first word from a Beny Moré lyric, meaning "life."
"¿Y tú?"	"And you?"
yanqui(s)	a mispronunciation of "yankee(s)"; Cubans much prefer *yanqui* as a pejorative for North Americans than "gringo," which is more Mexican—some say "gringo" comes from "green coat," in reference to the nineteenth-century uniforms of the North American cavalry along the Texas/Mexico border.
yuca con mojo	a traditional Cuban dish, made with cassava drenched in garlic and oil.

About the Author

Photo: Lisa Wax and Robin E. Johnston

ACHY OBEJAS is a widely published fiction writer, journalist and poet. Her first collection of short stories, *We Came All the Way from Cuba So You Could Dress Like This?*, was published by Cleis Press in 1994. Her work appears in *What We Write Now* (Birch Lane Press), *Feminisms* (Rutgers), *Latina* (Simon & Schuster), *Girlfriend Number One* (Cleis), *West Side Stories* (Chicago Stoop), *Discontents* (Amethyst), and *Woman of Her Word* (Arte Publico). Her poetry has appeared in dozens of anthologies and literary magazines.

In 1996, she received the Studs Terkel Award for journalism. She has also been honored with a NEA Creative Writing Fellowship, an Illinois Arts Council Literary award for fiction, a Barbara Deming/Money for Women grant, Peter Lisagor awards for journalism, and fellowships to the Virginia Center for the Creative Arts, Yaddo and the Ragdale Foundation.

She was born in Havana, Cuba, and came to the U.S. by boat as an exile when she was six years old. She has an M.F.A. in creative writing from Warren Wilson College and currently works as a writer for the *Chicago Tribune*.

Books from Cleis Press

Fiction

Another Love
by Erzsébet Galgóczi.

ISBN: 0-939416-52-2 24.95 cloth;
ISBN: 0-939416-51-4 8.95 paper.

Cosmopolis: Urban Stories by Women
edited by Ines Rieder.

ISBN: 0-939416-36-0 24.95 cloth;
ISBN: 0-939416-37-9 9.95 paper.

Dirty Weekend: A Novel of Revenge
by Helen Zahavi.

ISBN: 0-939416-85-9 10.95 paper.

A Forbidden Passion
by Cristina Peri Rossi.

ISBN: 0-939416-64-0 24.95 cloth;
ISBN: 0-939416-68-9 9.95 paper.

Half a Revolution: Contemporary Fiction by Russian Women
edited by Masha Gessen.

ISBN 1-57344-007-8 29.95 cloth;
ISBN 1-57344-006-X 12.95 paper.

In the Garden of Dead Cars
by Sybil Claiborne.

ISBN: 0-939416-65-4 24.95 cloth;
ISBN: 0-939416-66-2 9.95 paper.

Memory Mambo
by Achy Obejas.

ISBN: 1-57344-018-3 24.95 cloth;
ISBN: 1-57344-017-5 12.95 paper.

Night Train To Mother
by Ronit Lentin.

ISBN: 0-939416-29-8 24.95 cloth;
ISBN: 0-939416-28-X 9.95 paper.

Only Lawyers Dancing
by Jan McKemmish.

ISBN: 0-939416-70-0 24.95 cloth;
ISBN: 0-939416-69-7 9.95 paper.

Seeing Dell
by Carol Guess.

ISBN: 1-57344-024-8 24.95 cloth;
ISBN: 1-57344-023-X 12.95 paper.

Unholy Alliances: New Women's Fiction
edited by Louise Rafkin.

ISBN: 0-939416-14-X 21.95 cloth;
ISBN: 0-939416-15-8 9.95 paper.

The Wall
by Marlen Haushofer.

ISBN: 0-939416-53-0 24.95 cloth;
ISBN: 0-939416-54-9 paper.

We Came All The Way from Cuba So You Could Dress Like This?: Stories
by Achy Obejas.

ISBN: 0-939416-92-1 24.95 cloth;
ISBN: 0-939416-93-X 10.95 paper.

LATIN AMERICA

Beyond the Border: A New Age in Latin American Women's Fiction
edited by Nora Erro-Peralta and Caridad Silva-Núñez.
ISBN: 0-939416-42-5 24.95 cloth;
ISBN: 0-939416-43-3 12.95 paper.

The Little School: Tales of Disappearance and Survival in Argentina
by Alicia Partnoy.
ISBN: 0-939416-08-5 21.95 cloth;
ISBN: 0-939416-07-7 9.95 paper.

Revenge of the Apple
by Alicia Partnoy.
ISBN: 0-939416-62-X 24.95 cloth;
ISBN: 0-939416-63-8 8.95 paper.

LESBIAN AND GAY STUDIES

The Case of the Good-For-Nothing Girlfriend
by Mabel Maney.
ISBN: 0-939416-90-5 24.95 cloth;
ISBN: 0-939416-91-3 10.95 paper.

The Case of the Not-So-Nice Nurse
by Mabel Maney.
ISBN: 0-939416-75-1 24.95 cloth;
ISBN: 0-939416-76-X 9.95 paper.

Best Gay Erotica 1996
selected by Scott Heim,
edited by Michael Ford.
ISBN: 1-57344-053-1 24.95 cloth;
ISBN: 1-57344-052-3 12.95 paper.

Best Lesbian Erotica 1996
selected by Heather Lewis,
edited by Tristan Taormino.
ISBN: 1-57344-055-8 24.95 cloth;
ISBN: 1-57344-054-X 12.95 paper.

Dagger: On Butch Women
edited by Roxxie, Lily Burana, Linnea Due.
ISBN: 0-939416-81-6 29.95 cloth;
ISBN: 0-939416-82-4 14.95 paper.

Dark Angels: Lesbian Vampire Stories
edited by Pam Keesey.
ISBN: 1-57344-015-9 24.95 cloth;
ISBN 1-7344-014-0 10.95 paper.

Daughters of Darkness: Lesbian Vampire Stories
edited by Pam Keesey.
ISBN: 0-939416-77-8 24.95 cloth;
ISBN: 0-939416-78-6 9.95 paper.

Different Daughters: A Book by Mothers of Lesbians,
second edition,
edited by Louise Rafkin.
ISBN: 1-57344-051-5 24.95 cloth;
ISBN: 1-57344-050-7 12.95 paper.

Different Mothers: Sons & Daughters of Lesbians Talk About Their Lives
edited by Louise Rafkin.
ISBN: 0-939416-40-9 24.95 cloth;
ISBN: 0-939416-41-7 9.95 paper.

*Dyke Strippers: Lesbian
Cartoonists A to Z*
edited by Roz Warren.
ISBN: 1-57344-009-4 29.95 cloth;
ISBN: 1-57344-008-6 16.95 paper.

*Girlfriend Number One:
Lesbian Life in the '90s*
edited by Robin Stevens.
ISBN: 0-939416-79-4 29.95 cloth;
ISBN: 0-939416-8 12.95 paper.

*Hothead Paisan: Homicidal
Lesbian Terrorist*
by Diane DiMassa.
ISBN: 0-939416-73-5 14.95 paper.

A Lesbian Love Advisor
by Celeste West.
ISBN: 0-939416-27-1 24.95 cloth;
ISBN: 0-939416-26-3 9.95 paper.

*More Serious Pleasure:
Lesbian Erotic Stories
and Poetry*
edited by the Sheba Collective.
ISBN: 0-939416-48-4 24.95 cloth;
ISBN: 0-939416-47-6 9.95 paper.

Nancy Clue and the Hardly
Boys in *A Ghost
in the Closet*
by Mabel Maney.
ISBN: 1-57344-013-2 24.95 cloth;
ISBN: 1-57344-012-4 10.95 paper.

*The Night Audrey's Vibrator
Spoke: A Stonewall Riots
Collection*
by Andrea Natalie.
ISBN: 0-939416-64-6 8.95 paper.

*Queer and Pleasant Danger:
Writing Out
My Life*
by Louise Rafkin.
ISBN: 0-939416-60-3 24.95 cloth;
ISBN: 0-939416-61-1 9.95 paper.

*Revenge of Hothead Paisan:
Homicidal Lesbian Terrorist*
by Diane DiMassa.
ISBN: 1-57344-016-7 16.95 paper.

*Rubyfruit Mountain:
A Stonewall Riots Collection*
by Andrea Natalie.
ISBN: 0-939416-74-3 9.95 paper.

*Serious Pleasure: Lesbian
Erotic Stories and Poetry*
edited by the Sheba Collective.
ISBN: 0-939416-46-8 24.95 cloth;
ISBN: 0-939416-45-X 9.95 paper.

*Sons of Darkness: Tales
of Men, Blood and
Immortality*
edited by Michael Rowe
and Thomas Roche.
ISBN: 1-57344-060-4 24.95 cloth;
ISBN: 1-57344-059-0 12.95 paper.

*Switch Hitters: Lesbians
Write Gay Male Erotica
and Gay Men Write
Lesbian Erotica*
edited by Carol Queen
and Lawrence Schimel.
ISBN: 1-57344-022-1 24.95 cloth;
ISBN: 1-57344-021-3 12.95 paper.

**Women Who Run With
the Werewolves: Tales
of Blood, Lust and
Metamorphosis**
edited by Pam Keesey.

ISBN: 1-57344-058-2 24.95 cloth;
ISBN: 1-57344-057-4 12.95 paper.

SEXUAL POLITICS

Body Alchemy: Photographs
by Loren Cameron.

ISBN: 1-57344-063-9 34.94 cloth;
ISBN: 1-57344-062-0 24.95 paper.

**Forbidden Passages:
Writings Banned in Canada**
introductions by Pat Califia
and Janine Fuller.

ISBN: 1-57344-020-5 24.95 cloth;
ISBN: 1-57344-019-1 14.95 paper.

**Good Sex: Real Stories
from Real People,**
second edition,
by Julia Hutton.

ISBN: 1-57344-001-9 29.95 cloth;
ISBN: 1-57344-000-0 14.95 paper.

**The Good Vibrations Guide
to Sex: How to Have Safe,
Fun Sex in the '90s**
by Cathy Winks and
Anne Semans.

ISBN: 0-939416-83-2 29.95 cloth;
ISBN: 0-939416-84-0 16.95 paper.

**I Am My Own Woman: The
Outlaw Life of Charlotte von
Mahlsdorf**
translated by Jean Hollander.

ISBN: 1-57344-011-6 24.95 cloth;
ISBN: 1-57344-010-8 12.95 paper.

**Madonnarama: Essays on
Sex and Popular Culture**
edited by Lisa Frank
and Paul Smith.

ISBN: 0-939416-72-7 24.95 cloth;
ISBN: 0-939416-71-9 9.95 paper.

**Public Sex: The Culture
of Radical Sex**
by Pat Califia.

ISBN: 0-939416-88-3 29.95 cloth;
ISBN: 0-939416-89-1 12.95 paper.

**Sex Work: Writings by
Women in the Sex Industry**
edited by Frédérique Delacoste
and Priscilla Alexander.

ISBN: 0-939416-10-7 24.95 cloth;
ISBN: 0-939416-11-5 16.95 paper.

**Susie Bright's Sexual
Reality: A Virtual Sex
World Reader**
by Susie Bright.

ISBN: 0-939416-58-1 24.95 cloth;
ISBN: 0-939416-59-X 9.95 paper.

Susie Bright's Sexwise
by Susie Bright.

ISBN: 1-57344-003-5 24.95 cloth;
ISBN: 1-57344-002-7 10.95 paper.

**Susie Sexpert's
Lesbian Sex World**
by Susie Bright.

ISBN: 0-939416-34-4 24.95 cloth;
ISBN: 0-939416-35-2 9.95 paper.

REFERENCE

*Betty and Pansy's
Severe Queer Review of
San Francisco*
by Betty Pearl and Pansy.

ISBN: 1-57344-056-6 10.95 paper.

Food for Life & Other Dish
edited by Lawrence Schimel.

ISBN: 1-57344-061-2 14.95 paper.

*Putting Out: The Essential
Publishing Resource Guide
For Gay and Lesbian
Writers,*
third edition,
by Edisol W. Dotson.

ISBN: 0-939416-86-7 29.95 cloth;
ISBN: 0-939416-87-5 12.95 paper.

POLITICS OF HEALTH

*The Absence of the Dead Is
Their Way of Appearing*
by Mary Winfrey Trautmann.

ISBN: 0-939416-04-2 8.95 paper.

Don't: A Woman's Word
by Elly Danica.

ISBN: 0-939416-23-9 21.95 cloth;
ISBN: 0-939416-22-0 8.95 paper

*1 in 3: Women with Cancer
Confront an Epidemic*
edited by Judith Brady.

ISBN: 0-939416-50-6 24.95 cloth;
ISBN: 0-939416-49-2 10.95 paper.

*Voices in the Night: Women
Speaking About Incest*
edited by Toni A.H. McNaron
and Yarrow Morgan.

ISBN: 0-939416-02-6 9.95 paper.

*With the Power of Each
Breath: A Disabled Women's
Anthology*
edited by Susan Browne,
Debra Connors and
Nanci Stern.

ISBN: 0-939416-09-3 24.95 cloth;
ISBN: 0-939416-06-9 10.95 paper.

AUTOBIOGRAPHY, BIOGRAPHY, LETTERS

*Peggy Deery: An Irish
Family at War*
by Nell McCafferty.

ISBN: 0-939416-38-7 24.95 cloth;
ISBN: 0-939416-39-5 9.95 paper.

*The Shape of Red:
Insider/Outsider Reflections*
by Ruth Hubbard
and Margaret Randall.

ISBN: 0-939416-19-0 24.95 cloth;
ISBN: 0-939416-18-2 9.95 paper.

Women & Honor:
Some Notes on Lying
by Adrienne Rich.

ISBN: 0-939416-44-1 3.95 paper.

ANIMAL RIGHTS

And a Deer's Ear, Eagle's Song and Bear's Grace: Relationships Between Animals and Women edited by Theresa Corrigan and Stephanie T. Hoppe.

ISBN: 0-939416-38-7 24.95 cloth;
ISBN: 0-939416-39-5 9.95 paper.

With a Fly's Eye, Whale's Wit and Woman's Heart: Relationships Between Animals and Women edited by Theresa Corrigan and Stephanie T. Hoppe.

ISBN: 0-939416-24-7 24.95 cloth;
ISBN: 0-939416-25-5 9.95 paper.

Since 1980, Cleis Press has published progressive books by women. We welcome your order and will ship your books as quickly as possible. Individual orders must be prepaid (U.S. dollars only). Please add 15% shipping. PA residents add 6% sales tax. Mail orders: Cleis Press, PO Box 8933, Pittsburgh PA 15221. MasterCard and Visa orders: include account number, exp. date, and signature. FAX your credit card order: (412) 937-1567. Or, phone us Mon-Fri, 9 am–5 pm EST: (412) 937-1555 or (800) 780-2279.